TURNING CORNERS

Turning Corners

Published by The Conrad Press in the United Kingdom 2020

Tel: +44(0)1227 472 874
www.theconradpress.com
info@theconradpress.com

ISBN 978-1-913567-20-0

Typesetting by: Charlotte Mouncey, www.bookstyle.co.uk

The Conrad Press logo was designed by Maria Priestley.

Printed and bound in Great Britain by Clays Ltd, Elcograf S.p.A.

TURNING CORNERS

ROBERT E. WILLOCK

1

'Bye Robbie, best of luck with the paintings.'

'Thanks, Mr Young. In the nicest possible way, I hope I never see you again. But you've been good to me.'

'You don't realise how rewarding it is for us officers to see someone leaving this prison a reformed man.'

'I was a victim of circumstances,' I replied.

'Of course,' said Mr Young. 'Do you think your paintings would have been so popular, if the public had never discovered you were a resident of Her Majesty's Prison?'

I looked him in the eye. Well, almost; he was a very tall man.

'No chance. Most artists have ill-fated lives. You don't become popular by being normal. In fact, you're more likely to be famous after you die. I'm in no rush.'

'Robbie, you don't realise how lucky you've been.'

I smiled.

'There's been one or two times in those showers where I would say I was far from being lucky. Big Grace, and Mable, were formidable characters when they were on heat. It's no wonder people leave prisons in a state of depression.'

Mr Young, opened the large wooden door.

'See you, Robbie.'

I stepped out onto the pavement and took a deep breath. Fresh air I thought to myself. Well, there was no welcoming committee but I didn't care. I was free and even though there was the odd car passing by, it all seemed so quiet. In the prison there was the constant echo of metal doors being locked and unlocked. The mixed smell of disinfectant and urine. Usually the smell of piss was the stronger of the two.

A car stopped by the side of me.

'Would you be the ageing artist, Robbie Knottcut?' asked the driver.

'Casper, you bastard, I didn't recognise you with your new spectacles. Have you come to pick me up?'

'No, I was kerb-crawling and just happened to see this big strapping man walking down the road. Have you left your coat hanger on underneath your coat? What's happened to that fat gut of yours? Are you sure you spent the last four years in prison?'

'Three years three hundred and twenty days to be exact,' I said as I got into his car. 'It's amazing how many weights you can lift when you're angry,' I replied. 'And I was angry most of the time. The gym and the paint brush stopped me going mad. Most of my best paintings were just an extension of my anger. And please, Casper, don't say I was lucky there's nothing lucky about prison. Could you just stop at the nearest park? I just fancy a walk.'

'Okay,' said Casper, 'do you want me to stay in the car or walk with you and try and get that massive chip of your big shoulders? As far as I'm concerned, you're still ugly and your paintings are shit. You have women sending you love letters and you have your paintings hanging on the walls at art exhibitions. You could have easily been sentenced to ten years. So, stop feeling sorry for yourself.'

'Those love letters, as you put it, Casper, are mostly from

deranged old spinsters or people obsessed by God. As for the exhibitions, the local community hall isn't exactly big time.'

'You sold two paintings last year for over six thousand pounds,' replied Casper, 'That caused a stir in the local newspaper; is it right a prisoner should make money while serving a sentence for violent crimes?'

'Is that what it said on the front page?' I asked.

'Just milk it, Robbie. You even got shot and didn't realise it while people around you were being killed left right and centre.'

'That's all been a big exaggeration, and as for the paintings, it was only five thousand.' I said. 'And I donated a fair amount to charity. Are you still working for the council emptying dustbins?'

'Yes, Robbie, I've even been promoted. And I have a girlfriend and we have plenty of sex,'

'Don't rub it in, Casper. I've been incarcerated for almost four years and you start talking about sex. There's guys in that prison, it's a wonder their right hand didn't fall off all the wanking they were doing.'

'Oh, I suppose you didn't do any such thing; you just spent all your energy in the gym and painting abstract art.'

I paused for a few seconds.

'That's correct Casper, I didn't do such things; I always used my left hand.'

Casper, gave a short laugh.

'There's a guy from the local press who's been bothering me lately asking about you,' he said. 'He'll have a shock when he turns up at the prison tomorrow and finds you left a day early.'

'That's why they did it, Casper. They didn't want any sort of crowd. And I was more than happy to leave a day early. I must phone Reverend Percy, the local vicar and tell him I'm out of prison.'

'Have you become obsessed with God too?'

'No, I'm not walking around with a bible in my hand quoting stuff and all that. But he was very good to me, he gave me hope and has sorted out some living accommodation for me. So, who's this guy from the local press?'

'He wants to write a story about you. I just told him when you lived with me, you were just a moaning bastard who never paid any rent. Anyway, here you are. A nice little park for you to have a walk around.'

'This isn't a park; this is just a couple of acres of grassland. I wanted somewhere where there's a pond and ducks, flowers, a few trees, a nice play area for the kids.'

'For fuck's sake, Robbie, if you wanted the Botanical Gardens you should have said. You've become right arty-farty. Since when have you become interested in flowers?'

I grabbed Casper by the throat. 'Since the first night I spent in that shithole and cried myself to sleep. I'm not the same man I used to be. But I know beauty when I see it, and there's no beauty to be seen in prison. So, find me a proper park.'

'Take it easy, Robbie, there's no need to get physical.'

I let go of Casper's throat. I could see it had shaken him up.

'It's going to take a few months for me to become all sweetness and light,' I said. 'Take me to that nice park near your place. Just drop me off there. I just need a bit of time to myself.'

'I understand,' said Casper. 'I'll take you to a proper park.'

Then he gave me a mobile phone. 'That's my old mobile; take it. I figure your old one is really out of date. It's fully charged. If you have any phone numbers, I'll put them in for you.'

I gave him a list out of my pocket.

'Thanks, Casper. I shouldn't have grabbed your throat like that. Just as well I wasn't carrying a gun; I might have shot you.'

'That's not funny, Robbie.'

'Your girlfriend; is she nice?'

'Very,' said Casper.

'Good. I bet she doesn't know you're picking me up today.'

He looked a bit sheepish.

'No, she doesn't,' said Casper. 'She loves your paintings.'

'Poor girl,' I said. 'She loves my paintings, but you think they're shit.'

'I think you're having a laugh, but Christine, thinks they have meaning and tap into one's inner soul.'

'She makes me sound like a shoe repairer.'

'She'd love to meet you.'

'Well let me have a couple of days to myself, and then we'll have a little get together. First, I must buy some new clothes. Find my new dwelling and the nearest gym.'

'You intend to keep up all this weight training?'

'Yes, I do. You should try it sometime you skinny bastard.'

'No thanks, I'll just stick to the shagging.' said Casper, with a big smile on his face.

'If you open the glove box there's a few official-looking envelopes for you. I think they're from the bank.'

'You know damn well they are; you haven't been steaming them open have you?'

'No, I haven't. I did exactly as you said with any mail that was addressed to me with your name on it. I hid them away till you got out of jail. Are you all right financially?'

'I don't know till I open these envelopes. Some of them

9

should be bank statements.'

It was another fifteen minutes before Casper, dropped me off at the proper park.

'I'll wait for you here', Casper, said. 'You have a little walk round and get rid of some of that anger.'

I found a wooden bench to sit on. I'd never realised how nice this park was. Everywhere I looked was so colourful. I could smell the flowers; it was nice to hear the noise of toddlers and babies chuckling with their young mothers. There was one young baby bawling his head off. His mother was doing her best to console him, but he still kept crying. The spoilt bastard, I thought.

I walked back to Casper's, car and thanked him for the lift and the phone. He had kindly put all the phone numbers in for me and quickly showed me how to use it. Things had changed a lot over the last few years; you could use a phone for so many things these days, it was unbelievable.

'I need to set up a debit card,' I said to Casper. 'Can you help me? I been told nobody uses cash these days, not even taxi drivers. Bet that's fucked a few drivers up with their tax fiddles.'

'You should know Robbie. Will you go back to driving taxis?'

'No, I have a criminal record now. I'd like to go to America and meet this woman who's been sponsoring me. But the authorities wouldn't allow me into the country.'

'Do you want me to sort out your debit card now?' said Casper.

'No, don't worry. I'll walk down to the bank and get it sorted out.'

'Be careful how you walk in, they might see you and all dive to the floor shouting *don't shoot*.'

'Casper, am I a source of embarrassment to you? Do you feel uneasy being seen with me? If so just say and I'll keep out of your way. Otherwise any more jokes like that and I'll break your neck, do you understand?'

'I'm sorry, Robbie, that was in bad taste.'

'Thanks for the apology,' I said. 'You've been very good to me today, don't ruin it. I'll give you a call later.'

I walked around the town centre. Things hadn't changed much; a few more supermarkets and a newly-built old people's home that probably cost a fortune. Getting money out of the bank proved to be tricky. But eventually I managed to produce enough documents to prove that I was Robbie Knotcutt, slightly famous painter and gangster.

The different reactions from different people were amazing.

The first member of staff I spoke to responded in a really loud voice. So, it wasn't long before everybody in the bank knew who I was, and that I had forty thousand pounds in my account. Most of that had been acquired from an elderly American actress who had commissioned me while I was in the nick to paint several works of art. The manager, sorry I mean team leader, was looking nervous. Two elderly couples walked out of the bank immediately. One overdressed blonde asked me for my signature and gave me her address and phone number.

The next day, I phoned the number she'd given me and a man with a deep voice answered.

'Who's that?' he said.

I paused for a second then continued. 'Is that Clifton windows?'

'Wrong number, mate,' the man said then put the phone down.

Oh well, perhaps I was hoping for too much, a shag on my second day out. I really needed someone to help me with some clothes shopping. All the men were walking about with tight trousers, fancy haircuts and flowery shirts.

My phone rang. It was Casper.

'Have you heard the news? Pretty much everyone we know is talking about you being released and there's some art critic spouting bollocks about your artwork.'

'When you say spouting bollocks, what exactly are they saying?'

'It's ridiculous, he's saying your paintings relate to the pain and suffering of the working class. Then he's on about your use of colours and all that shit.'

'Casper, you've made your point, you don't like my work. How would you like it if I came around to your place and shagged your girlfriend? And then said, you know what that was the worst shag I've ever had, nothing exciting about it at all? You'd feel offended. So, could you please stop banging on about my work being shit.'

'That's a ridiculous comparison. Christine's a great shag,' said Casper.

'Well good for you, and long may it continue. I can't wait to meet her, but please stop calling my art shit. I can call it shit myself, but if anyone else calls it shit, I become offended. Please tell me you understand?'

'Okay, I won't say another word about it,' said Casper.

'I'll speak to you later.' I said

I managed to buy some clothes and have a good work out at the gym. There were one or two stares, but I took no notice. I felt good; you don't realise just how good freedom is until it is taken away from you.

There were some fit-looking women in that gym. I couldn't wait to see what Casper's flat looked like now he had a girlfriend. It used to be a right tip. I bought a bunch of flowers for his lady, Christine, and a bottle of Scotch for Casper, and myself. I felt a lot more relaxed with some new clothes. I knocked on Casper's door.

'Hello, Robbie, I'm Christine. Come on in. I'm so pleased to meet you.' She took my hand and gave me a kiss on the cheek. She was almost as tall as me, and I'm five eleven. She had dark brown eyes and long reddish-brown hair. The touch of her hand and the smell of her orange-scented perfume felt intoxicating after four years of being cut off from women.

'These are for you,' I said as I handed her the flowers. 'The Scotch is for my good friend Casper. He's a lucky man.'

Christine, smiled. 'Isn't he just,' she murmured.

'Come on in, Rembrandt,' Casper, shouted.

I walked through to the lounge, where Casper, was sitting on the settee, trying to look sophisticated, with his legs crossed and sipping wine from a large glass. He didn't look sophisticated in the least,

I gazed around the room. 'Casper, I think I've walked into the wrong flat.'

'Apartment if you don't mind, Robbie,' said Casper.

I looked at Christine.

'You've certainly knocked this man into shape This room used to be a dump; he would always bring home more rubbish from work than he left behind. He thought he could repair anything. This is an incredible transformation,'

'Well that was four years ago. We all change, Robbie, and

I'll be thirty soon,' said Casper.

'I'm so pleased for you, my younger cousin Casper, done good. I'm so pleased for both of you. Christine, how did you manage to transform this untidy bastard?'

'Oh, that was easy, I just told him, if he didn't get rid of the crap, the sex would stop.'

Casper, almost choked on his wine and spat most of it onto a small modern table.

'So, I imagined he removed it pretty quick.'

'Just two days,' replied Christine.

She was a truly elegant woman; it was difficult to tell her age but I'd say she was a few years older than Casper.

'I think you ought to tell Norman, your story,' Christine, said.

'Who's Norman?' I asked.

'He's the reporter who wants to write your story. It would be good to hear the truth,' said Christine.

'So, you think it's all lies? To be honest I'm not sure myself what is the truth and what is fiction anymore.'

'Why don't you give him a ring?' asked Casper, as he wiped the wine from his shirt and the table.

'Let him wait see how much money he's going to offer me.' I said, then looked at Casper. 'Since when have you been drinking wine?'

'Since I met Christine,'

'Don't you think it's a bit girlie?'

'We all change, Robbie, everyone drinks wine these days.'

Christine, was about to pour me a glass of Scotch, 'How do you like it?'

'Straight most of the time,' I replied. 'You do realise the last women who served me a Scotch, I was accused of shooting her in the head?'

'That's a hell of a chat-up line,' said Casper. 'You start off with a nice bunch of flowers and then you go and say a thing like that.'

'It's all right, Casper,' said Christine. 'Robbie didn't mean any harm I don't think he was trying to scare me. You can sit down if you want, I won't bite.'

'Thank you, Christine, I suppose it was a bit clumsy of me saying that. Anyway, I've had an offer from a journalist from one of the big nationals just a few hours ago. He's offered me a lot of money. He'll probably sensationalise most of it, but I don't care I'd like to get it off my chest.'

'Why don't you tell me your story?' said Christine. 'I'll tell you if it's worth listening too.'

'Why would you want to do that?'

'I write books, mostly kiddies' books and they're not that successful, but I think there might be a good book in you. Why don't you let me write it?'

'You little sneak,' I said, looking at Casper. 'Is this what this little meeting is all about,'

'Hold on Robbie,' Casper spilt his wine again.

'This is a big surprise to me. I didn't know Christine, was going to ask you that.'

I took a gulp of my Scotch.

'One of the reasons I ended up in jail was because I had too much faith in the women I was involved with.'

'You mean Doreen, and Gloria?' said Christine.

'You have been doing your homework,' I replied.

'I followed the case very closely, Robbie. There were a lot

of unanswered questions. Then suddenly it came to light that Robbie Knottcut, was the unknown artist who was painting all these wonderful pictures while serving a prison sentence.'

'Then shortly after that, I became famous selling all these paintings for a small fortune,' I said.

'Intriguing,' said Christine.

'And just by chance you happen to be going out with my cousin,' I said.

'It could be a great story Robbie,' said Casper.

'You only know half of it.' I said

'Exactly' replied Casper, 'I think I deserve to know the other half. I've always stood by you Robbie.'

'Deserve! I hate that word nobody deserves anything.' I took another slug of Scotch; it was going straight to my head. I looked at the pair of them. 'Do you think I could make money out of this, you crafty bastards.'

'That means he likes us,' said Casper.

2

The next morning. I woke up in a grotty outhouse of the Reverend Percy's grounds. This was my new home. I had a hangover that made a broken skull feel like a Christmas present. But I'd slept well and that was good. I looked round the room; it was a dingy little place with poor lighting and a kitchen the size of a phone box. I'd just managed to wash myself and get dressed when there was a knock on the door. My eyes bleary, I went to answer it still holding a saucepan I'd found in the kitchen.

'Hello, Robbie, long time no see. What are you going to do with that saucepan hit me over the head with it or boil an egg?'

'Both,' I replied. It was Detective Inspector Snipe, known as Sniffer, to everyone who knew him. He'd lost a lot of weight since I last saw him four years ago and he was skinny even back then. He had a walking stick in his right hand.

'Are you going to let me in to this dog kennel?' he asked. 'There's hardly enough room to turn around with your big shoulders. What the hell have they been feeding you on in that prison? You'll have to give me the recipe.'

I let him in an shut the door behind him. 'What do you want, Sniffer?'

'Don't get hostile, Robbie, I've just come to see how you're getting on. Prison can make a man very bitter and I'd feel better if you'd put that saucepan down somewhere.' He looked round the room in his usual way, like a bird of prey. 'I can get you better accommodation than this shithole.'

'Thanks, Sniffer, but this place is only temporary.'

'I know that, reverend Percy, sorted it out for you but if you're having problems, I might be able to help speed things up. Don't say no to help, Robbie. I know you might think you're tough and you don't trust anybody but the first few months out of prison can be difficult. Prison changes a man. It can make or break people; it makes them full off anger. I've seen enough ex-prisoners fall by the wayside. I do a bit of charity work with Reverend Percy, helping ex-prisoners. Trying to find them work, and somewhere to live, things like that.'

'You're joking, an old cynic like you doing charity work and helping ex-prisoners? You hate everybody.'

'It's true,' said Sniffer.

'What, you hate everybody?'

'No, it's true that I do charity work. I don't hate everybody, only some people and do you think I could sit down somewhere? I'm not using this walking stick as a fashion item.'

'I'm sorry Sniffer, take a seat. I heard you've retired.'

'That's right, a few months after they put you away. I'm sorry I couldn't attend the trial, but those butchers who work at the NHS decided it was time to saw my leg off. When that bastard who shot me gets released, I'll make sure no one helps him. I'll run the fucker over.'

'Oh, so you are a little selective who you try to help. Did the police ever find that money?'

'No Robbie, nothing. You do realise the police will be keeping an eye on you? To see if there's any change in your lifestyle? Don't go buying any big fancy yachts or anything like that.

Keep the receipts for all these strange paintings you're selling. So, what have you been doing with yourself since you were released?'

I explained to Sniffer, about Casper's girlfriend, Christine, asking if she could write about me.

Sniffer, smiled. 'You'd better be careful if you tell her the truth; you might get an extra ten years porridge. Can't you make enough money painting? Don't you think you might open up a few old wounds? You're edgy enough now opening the door with a saucepan in your hand. If I was you, I would just leave it alone.'

'I'd make it sound like you were a good copper; a bit of a hero. I'd even make out you were suave and handsome.'

'Don't talk crap. Saying I'm a good cop is bad enough, but suave and handsome – that's ridiculous.'

'Artistic licence and all that stuff,' I replied. 'They could make a TV series about you, *The Revenge of Sniffer*, or *Sniffer Strikes Back*, stuff like that.'

'You're taking the piss,' said Sniffer.

'Think about it, look at all the detective shit they put on telly at the moment.'

'You've picked up too much of that prison humour, one piss-take after another,' said Sniffer.

'It's up to you,' I said. 'You've got nothing to lose.'

'I hope not. I've already lost one leg.'

Just then my phone rang. It was Christine.

'Hello, Robbie. Have you thought any more about me writing this book?'

'That's a coincidence. I'm talking to one of the detectives who was on the case, although he's retired now.'

'Oh, would that be inspector Snipe?' asked Christine.

'You worry me. You seem to know so much about me and the people I've been involved with.'

'I could come around later on today, and we could start then,' she said.

'I'm not going to rush this idea, Christine. I still need time to think about it.'

Sniffer, looked at me.

'Tell her you'll do it,' he said, in a hissed whisper.

'I'll phone you later on today, Christine, after I've been to the gym,' Then I hung up.

'You be careful with those weights. You'll have those big, hard muscles popping out of your shirt,' Sniffer, said.

'Thanks, I'll bear that in mind. I'll speak to you later.' I gave a shrug.

'I'm not sure whether she wants to shag me or just write this book. And you soon changed your mind. One minute you're on about opening old wounds then the next minute you're telling me to do it.'

'Do what? Let her write a book or shag her? Is there something wrong with her?' said Sniffer.

'No,' I replied.

'Well don't flatter yourself. You might have muscles popping out all over the place but you're still an ugly bastard. So, don't think this young girl is going to fancy an old man like you.'

'She's not a young girl. It's hard to tell but I think she's about my age.'

'What fifty? And she's going out with Casper?'

'I'm forty-eight if you don't mind, and I'm not as old as you, Sniffer.'

'Well, I think you ought to keep it as a business arrangement. And don't forget, Robbie, there're still people out there that would be happy to see you dead. Anyway, I'm going now. I've heard enough shit and I couldn't possibly drink any more tea, you miserable bastard.'

'I don't have any tea and it's too early for Scotch.'

'I don't drink any more. I have enough trouble standing up on this artificial leg without getting pissed. Don't forget, if you're having trouble finding a new place, I might be able to help.'

'This is incredible. You've stopped drinking as well; nice to see you Sniffer, keep in touch. Let's face it you're like me; we haven't got that many friends between us.'

'You speak for yourself. Best of luck with the book and by the way, I can't stand the name Sniffer. It certainly doesn't suit someone who is suave and handsome.'

'How about The Hawk,' I replied.

'That's better.' He laughed. 'and not too much fucking swearing.'

I couldn't help but feel a little sorry for the old goat as I watched him walk slowly down the road. It was hard to believe he was helping reverend Percy, with his charity work He had aged badly over the last four years. A few minutes later, I phoned Christine.

'This book you're on about; let's go for it,' I said. 'Come around to my place tomorrow and we'll get started.'

'Great,' said Christine, 'and if you think of anything just write it down between now and tomorrow. I don't just want hard facts. I need to know what was going on in your head during that infamous few weeks of death and corruption, warts and all.'

'Fine. I'll see you at two.'

She seemed very excited; I hoped she wasn't going to be disappointed. I decided I'd better tidy the place up that would only take ten minutes, then I went down to the local café and had a good breakfast.

The next day, Christine turned up exactly on time, complete with her laptop, green teabags, and also a large canvas tucked under her arm.

'This is a present for you, Robbie. I'm sure you still want to carry on with your paintings,' she said, then gave me a kiss on the cheek.

'Thank you, Christine. I've been trying to find a suitable studio all morning. As you can see this place is far too small, and the natural lighting isn't good.'

'Any luck?'

'No,' I replied. 'Either too big, too small or too expensive.'

'Don't worry, I'll see what I can do about that. I'll just make myself a green tea and we'll get started.'

'Where do you want me to start?' I said, as we waited for the kettle to boil.

'I think it would be good if you gave me an idea of your day-to-day work as a taxi driver before you went into prison. And your relationship with your wife, Gloria. How you met big Martin. Was he really that uncouth? Did you and Gloria, really hate each other?'

'You seem to know enough already. I don't think you need me.'

'Oh yes I do. I've been going out with Casper, for two years and he's told me plenty of things about you. How you suffered with depression, financial problems, erectile dysfunction, lack of libido.'

'Casper, told you that?' I said in amazement. 'That erection thing was just for a few days.'

Christine, gave me a knowing look.

'It's nothing to be ashamed of. It can happen to anybody,' she said.

Well maybe it was a few weeks.' I paused. 'Possibly a few months. I can't believe that skinny bastard told you that. Wait till I get my hands on him. I'll tear him limb from limb.'

'That's my boyfriend you're talking about.'

'Boyfriend deceased,' I said. 'Forget the book. Take your laptop and your green tea with you and piss off.'

Christine was near to tears.

'You're a fraud,' she said. 'Underneath all that muscle, you're just a weak coward. Today's modern man would face up to his vulnerability and weaknesses.'

'That's bullshit. Life's bullshit.'

'You don't mean that. You're a very talented man and you've got the whole world at your feet.'

'Were you going to put that in the book; that my prick had stopped working?'

'It's essential that people know your state of mind.'

'Oh, spare me this analytical crap over the last few years I've been analysed how I felt when disposing of a dead body and what goes on in my mind with these abstract paintings of mine. The people that analyse me, they're more insane than anyone. Arseholes, the lot of them.'

Christine, took a deep breath,

'You're not insane. Why are you so afraid? Don't lock me out, Robbie.'

'What do you mean – physically or emotionally?' I replied.

'We all have our scars to bear,' said Christine, and put her hand out to touch my cheek. I quickly moved her hand away.

'Just go,' I said.

She walked to the door, then stopped and turned around.

'Don't worry,' I said. 'I won't harm Casper; do you want this canvas back?' I asked.

'No, you keep it it's a present. I've heard you do your best paintings when you're angry, so this one should be a master-piece.' I saw the tears in her eyes as she turned and walked out of the door, closing it behind her.

You bloody fool, I thought. I could be reading the signs wrong, but I think I've just missed my chance of bedding a stunning woman. I didn't mean to upset Christine. I have to get rid of all this anger; I was a far nicer man before I went to prison, or at least I think I was.

Later on, I phoned Reverend Percy, for guidance.

'Robbie, stay calm,' said Percy. 'We can get through this together. You know I only live yards away just come around to see me.'

How things changed. The first time I'd ever met the vicar, I was with big Martin. This was before I went to prison. He told me and Martin, that we were beyond help, and to just fuck off; mind you, Martin, did tell him to fuck off first.

My phone rang. It was Christine.

'I've had Norman, on the phone. When do you want to meet him?' she asked sternly.

'Just give me his number and I'll give him a call.'

'Are you going to let him write your story?'

'No, I've decided not to tell anyone. As Sniffer, said, it might open up a few old wounds. I'll get on with some paintings instead.'

'Okay. I'll text you his number.'

That was the end of the conversation. She's angry, I thought, very angry. I shouldn't have told her to piss off.

I decided to go for a jog, I passed the taxi rank but I didn't recognise any of the drivers. I wasn't surprised; taxi drivers come and go. They either go and work for another company or leave the trade altogether. I stopped jogging for a few minutes. This was where it all started, more or less.

'Robbie, is that you?' it was Scottie.

'How's trade?' I asked.

'Quiet. I'm thinking of giving it up. There's no money in taxi driving anymore. You did the right thing, leaving the trade when you did.'

'Well, it wasn't exactly voluntary,' I said.

Scottie, looked scared and embarrassed.

'So, you're painting pictures now?' he said.

'Yes,' I replied. I could see he didn't want to use the word prison or anything like that.

'If I remember rightly, Scottie, the last time we met you said you and I had a score to settle. You actually wanted to fight me.'

'That was a long time ago. I didn't mean it; I'm older and wiser now.'

'And a lot fatter,' I said. 'During the time I've spent in her Majesty's custody, you haven't noticed if anyone has become incredibly richer?'

'No one,' said Scottie.

'Are you sure?'

'Yes, I'm sure.'

'Okay, I'll leave you to your work. Lucky for you I don't bear a grudge. See you around, Scottie.'

When I got home, I lay on the bed, not feeling too happy about myself. I didn't want to spend my life frightening people; I knew I must get rid of this anger.

I phoned Christine, and asked if I could see her at her place.

'What, so that you can be rude to me again?'

'It depends what you mean by being rude,' I replied.

'You told me to piss off.'

'I'm sorry, I shouldn't have said that, I was just so angry. I'd like you to write the book. I'll tell you everything.'

'Everything? What made you change your mind?'

'Seeing you leaving the room crying. I felt bad about that. I was unreasonable.'

'You frightened me,' said Christine.

'I felt bad about that too. Look, if you feel uneasy about the two of us being alone together, I'll meet you in the pub. I'll even bring you some green tea bags.'

Christine laughed. 'You old smoothie. Just promise me you won't tell me to piss off again.'

'I promise. Give me your address and I'll see you in an hours' time.'

'Okay,' she said, then gave me the address and ended the call.

Christine, lived in an old town house; the lounge was big compared to where I lived. There seemed to be ornaments, framed pictures and flowers everywhere. She asked if I'd like to look around the place, but I declined.

'Maybe later,' I said. 'Let's get on with this book.'

We sat down at an old wooden table.

'Just relax Robbie, we don't need to rush this. You seem very tense. You're sure you don't want anything stronger than water?

'No thanks. What exactly is your relationship with Casper?'

'Why do you want to know?'

'Well, if you want me to tell you everything, that will involve Casper. Nothing serious, but it's possible you may not find it complimentary.'

'You're not trying to get your own back on him?' she asked.

'No, I wouldn't do that, Casper's a nice guy,' I said. 'But before he met you, he didn't have much luck with women. I'm not saying I was any sort of Romeo myself, but he was sexually naïve.'

'Don't worry, Robbie, he's told me about Martina, and the graveyard. As far as being sexually naïve, I showed him where the clitoris is and what to do with it. He's doing fine now. You look embarrassed.'

'No, I'm fine, that's okay. Three cheers for the clitoris, that's what I say. Now, moving on. Where do you want me to start?'

'Tell me about the customers you used to pick up, and about the other taxi drivers. Tell me how you met Sniffer, and the other characters in your life.'

I thought hard for a few minutes. Did she really say that about the clitoris?

'Are you sitting comfortably? Then I'll begin. Let's start with January four years ago. Am I talking too fast for you?'

'That's fine, Robbie, as long as you stay at that speed. Carry on. So, why January?' Christine, asked.

'I can just remember I started to wear a hat and everything from that time seemed to go downhill.'

'Why did you start wearing a hat?'

I paused for a moment.

'I had started to go grey, and I decided to let Gloria, dye my hair, and the bastard did it on purpose.'

'Did what on purpose?'

'My hair,' I replied. 'It was supposed to be black, but it turned out ginger, so I wore a hat to cover it up.'

Christine, started to laugh.

'Well it certainly isn't ginger anymore,' she said. 'Don't worry I think grey makes a man look very distinguished.'

'Silver, Christine, silver,' I said.

'If we're going to write this book, Robbie, you need to be less sensitive. There's an old saying amongst women. "Never let your angry sister comb your hair." you could say the same about an angry wife dyeing her husband's hair. So, let's go back to January. I won't mention the grey hair or the hat again.'

'It was cold; there's never much work after Christmas and those taxi drivers who can afford it usually go off to the Canary Islands for a few weeks. The rest of them stay at home moaning about how bad trade is. I was one of those, pissed off and broke. You would get the odd one or two telling you how well they were doing. But it was all bullshit; we'd be sitting on the rank waiting ages for a job.'

'I don't understand this rank thing,' said Christine.

'It's a designated area for taxis to park up and wait for customers. If there's plenty of work it hardly gets used. If it's quiet, there's usually about two dozen taxis parked up with miserable-looking drivers smoking or eating, waiting for work. Taxi drivers weren't supposed to eat or smoke in their cars but most drivers didn't take any notice. Big Martin, was always eating. In all fairness, he would get out of his car but he had this annoying habit of talking and eating at the same time. You couldn't understand a word he said, he'd end up with a face smeared with donor kebab, and anybody else that stood within three feet of him ended up covered as well. He always seemed to talk to me more than anyone else, so I used to carry a towel and a wet flannel in the car.'

'Why didn't you tell him to piss off?' Christine, asked. 'You're a big lad, muscular and fit.'

'I wasn't then, I was well out of condition,'

I drew a quick breath, then went on:

'Years ago, he used to work for some dodgy second-hand car dealer as a debt collector, and for one or two big-time gangsters. He wasn't the sharpest tool in the box, but he was still capable of throwing a punch and scaring the shit out of people. He had many nicknames; if he was in a good mood, he liked being called Killer, because it gave him a feeling of wellbeing. No one ever mentions the past to him, or how big his arse is.

Anyway, this one morning I was parked up on the rank like most of the other taxi drivers pissed off and cold. Martin, was parked up in front of me, and, as usual, got out of his cab to talk to me. It was always a struggle with his weight, and he had rheumatism in his knees. He started off with the usual conversation, and I had my towel and wet flannel ready.

'Quiet today, Robbie,' he said.

I was lucky, he wasn't eating anything.

'That's a nice-looking steering wheel cover,' he said, sarcastically.

'Christmas present from the wife,' I replied.

'It's very colourful,' said Martin, 'don't you think it's a bit

29

girlie? You'll be painting your car pink next.'

'No, I won't. 'I replied, angrily. Be careful I thought, I'm talking to the Killer.

'All right, Robbie, keep your hair on,' said Martin, he stared at me for a moment.

'So, what's with the hat, is that a Christmas present too?'

Christine, looked at me and said, 'I thought you didn't want me to write anything about the hat, and your silver hair?'

'Oh, just write it, it's all part of the story. Let's get back to Martin, taking the piss.'

'Okay,' said Christine. 'Carry on.'

'No,' I told Martin, 'I chose this hat myself.'

'Is that to hide your ginger hair?'

'What ginger hair?' I replied.

Martin snatched the hat off my head.

'Well, that's a miracle. Yesterday you were black and grey, and now you're the colour of an orangutan. How did you manage that?'

'Never you mind, just give me my hat back, you big, fat, ugly bastard.'

'Pardon?' said Martin. 'What did you say?'

'Give me my hat back, and just fuck off.'

Martin's face went red and I realised I shouldn't have said that. Martin, looked as though he was going to pull me out of the car. I quickly turned on the ignition and sped down the road as fast as I could. Trying hard not to shit myself whilst narrowly missing pedestrians and some guy in a wheelchair, who was that incensed with my driving that he got out of his chair and started to chase me down the road, shouting,

'Bastard!'

That was some miracle cure. I thought to myself.

'What happened next?' asked Christine.

'I parked up a few streets away, my heart was pounding. Suddenly there was a knocking at the window. I didn't recognise this madman. Shouting and waving his arms about, he was seriously out of breath.' I lowered the window slowly looking to see if he was in a wheelchair no, there wasn't one in site.

'Do you mind not leaning all over my car. I've only just had it cleaned' thinking, if he does cut up rough, he's so much out of breath any more trauma he'll just faint.

'You could have killed me, you, stupid bastard,' he gasped.

'You knocked me off my wheelchair, you didn't even stop. Left the scene of the crime, you're a maniac.'

'You seem to be doing all right without a wheelchair. You're not one of those benefit cheats that good honest hard-working taxpayers like myself have to subsidise,' I said, 'they cost a few bob those wheelchairs, you should be more careful. Anyway, what makes you think it was me? A lot of these taxis look the same?'

I was trying to remain calm, still confused about how he got this far without his chair.

'Oh, I know it's you alright.'

He'd regained his breath, and was starting to look menacing.

'One of the taxi drivers on the rank gave me a good description of your car, no loyalty there. He couldn't, remember the registration number, but if I wasn't sure there's was two obvious giveaways.'

'Oh, and what might that be?' I asked, trying to remain

calm and superior,

'That,' he said pointing at my steering wheel. 'That girlie cover and your ginger hair, you, big tart.'

'I'll have you know that was a Christmas present from my wife, you, fake 'disabled arsehole.'

'And this is a Christmas present from me, you big twatt.'

Bang! I never saw it coming; there was a sudden pain on my nose, then everything went hazy. I was half conscience as I could feel myself slumping to the side of my seat. Warm fluid dripping into my mouth, it was blood. The bastard had broken my nose with one punch. Everything was becoming painful and blurred, that wheel cover will be the death of me if I'm still alive tomorrow it's going in the rubbish bin, never to be seen again. Oh, shit the pain, then I passed out.

To say my wife was angry and deeply upset was putting it mildly. She just couldn't understand how a man in a wheelchair could break my nose and knock me out. I tried several times to tell her that at the point of contact there was no wheelchair in site. It made no difference. She felt humiliated.

'You've ruined the only shirt that fits you, I can't get rid of those blood stains,' she said angrily.

'Oh, dear that's very unfortunate.' 'Do you know my nose is throbbing like hell.'

'I'm surprised he didn't drag you out the car, and give you a good kicking,' she said, full of anger.

'He probably would have done if the local vicar hadn't been walking past at the time. That was the only bit of luck I had that day.'

'And what's happened to that lovely steering wheel cover I gave you for your Christmas present?' She asked suspiciously.

I knew whatever answer I gave to my beloved she wouldn't believe me.

'Maybe he took it for a souvenir and tied it on the side of his wheelchair.'

'Sometimes you talk a load of bollocks. My sister was right about you, she always thought you were strange.'

'Oh well you two are as thick as thieves what one says the other agrees. Don't you pair get fed up when people ask you where Cinderella is today?'

'How dare you talk about me and my sister like that.'

'I'm sorry, it's a weakness I have. I always follow public opinion.'

That was it. In no uncertain terms, she told me to find somewhere else to live as soon as possible because she couldn't stand the site of me. From there on it was the dreaded cold shoulder and that stare that was like a light sabre. Then there was the banging of doors. I've often wondered where the so-called weaker sex learnt to do that. Do they give them lessons at *Relate* or similar organisations? I can visualise a specially designed hallway with several doors. And a big arsed woman with a crew cut shouting out, 'Go on bang the doors as hard as possible, show that scrotum hanging shit head whose boss, give the bastard hell!'

Or maybe they just heard it on *Woman's Hour?* There was the odd comment now and again. The obligatory, 'Take your dirty shoes off. Put the toilet seat down when you finished and from now you can wash your own dirty underpants.' She knew how to hurt me, the bitch.

'What, was so difficult about washing your own underpants?'

asked Christine,

'It was just a question of principle,'

'Don't you think that's a bit childish,

'I thought you wanted to know everything about me, are you going to question me about everything I tell you.'

'No, I'm not said, Christine, but I do need to know your state of mind, it is so important. Why are you staring at me?'

'I just think Casper's a lucky guy,'

'Yes, and I'm a lucky girl,'

'Are you.'

'Yes, I am, we better continue with the book. Did Gloria, have a job?'

'Yes, she worked part time at a cake shop. She used to bring home a few cakes but that stopped. She was just being spiteful.'

'Anyway, a few days later, as the pain and the swelling subsided a couple of well-meaning cabbies came around to see me at my home. They were only being nosey.

I can't stand the bastards really. Freddie the Flirt, and his sidekick Scottie, he knew the name of every street and road in the town. But could barely put his shoes on the right feet.

'Why was he called Freddie the Flirt,' asked Christine. 'Was he good looking.'

'No' I replied, 'let's just say he was sexually active, and he was always sniffing round Gloria, rumour has it he's shagged half the women in town and half of them, wished they hadn't bothered.'

'You sound a bit envious, Robbie.' Said Christine.

'Mabey I was. Back then my life was shit, let's continue with the book,'

'Carry on big boy.'

3

'These guys just wanted to see how bad my face looked, have a good laugh. But it was good to see them as things were rather quiet and frosty in the house at that moment. They sat down looking around the room.'

'Very nice,' said Freddie the flirt. Scottie, was bouncing up and down as though he'd never seen a chair before.

'This is nice and comfortable,' he said. 'You've spent a few bob on this place.'

'Thank you, Scottie. But there's no need to be bouncing up and down on the chair like that. I'd, like to think it'll last me a few more years you big ape. Can't you take your finger out your nose. What are you doing up there, searching for your brain?'

'Excuse me, we only came here to cheer you up, no need to get shitty.'

'I'm sorry Scottie, it's nice to see you both I'm still a bit shaken up with recent events. I'm over-reacting to most things.'

'That's alright' said Freddie. 'We understand, don't we Scottie?'

'I guess so,' said Scottie, looking slightly annoyed when I handed him a paper tissue.

As Scottie, started to blow his nose, Freddie, started to explained the series of events that happened on the day I was knocked out.

It was incredible, I was so unlucky that day. These two

cabbies, started to tell me the history of the 'Wheelchair Man,'

Up to a couple of years ago before my friend was inflicted with this physical disability, he was a superb athlete.

He was just good at everything, not normal. He was seriously being considered for the triathlon at the Olympics.

So, I try to explain this to my wife, plus the fact this particular disability is spasmodic. Some days he wakes up and he's fine, other days he can barely get out of bed unaided. (I know quite a few people like that, but that's more to do with alcoholic poisoning). It just happened to be a good day for him, and an utter   disaster for me. It still didn't change anything as far as my wife was concerned.

'Your wife seems very upset,' said Freddie.

'Yes, it's been very upsetting and humiliating for both of us.'

Every time I spoke Scottie, and Freddie, started to laugh.

'Have you two just come along to take the piss? Bouncing up and down with laughter. This isn't funny my nose hurts like hell.'

'I'm sorry Robbie,' said Freddie. Quickly looking into the wall mirror, looking to see if his dyed hair looked okay.

'I never expected you to look like this with your black eyes and red nose and you're so hard to understand. You sound like a Brummie with a bad cold he must have given you a right slap'

'That's one way of putting it Freddie.'

'It's even turned your hair ginger,' said Scottie.

'I can't understand how super cripple got to my car that quickly.'

'Oh, that's easy to explain,' said Scottie, with his finger half-way up his nose again.

'Some kind old dear nearby, saw what happened, gave him

a lift minus his wheelchair. Followed you and dropped him off just around the corner. After he described to her what he was going to do to you, she didn't want to park any closer. The thought of seeing a full-grown man crying and bleeding to death would be too disturbing.'

'But she did find the chase, exciting and exhilarating,' said Freddie.

'Really, I'm very pleased for her that she's had so much excitement in one day. There's me having such a dull time half hanging out of my car. My nose splattered across my dull face not to mention my headache, and all thanks to an interfering old biddy. I should be gratefully indebted to her, the old bastard.'

Gloria, walked into the room holding a tray of tea and biscuits.

'There you are boys.'

'Thank you, Gloria, you look lovelier than ever,' said Freddie.

Gloria, smiled at Freddie, and Scottie.

I looked at my wife, but she avoided eye contact. I looked at Freddie, he was looking at Gloria's arse as she bent over to put the tray down. I knew what was going on in his mind, and it wasn't biscuits.

'Corr,' said Scottie, 'these biscuits are right posh. What are they called?'

'Petticoat tails,' replied Gloria.

'Whoever thought of that stupid name?' Scottie, asked, spitting crumbs all over his jumper.

Gloria, had left the room. Freddie's eyes followed her arse into the kitchen. I looked at the tray of biscuits, quickly disappearing,

'I'll be back in a moment,' she said.

Any other time she would have kicked these pair of prats out the house. What was she thinking offering them our best biscuits? They cost a fortune. The only other time Gloria, serves these biscuits is when her sister comes around, and as much as I loathe her being given anything in this house, she's so asthmatic, it takes her forty minutes to eat just one. These greedy pair of bastards, have eaten the equivalent of two and a half packets in a quarter of an hour.

'Don't they sell biscuits round your way?' I asked.

'What do you mean?' asked Freddie. 'We only live a couple of miles away, course they sell biscuits, might not be posh one's like these, though.'

'I just wondered the way you two were carrying on. They're extremely expensive you know you're supposed to eat them slowly not shove em down your throat all at once.'

'Hold on Robbie, me and Scottie, came here today with the best of intentions. To cheer you up that sort of thing, we know it's been a difficult time for you and your wife. But there's no reason to get all snobby and besides it's not me that's eaten all your posh expensive biscuits. It was old greedy bollocks over there,' said Freddie.

Pointing at Scottie, still chumping away.

Gloria, came back in the room with a restocked tray. 'Sorry boys only plain ones left.'

'Thank you,' said Freddie, 'your very kind.'

'Think nothing of it,' I said. 'I'm sure if you manage to eat all these, we've probably got a spare chocolate cake, or half a leg of lamb in the freezer, you can all have a chew at.'

My wife looked at me disgusted and walked out of the room.

Freddie, made sure Gloria, had left before he spoke.

'You can be sarcastic at times, it's unnecessary, can't you see, Gloria's very upset.'

'Yes, I can, but it's all very upsetting for me. I'm the one with the broken nose, aching head and black eyes, all I need is a pair of giant red boots and I'll look like Coco the Clown.'

'She's not talking to me and even worse she's refusing to wash my dirty underpants, the bastard, it's so inconsiderate.'

'Can't you wash your own underpants?' Scottie, asked.

'Piss off,' I replied,' a man has to draw the line somewhere. I just throw them away I bought some today at 'Primark,' the shop assistant looked at my face and asked me if they were to put over my head, cheeky get!'

'You'll regret buying those,' said Freddie. 'I bought half dozen pants from there last month waste of time. Takes you about twenty minutes to get your dick out, end up pissing yourself. I think they were made for the deformed, they're so uncomfortable.'

Well if it takes Freddie, twenty minutes to get his chopper out what chance have the rest us got? He's right though they are bloody uncomfortable, and I've almost pissed myself twice today.

'Who's Coco the Clown?' Scottie, asked.

'He's an old clown from yesteryear, before your time' replied Freddie.'

'Did he have a broken nose?'

'No Scottie, I'll explain later, when we have more time.'

'Things haven't been going too well lately my wife feels ashamed of me. Money worries, I'm shuffling the credit cards around like Paul Daniels, every month. That sister of hers is always filling her head with poison about me. She reckons I should be put away in an asylum. You know what, I don't need giant red boots to be a clown, I've already become one.'

The room went silent for a few seconds, neither Freddie, or Scottie, could look me in the face.

'Come on Robbie,' said Freddie,' 'get a grip, we all go through these tough times. In a couple of weeks, you and Gloria will wonder what all the fuss was about.'

'I doubt it, things were already bad enough with our marriage even before I got knocked out by a super fit cripple That really put the tin hat on it. Can you imagine how I felt, explaining to her, what happened that day, the humiliation, the pain? I just needed someone to comfort me. A kiss on the forehead, a loving arm around my shoulder. Instead all she did was stand there with her arms folded like a block of ice, she told me she was going to her sisters for the day. The underpants, you already know about. She recommended I should piss off and find somewhere else to live in the foreseeable future and don't come back.'

'Well you're still here.' said Scottie, eating the plain biscuits just as quickly as the last lot, 'she hasn't kicked you out of the house yet.'

'No, I suppose I should be grateful for that.'

I find it hard to believe,' said Freddie.

'Yes, it was a bit of a shock to me, to refuse to wash my underpants, the selfish bitch. At first, I thought it was just a bit of over-reaction, but there you are, "piss off," she said, after all those years we've been married, and here I am standing with one big red throbbing nose, and nowhere to go.'

'It probably wasn't much different on the first night of your marriage. I bet something else was red and throbbing on that night, and you definitely knew where that should go.' Scottie, said with a loud laugh.

'That's very funny,' said Freddie.

'No, it's not,' I said, 'It's not very funny at all, I have nightmares all the time.'

'I just can't imagine your wife actually telling you to piss off. I can understand it if she asked you to leave in a firm manner, because you can be a bit strange at times. The way you look at the moment with your broken nose you would scare the shit out of anybody at night lying in bed,' said Freddie.

'You know Freddie, you saying that hasn't made me feel any better at all. I could go to bed wearing a suit of armour and, Gloria, wouldn't notice.'

'Jesus Christ, I've heard of safe sex, but that's ridiculous,' said Scottie,

'Piss off, you insensitive bastard, is that the only reason you've come here tonight, to take the piss and eat me out of house and home.'

'Scottie, was only trying to lighten the situation,' said Freddie. 'Bit clumsy I know but he meant no harm. Listen, Robbie,' Freddie, looked round to make sure Gloria, wasn't about and continued to talk in a low whisper.

'If things aren't going too well in the bedroom there's always a little blue pill, I can get you some dirt cheap.'

Why, do you use them?' I asked. 'No, no, of course not, I have the opposite problem,' said Freddie.

'Why are you two whispering?'

'Just men's talk,' Freddie, said to Scottie.

'Oh, very nice, I must have had a sex change in the middle

41

of the night and the surgeon must have forgot to tell me,' said Scottie. 'You carry on whispering between yourselves while I go to the toilet and powder my nose.'

Freddie, watched Scottie, leave the room before he replied.

'So, do you want some of these pills? They're very good, so I've been told. They do solve a lot of problems.'

Scottie, came back into the room, 'don't mind me gents,' he said as he sat down. 'You carry on having your private little chat.'

'The problems not with me, it's Gloria, she's so frigid,' I said to Freddie.

'She's a very attractive woman,' replied Freddie, 'she's no spring chicken, but she must still have desires, and needs it's only natural, nothing worse than a loveless marriage.'

'Thank you, Freddie, I'm sure Gloria, would love to have it confirmed that she's no spring chicken.'

'There are people you can see, marriage guidance and all that bollocks. You can't continue like this, it's not fair to either of you.'

'Your right Freddie, I'm just sticking my head in the sand.'

'I lied earlier on, I have tried the blue pills, they don't work on me, they just give me indigestion, blurred vision and no hard dick. It's not Gloria's fault, the problem's not on her side,' I said, 'she does need fulfilment. The doctor's been as good as gold, I tried everything, nothing works, I have nightmares.'

'You've told me that already.'

'Yes, but I haven't told you what they're about, it's always the same one. I'm sitting in the doctors waiting room, full of sick people coughing, big scabs on their lips, old people bumping into blind people, deaf people shouting at everyone. Then suddenly the room goes quiet, a young shapely receptionist with bright red lipstick and magnificent looking breast, stands up and looks at me and shouts Mr Floppy, the doctor will see you now. All these sick people standing up and patting me on the back as I pass them shouting in unison like a bunch of mad football supporters.'

'Floppy, Floppy, Floppy.'

'Then as I walk into the doctor's room, he's holding a pair of scissors in his hand. It's usually at this point I wake up dripping with sweat, it's terrifying. I never manage to get a good night's sleep.'

'That's terrible, so what happens if you don't wake up at that point what does he do with his scissors?' Freddie, asked.

'For God's sake, use your imagination,' I said, 'he's not going to give me a haircut. It's all too graphic, gory and decisive,'

Freddie, looked really concerned, 'I'm sorry Robbie.'

'Yes, it's all one big mess,' I replied.

'Must be, blood on his scissors, all over the floor. Did he drop your dick in one of those kidney shaped silver trays? I've always wondered why they make them that shape.'

'I'm not on about my bloody nightmare you big twat I'm talking about my life, It's all one big disaster.'

'That's no way to talk to Freddie,' said Scottie, and then he asked.

'Is it the central heating?'

'Please explain to Robbie, and me, what you're talking about,' said Freddie.

'I'm trying to repair this man's marriage, and he insults me, and now you're going on about the central heating.'

'Well it's a bit difficult, with you two being in whispering mode' said Scottie. 'But I think I've heard enough to convince me you've been talking about the central heating. It's not very nice sitting here being excluded from the conversation just because you two decided it was men's talk. I probably know more about plumbing than you two put together, why all the hush hush?'

'Please, Scottie, there seems to be some confusion here, why do you think Freddie and me, were talking about central heating?'

'It's boring sitting here and nobody to talk too, and there's no more biscuits left. I'd be better off down the pub,' said Scottie, looking sorry for himself.

'Okay Scottie,' I said, 'go down the pub, there's fuck all left to eat here. But please explain, while I still have some breath left in my body, why you think we were talking about central heating?'

'I distinctly heard you say you've got a problem in the bedroom, and it's not on Gloria's side. I'm no idiot. I bet it's a problem with the radiator.' Scottie, said, with a big smile on his face.

'You're so wrong,' said Freddie. 'It was nothing like that at all.'

Scottie, was looking confused.

'I don't understand, why the whispering?' He shook his head.

Freddie, looked at me, he was angry.

'I'm sorry I called you a twat, Freddie. I'm just losing control.'

'That's it,' said Scottie, 'I know what's going on, I've just sorted it out.'

'This should be interesting,' said Freddie, 'explain.'

'It's was the same situation with my Uncle Bertie, he had

cancer and nobody would mention it neither the cancer or where it was. The family would say things like he's got problems downstairs, things are bad in the trouser department. Things like that it was weird. They would all be in the same room and talking about him as though he wasn't there.'

'Please Scottie, where are we going with this?' I asked, with some despair.

'Nobody actually says what they mean. They should get straight to the point. Say things like, "hi Bertie, you're looking good how's the cancer in your arse?'

'Don't you think that's a little blunt,' I said, 'and anyway we weren't talking about cancer.'

'That's the whole point nobody ever says what they mean,' said Scottie. 'He's dead now, poor man.'

'Was that the cancer?'

'No food poisoning his wife, my aunt, she was an awful cook nobody would eat there. Even the dogs would run away if she threw the scraps outside the house and believe me there was always plenty of scraps.'

This is beginning to be like the last scene of an Agatha Christie, novel, I thought to myself. I haven't a clue what's going on.

'You mentioned problems in the bedroom,' said Scottie, I thought you were on about the central heating, but what you meant was you're not doing it with your missus.'

Oh no, thought Freddie. Don't say any more.

'Gloria, you're unable to give her a good knobbing,' said Scottie.

'How dare you?' I replied.

'Just getting to the point', said Scottie, 'by the way, were you joking about that chocolate cake? I'm still hungry.'

'You bastard,' I shouted, as I grabbed him by the throat. Freddie, jumped on top of me, the table flew across the room.

'Stop it Robbie, your killing him!'

'That's the whole idea, die you bastard, die.'

'Don't Robbie,' shouted Freddie, as he was trying to pull me off.

'Don't you think you've got enough problems without you becoming a murderer?'

'It'll be worth it,' I shouted back.

Gloria' rushed into the room, and saved the day, and probably Scottie's life. With the assistance of a large broom and a shrieking voice it was amazing within a few seconds and several broken ornaments scattered across the carpet, she had all three of us standing to attention like naughty school boys.

I was still full of rage, but it didn't compare to the fury that hung-over Gloria's shoulders.

'What on earth is going on? Look at the state of this room you bunch of imbeciles.'

Freddie, was trying to tidy his hair with his hand. Scottie, was holding his throat every time he tried to speak, he sounded like a squawking chicken.

'What's wrong with his throat?' Gloria, asked, expecting an answer straight away.

'He's probably eaten to many biscuits,' I said.

'Don't be stupid.'

Things are looking up, she's talking to me, albeit in a rather brisk manner.

'Freddie, what have you got to say for yourself? I expected

better behaviour from you.' Freddie, was looking awkward and sheepish, his underpants probably choking everything in sight.

'You see Gloria, I was just trying to stop Robbie from strangling Scottie.'

'Oh, is that all, and stand still while I'm talking to you.'

Every time one of us moved there was the crunching of broken crockery beneath our feet.

'Is there anything else I should know?'

'I'm sorry Gloria, it was my fault.' I said, 'thing's just seem to be out of control. Freddie, was right, he was only trying to stop the fight everything seems to be getting on top of me.'

'Apart from Gloria,' squawked Scottie.

'Oh, bollocks,' said Freddie,

'What do you mean?' said Gloria.

'Come on Scottie,' said Freddie, 'Let's fu… let's go home, I think we've caused enough damage for one afternoon.'

Freddie, grabbed Scottie, by the arm. Scottie, wouldn't move.

'Your husband tried to strangle me, he's a lunatic.'

'It seems my husband has been taken over by some form of madness but why would he try to strangle you?'

'Because Scottie's an arsehole' I said. 'I've had to spend the last hour, being laughed at and demoralised, watching all my best biscuits being gobbled up by these two-greedy bastard's.'

'Hang on Robbie, it wasn't me that eat all the biscuits, said Freddie.

'If you continue to behave like this, I'll have you kicked out of the house now. I can't believe a fight started over a packet of crummy biscuits.' Said Gloria. 'What sort of people are you?'

'It was two and a half packets,' I said, 'that would have lasted your sister for a whole year.'

'It was more than just the biscuits.' said Scottie, holding his throat, 'I just upset your husband, because I told him straight, he was trying to blame you at first, but I told him.

'Told him what exactly?' Gloria, asked.

'That he was incapable of giving you a good knobbing.'

Me and Freddie, looked at each other, open mouthed hoping for the ground to swallow us up. What happened next was hard to define. Whether it was fear, the distress of the fight the mayhem in the room, or just the complete inability to understand and deal with the situation. Gloria, looked puzzled as she looked at Freddie. Then she spoke.

'What's a good knobbing?'

'Pardon,' said Freddie.

'A good knobbing, what is it?'

'Come on Gloria, you're having me on surely you're not that naïve?' a slight smile appeared on his face.

'If I knew I wouldn't be asking, what's a good knobbing?'

Freddie, started to laugh, even Gloria, started to smile.

'I suppose it's the opposite to a bad knobbing,' said Freddie, now crying and in a fit of uncontrollable laughter. Scottie, started to laugh, it even made me smile.

'I've got a feeling this is something rude,' said Gloria, still smiling,

'Is it something you can buy from a shop, and I suppose a bad knobbing is something you send back?'

'Please stop it, Gloria, if only it was that simple,' Freddie was doubled up.

'Well, if you won't tell me, I'll ask Scottie.'

'No, NO, 'Don't do that.'

Too late, Scottie explained in his usual blunt way. Gloria, and

everybody else stopped laughing, good knobbing or bad knobbing another fight broke out. But this time it was started by
my dearly beloved. The police turned up, not at all impressed,
they've had enough of me from last week. They arrived at the
house in extra quick time, I checked to see if one of them was
in a wheelchair.

Scottie, was doubled over and talking in a high-pitched
voice, a swift kick from Gloria, in the groin no doubt Telling
him his knobbing days are over. Somebody had punched me
on the nose, the pain was that bad I pissed myself.

The front of my wife's dress was, badly torn and her hair
looked like she'd had an electric shock. Apart from the front of
his shirt hanging out over his trousers, Freddie, looked in one
piece, combing his extra black hair and looking at my wife's
tit's half hanging out of her dress. He doesn't miss a trick, the
two of them look more like they've had a quickie, instead of a
punch up. I must stop thinking like this, my nose is throbbing
like hell. My pants are wet, I did notice Freddie, was going a
bit thin on top. That's made me feel better. As for Scottie, he
can go and fuck himself.

The police gave us all a bollocking, told us if it happens again,
they'll lock us all up. (they always say that.) The younger police
constables where whispering and tittering about my wife's tit's,
it seems the general opinion, was not bad for an old biddy.

The police sergeant suggested that I change my trousers,
because I smelt of piss. My wife was more emphatic, she told
me while I was upstairs to pack my bag, and piss off somewhere
else to live.

On questioning her about this, she replied, 'If you stay, I'll
cut off your nuts while you're asleep in the middle of the night.'

Apart from the pain and the risk of infection, this won't make any difference to our relationship I thought, it's still loveless.

A crowd of nosey neighbours stood outside the house, hoping to see a full body bag or a severed head, something like that. A group of young lads walked past,

'Probably drugs or a brothel for old people' one of them said.

'Goodbye Darling,' I shouted, as I walked out the door, suitcase in my hand.

'Make sure you wipe the blood off the chainsaw before it dries. And see if you can find out who that severed arm belongs too and by the way, the police love your tits.'

I was lucky her favourite vase, one of the few remaining items intact had just missed my head, landed on the ground and shattered into pieces. Just like my life.

Her parting words will stay with me till my dying days.

'Fuck off arsehole, and don't come back.'

My nose is throbbing more than ever, a big lump has appeared on my head a big bruise on my cheek and the clothes I possess are creased and damp and smell of piss, isn't life fun?

'Did you and Gloria, ever think about going to marriage guidance, or something like that,' asked Christine.

'I can see what you're saying, and looking back perhaps I should have tried harder' I was a weak broken man, Christine, it's difficult when your financially broke, tired and depressed,' I paused for a moment, I was finding it hard to speak.'

Christine, looked concerned are you all right, Robbie.'

'I'm all right now, I wasn't back then, It's no fun when you can't even fuck your own wife, I know you said earlier on that

I should face up to the fact that I couldn't get it up, but no woman on the planet would ever understand just how bad and demoralising this can make a man feel.'

'Do you want to carry on with this Robbie, do you want a drink, I didn't mean to upset you.'

'Christine, just get me a Scotch please, and then let's get on with the book.'

4

It had been two days since Gloria, had kicked me out the house I feel and look worse than ever. I shouldn't be back at work really. I feel crap, and I'm likely to scare the shit out of the customers. I tried phoning my wife, but there's no answer.

She's probably having a chin wag with her ugly sister in one of those little restaurants that doesn't sell beer full of old fat women eating chocolate cakes, unable to drink their tea because the handles on the cups are too small. Her sister's probably telling Gloria, it's the best thing she's ever done getting rid of me she should have done it years ago. Filling her head with poison I'm just amazed how vicious these two can be.

However, being self-employed and living with my younger cousin, Casper, is a great incentive to go out to work. One, it's a shithole, and two I'll starve to death.

So, here I am, back on the rank looking like the living dead and trying to avoid Martin.

It was no good, Martin, appeared from nowhere, he slumped himself over my car door.

'I heard you been kicked out the house, Ginger, with your suitcase badly packed, coat sleeve hanging out and some woman chasing you with a chain saw, threatening to cut your nuts off. Added to which your face is in a bit of a mess, things aren't going to well for you at the moment,' said Martin,

'You could say that,' I replied. 'Who told you that?

'Piddling Pete.' said Martin.

'Well, as usual he's got that all wrong,' I replied. 'It didn't happen like that at all.'

'Well I had my doubts,' said Martin. 'It seemed a bit far-fetched to me. I've always thought of you as a tidy person, I can't imagine you having your coat sleeve hanging out of your suitcase.'

I can't imagine myself walking around without my nuts, but that's become a distinct possibility over the last forty-eight hours. I thought to myself.

'That wasn't very nice, what you said to me the other day.'

'I'm sorry Martin, I was wrong to call you all those names.'

'So, who was chasing you with a chain saw?'

'No one.' I replied, 'Piddling Pete's got it all wrong.'

'Oh, that's a shame,' said Martin, at that point he pulled the handle off my car door.

'Oh, dear me Ginger, look what I've done,' he stared at me. 'Next time it'll be your neck.'

'Martin, I said I was sorry.'

'That's okay,' said Martin, 'we're all square at the moment. I don't bear a grudge.'

Not much you don't I thought to myself.

'So where are you living at the moment, at your sister in laws?'

'No way, we can't stand the site of each other, she's caused so much trouble between me and Gloria.'

'How's the wife?' somebody shouted from a passing car, it was Scottie, giving me the 'V' sign.

'Does she, need any help in bed?' He shouted at the top of his voice.

'What's Scottie on about?' asked Martin. 'Helping your wife in bed?'

'The little shit was just being sarcastic I think I'll just go down to the sandwich bar; I'm feeling a little peckish.'

I can't believe Martin's just pulled my door handle off, the fat bastard, I thought to myself. I wasn't really hungry I just wanted to get away from Martin, and get my car door fixed. I phoned up Casper, he was always good at that sort of thing.

'There you go Robbie, all done.'

It took him ten minutes. '

'Try not to upset Martin, anymore, you know it's not good for your health, you look terrible. No chance Gloria's, asked you back then?'

'No, she can be a hateful bastard,' I replied.

I thanked Casper, and popped into the sandwich bar, sat down and ordered a mini breakfast. Big Vicky, served me.

'You look tired.'

Vicky, had blonde hair and wore bright pink lipstick that matched the colour of her tight-fitting cardigan.

'Still not back with the wife then? It's not right for a man not to have a woman to look after him, sleeping in a cold bed on his own.'

'I suppose it's not,' I said, trying to avoid looking at her large breasts as she thrust them over the table.

'Are you still with Barry?' I asked.

'No, that didn't work out I didn't realise he had false teeth. He used to leave them all over the place it could be quite disturbing at times. You haven't got false teeth have you Robbie?'

'No Vicky,' I said.

'He used to fart and snore a lot, we just weren't compatible.'

The mini breakfast was very tasty, and seemed to contain more eggs, sausage and bacon than I expected. I thanked Vicky, and paid her, she gave me a couple of rounds of toast wrapped in paper and placed it in my hand.

'There you go Robbie, that should keep you going for a couple of hours, you're always welcome here.'

I could hardly move, the amount of food I had just eaten but I managed, to drive back on rank, it was still very quiet.

'You missed your chance there Robbie,' said Christine, 'I'm sure Vicky, would have looked after you better than Casper.'

'You could be right but Casper, is very good at repairing cars. He's very good with his hands. Anyway Christine, let's get back to the book.'

'I decided to go down to the job agency, try something different, but it was a waste of time.'

'Why don't you want to do taxi work anymore?' asked the receptionist. 'The money you guys charge you should be making a fortune take a seat and someone will see you shortly.'

She picked up the phone and continued talking to someone about her new boyfriend and how lovely he is.

It was a dull room that looked in desperate need of T.L.C. On one side of the room was a large glass window, which was more or less from the floor to the ceiling and overlooked the main road. There was a mad dog trying to eat a bag of chips and meat pie that someone had discarded on the pavement the night before. It was half flattened by a big footprint he must have been very hungry, he barked at everyone that walked past, you could see people swerving past him, telling the dog to 'fuck off.'

There was an out of date calendar of a youthful Cliff Richard, in swimming trunks hanging up by the receptionist's desk, someone had drawn pubic hairs growing out of the side of his pants.

'I bet you did that Robbie, you were always drawing dirty pictures at school,' said the fellow sitting next to me.

'You don't recognise me, do you? We were in the same class at school,'

'That was a long time ago,' I said, 'and I don't remember any one with a bald head and a beard.'

He started to laugh.

'You're still a sarcastic bastard I can't remember you having ginger hair, and you've certainly put on some timber.'

'Go on, you'll have to tell me, who are you,'

'Sammy, Sammy Blick,' he replied.

'Good God, Sammy, great to see you, what are you doing here?'

'Looking for a job, why else would I be here? I used to work at the local abattoir but they caught me nicking a leg of lamb. I used to steal meat for my mates and family, they'd pay me a few bob or buy me a drink. I was unlucky really, just as I had finished my shift, they called an emergency staff meeting about someone that had died on the premises. I had the leg of lamb stuffed down the front of my trousers and it had begun to thaw. We had a new female security guard who wasn't corrupt like the rest of the officers. When she asked me, what was the lump at the front of my trousers I tried to joke it off. I'm just a bit bigger than most men,' I said.

'That didn't go down to well, within seconds she had my trousers down to my ankles and the leg of lamb in her hand,

I didn't know she was a black belt in origami.'

'Origami, isn't that something to do with folding paper?'

'Well some name like that, she made me look a complete idiot.'

Just then, the hungry dog outside gave a loud yelp as he flew past the window eight foot in the air.

'Someone out there obviously isn't a dog lover,' said Sammy.

We had a good chat about our school days. Sammy and I gave the agency all our details Sammy, lied a little about his quick departure from the abattoir. Some dear old lady brought the dog inside the office,

' I think this poor thing has had an accident.' As he laid there in her arms looking distinctly cross eyed and his tongue hanging out. I left the agency not feeling too hopeful, but it was good talking to Sammy hope he finds work the thieving little get.

I jumped back in my taxi and drove back on rank.

So, your wife's okay?' Asked Martin.

'She's bruised her knee and broken a fingernail, but she's okay. I don't think she's traumatised or anything like that, I believe there's been plenty of talk down at the police station about how nice her tits are for an old un.'

'Traumatised, said Martin, 'that's when they're fucked up in the head, is she just lying their tongue hanging out staring into space saying nothing?'

'My wife may not be saying anything to me, but I'm sure she's talking to most people as we speak, she's probably on the phone inquiring about medical appliances that specialise in castration. The only thing that was hanging out last time I saw her wasn't her tongue, just her tits.'

'No, she's not traumatised or anything like that in fact with me out of the house she's happier than she's been for years.'

Martin, looked puzzled, again.

'let's change the subject.' I said

'You do look like a bag of shit.'

'Thank you, Martin,' I said, angrily.

'There's no need to shout,' said Martin.

'My nose and face hurts and that's one big laugh, I have no money in the bank, the manager is really pleased about that and then you tell me I look like a bag of shit. Well let me tell you Martin, have you looked at yourself lately? It's a wonder you can get in and out of the car with your big arse'

'Just shut the fuck up, said Martin.'

He grabbed me round the neck, oh shit this is it.

'Let him go Martin,' it was Freddie. Where the hell did, he come from, maybe Freddie, is God in disguise? God with dyed black hair. Somehow that doesn't seem right.

'Let him go,' said Freddie. 'Robbie, doesn't know what he's saying at the moment, breaking his neck won't make things any better.'

At this moment I was incapable of saying anything, I was chocking.

'The bastard's been insulting to me; I've got my reputation to think of.' said Martin.

'Your reputation won't mean much by strangling a mad man,'

Thank you, Freddie, I thought to myself, I might be going dizzy through a lack of blood but I can still hear. A nervous breakdown sounds better than a madman.

'Anyway, 'said Martin, 'what the fuck has this got to do with you Freddie?' you two aren't exactly the best of friends and your mate Scottie, doesn't seem too fond of Robbie boy, either.'

'I just don't think it's right to kick a man when he's down,' said Freddie.

'Well I've done that for years, made quite a good living from time to time,' said Martin.' He released me from his grip and I fell to ground on to my hands and knees. although I felt like shit it was nice to be able to breathe again.

'You all right, Robbie boy, I've known you too long to really hurt you,' said Martin.

'But if you insult me again, I'll insert your balls right down your throat, you'll be spitting pubic hairs for months.'

Martin, looked at Freddie.

'Well Freddie, the shows over Robbie's still alive you can piss off now.'

'Can I have a drink of water Christine; all this talking has made my throat dry.'

'Help yourself, you're sure it's not the thought of Martin, trying to strangle you. Was there anything nice about the man.'

I thought for a moment, 'No there was nothing, I'm sure Casper, must have told you that.' I took a sip of water.

'I hope you're not getting bored writing this book' I asked Christine.'

'No, I'm fine. I'll just cut out the boring parts, why are you staring at me like that.'

'I'm sorry I didn't mean to, it's just that you seem to know so much about me and apart from the fact you look great in tight blue jeans I know hardly anything about you.'

Christine, smiled.

'That's very kind of you Robbie, you don't think they make my bum look big.' I paused for a moment.

'I think they make your arse look massive.'

'What.' Christine, shouted with disgust.

'Take it easy, I was only joking.' I started laughing.

'You bastard, fancy saying a thing like that.'

'Christine, it was a joke. You know very well your arse looks great or you wouldn't have asked me the question in the first place.'

'I still think you're a pig.'

Christine, started to laugh.

'If it's any consolation,' you looked gorgeous' the first time I set eyes on you.'

'Shall we carry on with the book said Christine, I think Martin, had just dropped you on the ground, after half strangling you, that would have been worth seeing.

'let's calm down.' I said, 'Martin, I'm sorry if I offended you and Freddie, thanks for trying to calm things down, even though I'm not too happy about being called a mad man. I know I'm not myself at the moment and it doesn't help me when things are mentioned about me and my wife. So, can we just change the subject, please.'

Everything went silent.

Thanks Freddie, I thought, he did try to help me I just hope the bastard keeps away from my wife.

'I'm glad Freddie, poked his nose in when he did,' said Martin, 'the revolting little shit. I would have felt terrible if I'd have strangled someone who was completely barmy.'

'Now Robbie boy, don't speak to me like that again,

understand.'

'I'm sorry, Martin, I promise I won't do it again.'

'That's fine,' he replied, 'we're all the best of pals, I'm glad about that.'

'So am I, Martin, so am I,'

'Well let's hope it's taught you a lesson,' said Martin. 'All for some and some for others, as they say in *The Three Musketeers.*'

I couldn't be bothered to tell him the correct saying.

'Thank you, Martin, we must have more of these meaningful little chats,'

'Go on Robbie boy, piss off, clean yourself up and do some work, and try not to frighten the customers with that lumpy head of yours.'

Martin, really amused himself with that last comment, and burst out laughing. Suddenly it started to snow oh no, I thought, please God, no white shit.

Taxi drivers hate Snow, maybe it's just a slight shower, no it wasn't, it just snowed and snowed. After three days of snowing, the weather decided to freeze, sub-zero temperatures for the next two weeks. The roads were impossible to drive. So, I'm stuck, in this two-bedroom flat with my cousin Casper. Bollocks, shit happens at the worst of times, even though this gives me time for my face to heal I need to be out working I hate this snow. It was good of Casper, to let me stay here for a while and it's fair to say it's not a small flat, at least it wouldn't be if it wasn't full of rubbish he brings home from the tip.

He has this obsession with bringing anything home that will fit in his car and repairing them (most of the time).

At the moment we have several kettles, vacuums, laptops, car parts, a manakin, large empty bottles, a pink corset, two toilet seats, a broken condom dispensing machine, and many more items.

'Christine, are you sure you want me to continue about living with Casper, or has he told you enough already.'

'No, I would like to hear your version of events.'

'Casper, may have had all this rubbish but I was in desperate need of an iron. He would always say don't worry about the creases in your shirt just wear it, after ten minutes the heat of your body will get rid of all that.

'You'll look fine.' Casper, use to say.

'Just like one of those male model's you see on the telly wearing after shave, or some shit like that.'

'Casper, I need an iron.'

'Oh, stop moaning,' said Casper, I might not have an iron but a lot of this stuff is useful'

'Like what?' I asked.

'Sometimes I sell car parts that I repair often for your lot,'

'Who's my lot?'

'Taxi drivers.'

'I do a fair amount of business with them, Freddie the flirt, is one of my best customers.' said Casper. 'He's bought that condom vending machine off me and the gentleman's abdominal support,'

'The condom machine,' I said,

'I can just imagine the scene.' I said, 'Freddie, showing his latest girlfriend his bedroom providing her with change and quickly discarding his corset and kicking it under the bed while his latest conquest decides what type of condom to go for, all very romantic.'

'I think your jealous of Freddie,' said Casper.

'Me, jealous of him, of course not.'

'He gets plenty of girlfriends that's why he needs a corset, all this sex has weakened his back' said Casper. 'He gets more pussy than you or I get put together.'

'Well that's not hard to do, and anyway have you seen some of the old tails he knocks about with?'

'Well he's been shagging that barmaid with the dark hair and big tits, you know, the one you fancy.'

'I don't fancy her; I just think she's a nice girl that's all. I don't believe she'd be going out with an old man who dyes his hair and wears a corset she must be half his age,' I said.

'I don't think you should be talking about people who dye their hair,' said Casper.

'Anyway, Freddie's younger than you,' he added.

'Listen, I don't fancy her, the thought of that poor innocent girl being groped by that slimy oversexed maniac makes me feel sick.'

'Listen Robbie, I don't think she's that innocent.'

'I gave her a tip last month, the bitch'

'Well, that sort of gave the game away you never tip anybody.'

'That's not true I gave old Gracie, a tip last Christmas.'

'Well done,' said Casper,' Two tips in twelve months that's very generous of you.'

'Well; Christmas spirit, that sort of thing. Come to think of it I haven't seen Gracie, for ages,' I said.

'I'm not surprised they buried her shortly after Christmas day.' 'said Casper.

'She's dead?'

'I hope so, they may do some strange things in this town,

but I don't think they've started burying people alive yet. She went home after working Christmas day and had a massive heart attack it was probably that tip you gave her; it was too much of a shock for the poor old dear.'

'That's not funny.'

'I guess not, the landlord was deeply upset,' said Casper.

'Were they close?'

'Not really, he couldn't get anybody to cover her shift, he had to work behind the bar himself. He was furious, swearing at the customers, sweating away with his bright red face telling them to fuck off if they questioned him about overcharging.'

'Was he?' I asked, with mock surprise.

'Not exactly,' said Casper, he was just short changing everybody. It didn't help that his wife was standing at the end of the bar wearing her blonde wig telling him who to serve next while she was eating a big chocolate Gateaux and flirting with the local rugby team.'

'Perhaps she was hoping for a game,' I said, 'anyway Casper, all this talk isn't going to sort my iron out.'

'Sorry Robbie, I never thought you'd be so fussy.'

I looked out of the window everywhere was still covered in snow. I'll go mad if I stay here much longer, I thought to myself. I even phoned Gloria, and I pleaded with her to have me back I told her that I loved her very much and I've seen the error of my ways. I told her that I am now a better man; I even promised to be nice to her sister.

Gloria, paused for a moment, and in a most sarcastic manner she said,

'What's up, run out of clean underpants? goodbye. And don't bother me again.'

Yes, I was disappointed with her ice-cold reply but I won't let it get to me. The shallow bastard I'm a better man now my face is healing nicely. I can rise above this and besides I've still got four pair of pants left you cold hearted blood sucking bastard, I hope you and your self-righteous sister fester in hell.

As for me, I'll just ride out the storm and stay with my industrious little cousin. It's a little like living with 'Santa Clause,' He brings home a present every day apart from an iron

'Listen Casper,' I said, 'girlie or not I'm going down to the local stores and I'm going to buy myself an iron.'

'The store is closed,' said Casper, the central heating broke down, it is too cold for the staff to work.'

'Marvellous,' I said, 'a bit of snow, and the whole country comes to a standstill. Nobody cares anymore.'

'Well you're not working,' said Casper.'

'That's different,' I said, 'it's dangerous on the roads, it doesn't matter how carefully I drive, some prat will skid into me and, 'bang', I'm off the road for weeks.'

'I saw Martin, driving down the road yesterday,' said Casper, 'he was driving very slowly. I'm not certain if that was because of the road conditions or the fact that he was trying to consume what looked like a giant kebab.'

'It was probably a dead cat' I replied.

'You wouldn't say that to his face,' said Casper.

'I might, I told him he'd got a big arse the other day.'

'You told Martin; he's got a big arse. Fuck off, I don't believe that.'

'I did, in fact I can't remember if I said he had a big arse or a huge one I was in such a fit of temper at the time. You know I think I scared him a little. Martin, respects me.'

Casper, looked at me for a short while. 'Is that why he had your head in an armlock? That's a funny way of showing respect.'

'We were just mucking about,' I replied, 'I was just showing Martin, a few wrestling moves.'

'Oh really, it all sounded very realistic to me. So, when you dropped to your hands and knees was that because you were in fits of laughter? and was Freddie the flirt, pretending to be the referee? I always thought his physical attributes were of a slightly different nature.'

'Did that ageing Romeo tell you all this?' I shouted, 'you can't believe a word of it.'

'I don't need to I know Martin, and I know you. Martin, doesn't respect you or anyone else so spare me this crap.'

'Oh, very nice,' I said. 'Well, respect or no respect, if I don't see an iron in this flat in the next twenty-four hours, I might tell him about a certain kleptomaniac who works for the council has been sniffing around his daughter.'

Casper, stared at me, 'you know Robbie, you can be a hateful bastard at times.'

'Only at times,' I replied, 'I must try harder.'

'I take you in and spoil you when nobody else cares a shit about you, I give you some useful hints how you should dress and you start threatening me with heavies,' said Casper, 'anyway that's history and Martin's not the thug he used to be.'

'He can still handle himself regardless of what I've just said, 'that's why he's still driving around in this ice and snow.'

'I Don't follow.' said Casper.

'If Martin, has a bump, it won't be a question of apologies exchanging insurance policies admitting blame. Nothing like that, he just threatens the driver of the other car to accept blame and pay for all the damage within hours, or suffer the physical consciences.'

'You're exaggerating,' said Casper, 'If things where that bad, he wouldn't be driving around in a taxi, the council wouldn't issue him a licence.'

'Fear Casper,' I said. 'The council's shit scared of him. Martin, just takes his car to the council garage for his taxi MOT, they don't even open the bonnet. They just give the seats a wipe issue him with a certificate wish him the time of day and tell him they'll see him again in twelve months' time. I don't know why they bother; they may as well just send it through the post.'

'But he still has to apply for a taxi driver badge,' said Casper.

'You're very knowledgeable about all this,' I said. 'Did his daughter tell you about all this while you were fondling her that night at the back of the tip?'

'I've told you Robbie, that's history and besides it was in the graveyard at the back of the church.'

'The graveyard,' I replied, 'How romantic you certainly know how to show a girl a good time.'

Then Casper, started to tell me about his night of hot passion and how he persuaded Martina, to see were his favourite uncle Frank, was laid to rest. How Frank, had brought him up after his mom and dad died when he was a young boy if it hadn't been for his uncle, he would have been a broken young man, suicidal and in desperate need of a woman's love.

Then Casper, continued to tell me how he could feel the passion between him and Martina, as they lay down next to his uncle Frank, she was turned on by his fragile vulnerability.

He said she whispered in his ear, take me Casper, you have

me to look after you now, I will always love you, Casper, said he was going dizzy with excitement.

I looked at Casper,

'I have never heard so many lies in my life.' I said to him, 'your uncle spent most of his life in prison and both your parents are alive and well.'

'Come on Robbie,' said Casper, 'You know what it's like when the urge takes over.'

'What happened next.' I replied

Casper, looked at me with anger.

'My fucking mother phoned me up. and that just completely ruined the night.'

'At this point I had my hanky in my mouth, trying desperately not to laugh.

'Go on,' said Casper, 'You have a good laugh at my expense, that was the last time either of those women spoke to me.'

'Please Casper, no more,' I said, 'I'll have a heart attack. 'So, I suppose Martina, went home and told her Dad? Honestly Casper, it was a good job you didn't shag her you would have ended up lying next to Uncle Frank, with your balls in your mouth. Didn't you realise who her dad was?'

'No, not at all I heard about some hard case taxi driver with a big arse but I didn't realise I was messing about with his daughter.'

'He came banging on my door the next night.'

'Did he kick the shit out of you?'

'No, when I answered the door, he just looked at me, pushed me aside, walked into the room and looked around. I'd never seen him before, but I knew who he was.'

'Was that because you could feel the evilness about him, that threatening look in his eyes?' I asked

'No' said Casper, 'I recognised his big arse, Martina, had told me about that. When he finished walking around the room, he walked up to me toe to toe. I must admit at this stage I was getting really scared and then as he spoke, he grabbed me tight by the balls.'

'Oh no, what did he say?'

'He told me to keep away from his daughter, or he'll rip my balls off and shove all the rubbish in this room up my arse.'

If there was as much rubbish in the room then as there is now, losing your balls might be the lesser of two evils, I thought to myself.

'You were lucky,' I said to Casper. 'Don't you think you should have got rid of some of this rubbish just in case Martin, had a change of heart?'

'I did at first it all felt very lonely I could see all four walls, but after a few months I got back to my old self.'

'I can see that,' I replied

'That was the last time I had any sort of sex,' said Casper.

5

'Well,' said Christine, 'That's a slightly different version to the one Casper, told me, still let's carry on with the book, tell me what happened next.'

'Suddenly there was a knock-on Casper's door, it was Freddie.'

'Hello, Robbie boy, your face is looking a lot better, I didn't realise you were staying here with Casper. Piddling Pete, told me you were staying at your sister in law's.'

'Piddling Pete', I said 'Does he ever get anything right, the big twat?'

'Well, I knew you didn't get on to well with her,'

'That's putting it mildly,' I said. 'Have you ever met the old cow?'

'No, I can't say I have,' said Freddie. 'Is she married?'

'Used to be, her husband Horace, saw sense one day and pissed off with a young girl who worked in the local fish and chip shop. She had the worst squint you could ever wish to see.'

'Who had the squint, your sister in law, or the girl who worked in the chippy?' Freddie, asked.

'The girl that worked in the chippy.' I replied. 'You could never be certain if she was looking at you or someone else halfway down the street but she always had one eye fixed on Horace. Tessa, the sister in law never got over it.'

'Since that day she hated men especially me and very rarely

would she eat a bag of chips. A battered sausage is completely out of the question.'

'So apart from hating men and battered sausage, what exactly is wrong with her?' Freddie, asked.

'Everything' I replied. 'She's just horrible, even you wouldn't fuck her.'

'Blimey,' said Casper. 'is she that bad?'

'Yes, she is.'

'I think I know this girl who works in the chip shop.' said Casper. 'She's a nice girl really, she just gets a bit confused if the customers are standing to close together.'

'You try telling my sister in law that the girl who took her husband away is nice' I said. 'So, tell Piddling Pete, to get his facts right,' I told Freddie, 'there's absolutely no way I would be staying at my sister in laws.'

'I was down at Piddling Pete's this morning,' said Freddie. 'He's still got that mad dog of his. Everywhere you walk he's trying to bite your leg off. And if you sit down on the wrong chair he jumps on your lap and tries to bite off your dick. He must be one of the oldest dogs I've ever seen, the mad little bastard.'

'Dear me, Freddie, that would be a disaster you with your dick in tatters. The local lasses would be distraught, they'd have to take up knitting or play bingo, something like that. Perhaps he was just jealous?'

'Jealous, I don't follow,' said Freddie.

'Well maybe he could smell some old dog that's had their nose up there before, he was only trying to get rid of any competition by biting your dick off and burying it in the garden.'

Freddie, looked angry, 'are you suggesting I fuck dogs?'

'Sarcastic. He's always sarcastic,' said Casper, 'Take no notice of Robbie, what can I do for you Freddie?'

'I just wanted a word with you in private Casper.'

'Private is it?' I said. 'If you like I'll stand over here out of the way so you two can discuss things.'

While Freddie, and Casper, were having a quiet chat I looked out the window and to my surprise the snow had started to thaw. Thank God for that I'm desperate for some cash.

'Oh, by the way Freddie, thanks for calming things down the other day between Martin, and myself, I do appreciate it.'

'That's okay Robbie, I know things have been a little tough lately, nobody likes to see anyone get a good hiding.'

'Yes,' I said, 'Martin, was lucky that day, only joking.' Freddie, laughed.

'Come on let's go down the boozer, I'll buy you and Casper, a drink.'

'Have you and Casper, finished your little business chat?'

'Yes, I needed a part for my car but Casper, can't help me.'

'Oh, nothing else?' I asked, thinking he might need a condom vending machine for each room or a spare abdominal appliance.

Freddie, looked at me and stared. 'No, nothing else,' he replied. Let's go and have a drink before I change my mind. Haven't you a decent coat to wear?' Freddie, asked me.

'I haven't a decent anything to wear,' I replied. 'Perhaps I'll just stay here like Cinderella, and let you two go to the ball.'

'For fucks sake Robbie, don't start all that self-pity shit again,' said Freddie. 'The snow's started to thaw you'll soon be able to earn a few bob again.

Get yourself a dozen new underpants your face is healing nicely. Well within reason everything is tickety-boo, you'll be fine.'

'Freddie's right,' said Casper, 'I've got a nice coat you can borrow.   I found it on the rubbish dump the other day it will make you look a lot smarter. Just keep your left hand in your pocket, there's a big rip under the arm you're right-handed so it won't matter, you'll look the dog's bollocks.'

'More likely, I'll smell like the dog's bollocks.'

'There you go again, all these negative thoughts,' said Casper.'

'What the hell, let's go for it,' I replied, 'but I don't won't to get pissed. With a bit of luck I'll be back on the road again tomorrow.'

'We'll see,' said Freddie.

So, there I stood in an overcoat that was three sizes too small for me with a big rip under the arm. I'm hardly able to pick up my pint of beer because the sleeve was that tight it was almost impossible to bend my arm. I was sweating like a pig and smelt like one.

'Alright Robbie boy, the coat looks great,' Casper, said. 'Like it was made to measure. He took a big sip of his beer.

'Piss off Casper, I look ridiculous.'

'No, you don't, I've told you before tight fitted clothes are all the fashion these days. A few pints down your neck and you'll be fine,'

'It smells,' I said.

'Everything smells,' said Casper, 'But in different ways.'

'That's very true Casper, and this coat smells of shit.' Freddie, was busy talking and laughing to some big girl he'd never met before with a tattoo on her forehead.

'Freddie, doesn't waste any time with the women, said Casper.

'No, the old smoothie, is he wearing his corset tonight,' I replied.

'I told you, it's a gentleman's abdominal support appliance,' replied Casper.

'Every time I mention this subject you give it a different name. It's a corset and if I don't get this coat off soon, I'm going to faint.'

'Help me take it off Casper, I feel really ill.'

'Robbie, you don't look too good you're all pale and sweaty. Freddie, give me a hand,' Casper, shouted. 'Robbie's, dying we need to get his coat off.'

'Do you mind Casper,' said Freddie, 'I'm having a meaning-ful conversation with Belinda.'

· 'Freddie just help Casper, get this damn coat off me it's that bloody tight we might have to call the fire brigade.'

'Oh, all right,' said Freddie, 'I'll give you a hand. My word you do look ill.'

'I think it's that tight, it's stopped the blood going to my brain.'

As the two of them were trying to get my coat off, Freddie, said 'This coat smells a bit earthy.'

'It shouldn't do, I gave it a good spray with toilet cleaner before I put it on Robbie,' replied Casper.'

'I feel sick, my legs have gone weak,' I whimpered.

'You better get that drunk out of here!' It was the gaffer's missus.

'We don't tolerate drunken old tramps in this establishment look at him, he can barely stand.'

'He's not drunk, he's ill, he's had some sort of funny turn,' said Freddie.' He hasn't even finished his first drink.'

'Please get me out of here I feel awful.'

'They all say that,' replied the landlady, 'he's probably been drinking meth's all day now just piss off all three of you.'

'I don't think I like your tone Madam,' said Freddie.

'You tell her Freddie,' said Belinda, 'the snotty nosed old cow you wouldn't be talking to us like that if we were one of your lover boys from the rugby club.'

Freddie, and Casper, were still trying to get the coat of me when suddenly Belinda, and the gaffer's wife were grappling on the floor pulling each other's hair. The room was swaying. It was difficult to define whether Casper, and Freddie, pulled the coat off me or I just popped out of it.

Please get me out of here, I thought to myself as I slumped on my elbows sliding down the bar.

Freddie, and Casper, just stood there in shock, watching Belinda, with her arm held high with a wig in her hand, running around performing a red Indian war dance being chased around the lounge by a bald-headed landlady!

'I didn't realise they did live entertainment,' said Casper.

'Only on Tuesdays,' said Freddie.

I suddenly threw up all over the bar.

'Let's piss off,' said Freddie, as Belinda, kneed some muscular young man in the balls.

'You grab Robbie one side I'll grab the other, let's go quickly.'

'What about Belinda? Casper, asked.

'She's seems to be doing all right to me,' said Freddie, as another young man fell to the ground in pain holding his testicles.

'Come on Robbie, try to walk. If the rest of the rugby team turn up, we're fucked. Move those skinny legs of yours.'

'I'm trying Freddie, I just feel so ill.'

'We'll all be feeling ill if we don't get out of here now. You've just thrown up over a couple of the bar staff and Belinda, castrated two of the rugby team. She's really pissed off the gaffer's missus and you smell worse than ever.'

Fresh air, thank God, I thought to myself.

'That's its Robbie boy,' said Casper, 'keep running,'

'I can't keep running I need a hospital.'

'Listen,' said Freddie. 'Me and Casper, are holding you up on both sides, but we need you to use your legs. I've got a bad back.'

Suddenly the three of us fell over in the snow I laid on my back. I had banged my head; I could feel it bleeding. I could hear Freddie, groaning.

'I've broke my leg, I can't move it,' Casper, was silent.

It was dark, but standing over me, I could see the silhouette of a large figure with a blonde wig in her hand.

'Your mate just fucked off; I hope you two weren't thinking of leaving after all I've done for you tonight.' It was Belinda.

'The lads were just trying to get me out of harm's way. I don't know what's wrong with me I just feel very ill we need to get away from here.'

'Oh, don't worry about anybody in the pub. One or two of the locals started laughing at the bald landlady and the fact you vomited over some of the bar staff caused a few more laughs. So, they ended up fighting amongst themselves, bunch of wankers.'

As she was talking, I could hear Freddie, moaning about

his leg,

'It's broke,' he said.

I started to go dizzy.

'That's a bad gash on your head,' said Belinda, her voice was becoming fainter.

'Don't let me faint,' I said.

'You know what' said Belinda, 'I love a good fight I find it exhilarating. If I sat on your face right now there would be nothing you could do about it.'

'I suffer with asthma,' I shouted, 'try Freddie, he has more of an appetite for that sort of thing. I heard he can breathe through his ears.'

'Appetite? I don't want you to eat it, maybe a bit of a soft chew,' replied Belinda, 'anyway you smell like shit.'

I fainted, whatever happened in those next few minutes I dread to think. I woke up in an ambulance and my head was aching. I think there must have been a problem with the paramedic. He kept asking me what day it was, how many fingers were on his hands and repeating my name several times. That must be terrible to have such a bad memory for someone in such an important job. I looked round the ambulance. Freddie, was lying next to me.

'You're awake, you bastard, you've really fucked me up this time, you shit head.'

'Freddie, what do you mean?'

'Now, Now, no arguments please,' said the paramedic. 'I know you are both stressed it's only natural, but you must calm down. Once we get you both to hospital, we'll get you sorted out. I'm sure a good bath wouldn't go amiss,' he said, looking me up and down his hands were clenched together, as though he was going to pray for us.

'I've never been so humiliated in my life,' said Freddie, and you pretending to faint and what happened to Casper? He's younger and fitter than either of us, the bastard just fucked off.'

'Self-preservation I suppose. Listen Freddie, I genuinely fainted.'

'How very convenient,' said Freddie.

'What happened to Belinda?'

'She did her best the rest of the rugby team turned up, well most of them. She managed to knock a couple to the ground but in the end, there were too many of them. I couldn't do anything with my bad back and broken leg. Mind you she must have a chance of getting a game next week she was pretty impressive.'

'We're not certain if it's broken yet,' said the paramedic as he looked at Freddie's leg.

'What's' your name?' Freddie, asked.

'Gus.'

'Okay Gus, is this my leg or some other fucker's leg we're talking about? We're not talking about your leg or Robbie's leg or even the driver's leg, it's my leg so I should know if it's broken or not, okay Gus.'

'Don't take it out on Gus, Freddie, and anyway let's suppose if your leg hadn't been broken and you hadn't got a bad back. Are you saying you would have gone to Belinda's rescue?'

'Fuck that,' said Freddie, 'I would have run down the road quicker than shit through a goose. Those rugby players are big bustards I should have pretended to have fainted like someone else I know. I wouldn't stand too close to, Robbie,' said Freddie, looking at Gus. 'He has a habit of vomiting over people. I'll be off work for weeks with this leg I can't afford that, I'll end up a broken wreck like you Robbie. That's a bad looking dent in your head I hope it hurts like fuck.   I go out for a quiet drink and all hell breaks loose.'

'You can't blame me for that,' I said, 'you were the one talking to mighty woman. She caused all the trouble pulling off the landlady's wig,'

'Then you threw up over the bar staff,' said Freddie. 'You're a right Jonna, every were you go you cause problems. This is the third punch up you've been involved in as many weeks. I couldn't believe it when we were all lying there in the snow,' said Freddie. 'I saw Casper, get up and run off holding his arm, I'm begging for somebody to help me up. That Belinda's is never right, I saw her standing over you as you were shouting for help,'

'Oh no, what happened then?' I asked, in sheer panic.

'Then she came over to me,' said Freddie.

Oh, thank God for that, I thought to myself.

'She stood over me,' Freddie, continued, 'saying a good fight makes her horney and is it true, can I breathe through my ears?'

'She sounds a bit sassy,' said Gus.

'Mental,' said Freddie.

'So, was she the one that !?'

'That's enough,' said Freddie, starring at Gus. 'I don't won't to talk about it, it was so humiliating and painful. I'll tell you this you certainly find out who your real friends are in times like this. One pretends to do a girly faint and the other just fucks off.'

'Freddie, I have got the most painful headache,' I said, 'let me just go to sleep.'

'No, don't go to sleep we will be at the hospital soon' said Gus, 'you need to stay awake.'

'Freddie, I swear I passed out. I can't remember anything after we all fell over apart from Belinda, standing over me, everything went dark.'

'You honestly can't remember what happened next?' Freddie, asked.

'Nope not a thing, I can only imagine the police turned up and saved the day.'

'They took ages,' said Freddie. 'Belinda, ran off minus her dress I was just left there on my own. The lynch mob left you alone, probably because you smelt of spew and pretending to be dead.'

'Well apart from a broken leg, you don't look to bad, no cuts and bruises', I said. 'I think you've been very lucky.'

'Lucky! shouted Freddie, 'do you want to know what those big bastards with their deformed necks and shoulders did to me?'

'A few minutes ago, you said you didn't want to talk about it.'

'Well I've changed my mind,' said Freddie, angrily. 'They pulled off my shirt and coat.'

'Wouldn't it be the other way around? 'Gus, inquired.

'What?' Replied Freddie.

'You said they pulled of your shirt and coat, it would have to be coat and shirt they wouldn't be able to take your shirt off before your coat.'

'Young man, these bastards did.'

'And much to their delight they discovered I was wearing an abdominal support appliance and before anybody say's anything, no it is not a corset. All the time I'm screaming in agony with my broken leg. They all took it in turns to wear it then they put it back on me and tied me to a lamp post, pulled my trousers down and shoved a carrot up my arse.'

'How did you know it was a carrot?' I asked. 'You wouldn't know if you were tied to a lamp post looking the other way.'

'I told him,' said Gus, 'as I pulled it out.'

'Okay that's enough of that,' said Freddie. 'It was painful. How anyone can become gay, is totally beyond me.'

'Well, they would usually use a lubricant,' said Gus. There was a slight pause,

'I think we better change the subject.' said Freddie.

'So, what where the police doing?' I asked.

'The bastards' said Freddie, 'they were taking selfies standing next to me, they thought it was hilarious. Between the laughter they just about managed to tell the rugby players to piss off. Gus, convinced the police that even though you smelt like a rotting corpse you were still alive. Meanwhile, the gaffer's wife was walking about looking for her wig, wearing a big hat that she must have used for Ascot. I suppose you could say it was a very eventful few minutes it's a shame you and Casper, missed all the fun, you pair of bastards.'

'We're at the hospital now,' said Gus, 'They'll soon sort you out here. Cheer up Freddie, you're in good hands, and Robbie, with a bit of luck you might even get a nice shower.'

After several hours of waiting, a few test and examinations, it was decided I should stay in the hospital overnight. They sent Freddie, to another part of the hospital as soon as we were taken through the main entrance, so that was nice. He was still moaning as he was wheeled out of site down one of the many corridors. I don't think he'll ever believe that I really fainted.

Gus, had put my coat in a plastic bag and started to call me Joseph, because it was a coat of many colours, and unbeknown to me a blonde wig was stuffed in one of the pockets!

'Very fetching,' he said, 'is there something you're not telling me, Robbie? Have you anything else stuffed in any of the other pockets? Like a pair of knickers, suspender belt, anything like that? I did wonder where that carrot came from, there wasn't' a supermarket in site.'

'Haven't you got fuck all to do?' I asked. 'Why don't you go and take the piss out of Freddie, with his corsets? I thought you ambulance people, were rushed off your feet.'

'Paramedics, that's what we're called, not ambulance people if you don't mind,' Gus, said with a certain amount of indignation. 'I've trained years for this job, I'm highly qualified.'

I bet Freddie, didn't think that when you pulled that carrot out of his arse. That would make his eyes water.   You don't even know how many fingers you've got. I thought to myself.

So here I am, lying in a nice clean hospital bed. The staff allowed me to have a shower, well they insisted, as long as I kept my head dry. I have several stiches in my forehead, I feel a little groggy, but I'm in no real pain. I keep asking about Freddie. But nobody seems to know anything about him, perhaps the nurses became so fed up with all his moaning they may have thrown him in one of the incinerators!

I've had a decent night's sleep, only to be woken up at some ridiculously early hour in the morning, with a cup of lukewarm tea. The nurses said I should stay in bed and they had no idea what time the doctor would be coming around but he shouldn't be too long. They said they couldn't serve me a hot cup of tea because of health and safety reasons. I don't care really, after living a few weeks at Casper's, this is luxury.

'I know you,' said some young lad opposite me, lying in bed with both wrists wrapped in bandage.

'Your face is a bit of a mess; how did that happen?'

'Have you got all day? 'I asked, in reply.

The young man looked round the ward, 'yeah. Course I have, I'm in hospital, I've just realised who you are. You're a taxi driver. You've picked me up loads of times haven't seen you lately though.'

'Well the weather's been crap, haven't you noticed there's been a lot of snow and ice about lately?'

'Tell me about it, that's how I broke both my wrists, building a snow man in the front garden.'

'What, did the snowman attack you?' I replied.

'Don't be silly, oh your having a joke, that's very funny. I remember now, you've always been sarcastic, that's probably why you've got that big dent in your head. Did you upset one of your customers?'

'Not really I just happened to be a victim of circumstances.' I said.

'They all say that,' said the young man. 'I bet you were in that big punch up in "The Crown" that spilt over into the High street yesterday. I've heard some funny stories about that fight.'

So, for the next few minutes, Conner, that was the young man's name, and I started to exchange details of events that brought us into hospital. I think I told the story more or less correct, I left out the bit about the carrot, I didn't think it was fair on Freddie, to bring that up. It's a small world, it turns out that Belinda, is Conner's, cousin.

'She's mad,' said Conner.

'That tattoo on her forehead what does it say?'
I asked.

'I'm not sure if its Latin for 'fuck it, or fuck off,' 'said Conner. 'It's not the best thing for a job interview.'

'Yes, you can just imagine the interviewer asking, "What's that tattoo say on your forehead young lady? and her replying 'oh just fuck off, have I got the job?' We had a good laugh about that.

'So, come on Conner, tell me how you damaged your wrist building a snow man, were you arm wrestling or something like that.?'

'No this was one of the biggest snow men you've ever seen. It was massive. We couldn't get his head on because he was so tall, and we couldn't scrounge a pair of ladders from the neighbours because they're miserable bastards, and they think we're a barmy family.'

'Really, so what did you do next?' I asked.

'Well the snowman was very close to the bedroom window minus his head of course. So, we made a big fat head in the garden and I rushed up stairs with it in my hands and leaned out of the window to place his head on top. That was the plan anyway, but 'Mr Snowman' wasn't as close as I thought. I fell straight out of the window breaking both my wrist, and ended up covered in snow.'

We both had a good laugh at each other's misfortunes, I started to call Conner, 'Snowy' and he called me 'Scarface,' I'm not too sure how I felt about that.

A little later on the consultants came around and informed me that they weren't certain what was wrong with me.

They told me that I was run down and they would like me

to come back for more tests in a couple of weeks. In the meantime, they said I should take it easy and they asked me if I had someone to collect me and look after me for a couple of weeks.

I insisted I felt fine and I told them I had no one to pick me up. And as a self-employed taxi driver I needed to go out to work, because I'm broke and have no one to look after me.

They told me to 'pull myself together.'

They said that there must be someone out there to pick me up. Look after me and with the extortionate prices taxi drivers charge these days and the tax dodges, I must be worth a small fortune.

'Arseholes.'

I've tried several people on my phone to take me home, Casper, seems to have disappeared off the scene. Conner, said Belinda would be visiting later.

'She would give you a lift home, That's if she's sober.' He also told me that she could get me a mobile phone for twenty quid, far better than the crappy old thing I'm using now.

'I'll keep it in mind.' I replied. I tried a few more numbers, I even tried Martin, I was quite surprised he sounded a little concerned even though he was difficult to understand him, I think he was trying to eat something while it was still alive.

'Well, Well, what have we got here? The Robbie, and Conner, rest home.

Don't you two look sweet, tucked up in your nice clean beds fully paid for by the hard-working taxpayer?'

'Oh, hello, Sniffer.' Conner, said, nervously.

'Inspector Snipe. to you, let's have a bit of respect you little shit.'

Sniffer, or Snipe. was a tall man with hawk-like features.

85

He was lean and wore a dirty mac that fitted badly. He looked round the ward, I noticed half of one of his ears was missing. I bet he didn't lose that at the barbers, I thought to myself. He sat on the side of my bed.

'Your mate Freddie, he's really pissed off with you.'

'I'm sorry but do I know you.' I said.

'No but I know you I keep getting silly reports on my office desk about you and lover boy Freddie. Stupid reports about silly little fights, wasting police time. I think to myself is this some new troublemaker on the block or someone who is completely stupid and deranged?'

'The fight that took place yesterday was not my fault, and could have ended up with serious injuries, even death. I don't consider that a silly little fight. Poor Freddie, the moaning bastard could be traumatised for the rest of his life. I don't think either of us could stand the site of another carrot again.'

Conner, burst out laughing.

'Shut it Conner, or I'll re-arrange your wrist.' Said Sniffer.

'Don't do that, I need a dump any minute now and the nursing staff wouldn't be too happy if one of them has to wipe my arse because of some bullying detective.' Sniffer, walked over to Conner, looked round the ward then grabbed his ear. Conner, winced.

'We're looking for your mad sister Belinda, the big girl with the tattoo on her forehead.'

'She's not my sister, she's my cousin. Let go of my ear, I'll call for the nurse.'

'Silly me,' said Sniffer.

'Sister, cousin, auntie, it doesn't really matter your all shit bags and thieves rotten to the core. So, do you know where she is? I know she started the fight yesterday. She assaulted the licensee's wife stole her wig and as good as castrated two of the rugby team. So, if you could tell me where I could find the little princess, I would appreciate it.'

'Oh, so you know I didn't start the fight?' I said.

'That's right' said Sniffer, 'you were far more subtle. You just vomited over two of the bar staff. Is this one of your little party tricks?'

'I was ill, and your police officers were a disgrace taking selfies with Freddie, tied to a lamp post with his leg broken and underpants down to his ankles.'

Sniffer, walked back over to my bed. 'What I've been hearing about Freddie, that was quite a regular thing with his underpants. Anyway, I thought you were supposed to be unconscious while all this was going on. Freddie, was right you were just pretending.'

'He told me when I gained conciseness in the ambulance.'

'The staff here say your suffering with depression and you need plenty of rest. 'You're not having a break down, suicidal that sort of thing?'

'I'm just run down that's all.'

'Where's the wig Robbie? Is it in your little locker? Just give me the wig and I'll let you rest in peace.' Sniffer, put his finger on my head wound.

'That's a nasty cut, does it hurt when I press hard.'

'Nurse, nurse,' Conner, shouted, 'there's a mad man in the ward, he trying to kill someone.'

'Shut the fuck up Conner, I'll come over there and you'll never be able to wank again,' shouted Sniffer.

'What on earth is going on?'

Sniffer, stood up; he was several inches taller than the nurse who had just entered the room.

'Are you a relative of either of these two men? She asked sternly.

'Do me a favour, if I was related to these pair of retards, I'd shoot myself.'

'Has anyone got a gun?' Conner, shouted at the top of his voice.

'I'm a police officer, just doing my job, I'm looking for a blonde wig.'

'Don't be ridiculous, a blonde wig wouldn't suit you at all.' Me and Conner, started sniggering under the sheets.

'Tell him nurse,' said Conner, 'he's a big bully he threatened to pull my head off.'

'Will you two be quiet while I deal with this man.' she ordered.

'Dishonest appropriation of property belonging to another.'

'What?' asked the nurse, looking confused.

'The blonde wig it's been nicked, and I have every reason to believe it's in this gentleman's locker.'

'Well I'm just doing my job' said the nurse. 'I am responsible for these two young men who at this moment are suffering with acute trauma, so I must ask you to leave.'

'I'm not leaving till someone opens this locker.' said Sniffer, after a few more cross words, the nurse, whose last name was Fisher, walked off.

'She's gone to get the keys,' said Sniffer, 'so this could be interesting. Are you denying you have no knowledge of this blonde wig?'

'What's so important about a blonde wig? I could have

died yesterday. Freddie, had a carrot shoved up his arse while tied to a lamppost, surely that must be some form of sexual harassment?'

'Only if you're a vegetarian,' said Sniffer.

'The wig's been stolen, and the owner wants it back. She's made a complaint it's ridiculous really, I told her, if you're running a pub it's a crash helmet she's needs on her head, not a wig the ugly fat cow.

But her husband's in the same lodge as my boss, so I need to get this wig back.' 'Same lodge, what'd you mean, one of those holiday camps?'

'No, you moron, the Free Masons. They're a bit like the Mafia, but they wear aprons instead of guns,' said Sniffer.

'When they join, they roll their trouser leg up and get escorted around a darkened room blindfolded.'

'There's no carrots involved is there?' I asked. 'So, what do they do for the rest of the night, tell their new recruit what a lovely leg, he's got?' I added.

'You know what,' said Sniffer, 'you've got this irritating way about you I can see why you're always getting involved in fights, you sarcastic bastard.'

The nurse returned with a key and promptly opened my locker, there was no blonde wig, just a pair of shoes.

'Where's all his clothes?' asked Sniffer.

'They were sent off to the laundry. It was either that or we sent them off to be incinerated, they were in a right state,' she said.

'You were expecting me to go home in just my shoes?' I asked in amazement.'

'Oh, that would have been a lovely treat for the local females, they'd all turn into lesbians overnight,' said Sniffer.

He turned around to the nurse,

'I'm beginning to lose my temper with all this nonsense, was there a wig amongst all his belongings?'

'No, there wasn't, and I must ask you to leave now, you have become a disruptive influence.'

He looked round at me and Conner, and sniggered, 'I'll be back,' and walked away.

'Listen to him, he thinks he's the Terminator,' said Conner, 'the lanky twat.'

'I heard that Conner,' shouted Sniffer, as he disappeared down the corridor.

'He's a bit scary,' I said to Conner.

'He's always had it in for me.' He replied. 'Ever since Belinda, knocked him out flat. She used to do some boxing; she was very good but very undisciplined. If she lost on a points decision, she would knock out the referee, and the judges, if they couldn't run away quick enough.'

So, now I was phoning round for someone who could get me some clothes that I don't have, and take me home to somewhere I don't live. Suddenly, my guardian angel appeared, well two of them actually, Casper, with his arm in a sling and big Martin, with a bunch of flowers. Well not so much a bunch, but almost.

'I'm sorry' said Casper, 'I'm a physical coward, I was frightened shitless when all those rugby players came rushing out the pub yesterday. I just didn't know what to do.'

'So, you fucked off?' I was furious.

'Well, yes, but I did phone for the police and ambulance.'

'I bet that was difficult for you,' I said.

'It was, I could only use my left arm, the other one's badly bruised, and I think I've broken a few fingers.'

'Badly bruised, how awful.'

'We've just been to see Freddie, and he told me to fuck off.'

'Oh, so you've been to see Freddie, before you came to see me.'

'Knock it off,' said Martin, Casper, feels bad enough about all this.'

'If you hadn't spewed up over the counter and collapsed outside the pub, dragging me and Freddie, down with you,' said Casper, 'none of this would have happened. It's a bad break on his leg, all you've got is a slight bit of concussion.'

'Oh, slight is it? I, could drop down dead any minute with this injury and if I remember rightly the girl Freddie, was chatting up started all this. 'Grappling on the ground with the licensee's wife and pulling her wig off. Freddie, can certainly pick his women.'

'Are these your friends, Robbie?' asked the nurse. 'He's fit and ready to go home, but apart from his shoes, he has no clothes to wear.' She took the flowers from Martin, who looked deeply embarrassed. There was a little note with the flowers, which Martin, gave to me.

'I know what it's like being stuck in hospital,' he said. 'It's happened to me a few times, and it can get very lonely.'

This was a sensitive side of Martin; I'd never seen before. How come he and Casper, are friends?

'What exactly where you in hospital for?' I asked.

'Once for an appendicitis and another time when a client ducked, and I broke my fist hitting a brick wall. Another time, the floorboard gave way when I was chasing someone on a building site.'

'I bet that was painful,' Casper, said.

'It was when I was lying there, and he came back with four of his Irish mates, they gave me a right good kicking.'

'Don't worry about your clothes,' said Casper. 'I knew, after the vomiting event, your clothes possessed a certain odour.'

'Why don't you get to the point? I smelt like shit, even before I threw up.'

'Yes okay, whatever, I've got you some clean clothes, said Casper, so stop banging on about what happened yesterday.'

'Oh, that's very thoughtful,' I said.

'Yes,' said Martin, 'we popped down to Gloria's last night and managed to persuade her to give us some of your clothes after we explained the events. She seemed quite shocked.'

Casper, gave me an envelope with a letter in it. 'She told me to give you this. And here is a get well note from me and Martin.'

'Thank you, lads for thinking of me, I don't know what to say. Half an hour ago, I had nowhere to go and nothing to wear. Martin, thanks for the flowers.'

'I was going to buy you some chocolate,' said Martin. 'But I knew you were getting to be a bit of a fat bastard, so I thought flowers would do the trick.' 'Thank you, Martin, thank you Casper. All these little notes. The only notes I get these days, are usually final demands from the bank manager.'

'Yes, we lost the original note, so we had to improvise,' said Martin.' He gave me a note, it was impossible to read, Martins, spelling left a lot to be desired,

I think it said get well soon.,

'Thank you, Martin. It's very good of you.' I said. I noticed the message was on the back of a taxi receipt, but I didn't make any comment.

'That's okay,' said Martin, 'that's what friends are for.'

He put his arms around my shoulders, oh no more head-locks, I thought to myself.

'I know there might be a few spelling mistakes, but Casper's still a bit shook up, so I insisted on writing it'

'No that's fine,' I said, 'I'm very impressed.'

It must have been difficult for Martin, at school trying to write with his boxing gloves on, I thought to myself.

'Like they said in *The Three Musketeers*, all for some and some for others,' said Martin, looking very pleased with himself and shaking me hard around the shoulders.

'The course is working then,' I said.

'What course?' Martin, asked.

'Open University,' I replied,

Casper, looked up in the air in despair.

'I'm sorry Martin, I was just being sarcastic, I shouldn't do it, it's like a defence mechanism, I really am touched by your concern for me,'

I started to cry.

'Don't do that said Casper,' looking embarrassed.

6

Christine, looked at me.

'Have you had enough Robbie, you look tired,'

'Yes, I have it's hard work talking about oneself, I'm still conditioned to go to bed early, how does Casper, feel about me being here today, just the two of us.'

'Your point is,' said Christine.

'I think what I am trying to say, what exactly is your relationship with him, do you intend to live together.'

'No we don't, we are happy with the situation as it is, are you okay to continue with telling me more about yourself tomorrow, I must say the man that is sitting in front of me at the moment bears no resemblance to the to the man I am writing about.'

'Do you think I'm telling you a pack of lies.'

'No, said Christine, 'but you've changed.'

'Did you want something to eat, another drink perhaps.'

'No Christine, I'm fine, I just need to go home and sleep.'

I was finding it hard not to say what I was really thinking. I found it difficult to sleep that night, all I could think off was Christine, stop it I thought she's Casper's girl.

The next day I arrived at ten, Christine, was all ready for me with a cup of tea and her laptop open. She was wearing a dress.

'Are you all right Robbie, you seem a little uneasy today.'

'I didn't sleep to well last night; I'll be fine once we continue with the book and hopefully finish it today.'

'Fine let's get started,' replied Christine, where did we finish last night.'

'I was in the hospital, I became a little emotional when Casper, and Martin, came to visit me, we all became a little tearful.'

'What's going on?' asked the nurse, angrily.

'You two aren't from the police, upsetting my patient? This man is still emotionally fragile and needs care, what have you been saying to him?'

'It's not what you think,' said Casper, as he put his handkerchief to his face, 'this has been upsetting for all of us.'

'Yes, it has,' said Martin. 'We're all a bit upset, and you come along and start shouting at us, have you no feelings at all?'

By this time all three of us were sobbing and crying.

Conner, looked on in disbelief.

'Does anyone want to buy some tampons or are you all too old for that sort of thing? Pull yourselves together you bunch of tarts.'

'That's enough of that!' said Nurse Fisher, 'that sort of talk is totally inappropriate.'

'Let me wipe the tears from my eyes, and I'll go over and deck him. 'said Martin.

'Security, someone call security,' shouted the nurse.

Too late. Martin, with a quick jab with one hand and hanky in the other, knocked Conner, to the ground. He lay at the side of his bed with a broken nose, blood every were, and crying like the rest of us. But for a very different reason.

It was quite frightening really, not so much the blood, but the clinical accuracy. Martin, might be fat and old, but he could still throw a punch.

'You've broke my does', shouted Conner.

'Well you're in the right place then,' Martin, replied.

'I'm going to tell my Uncle Billy, about you,'

'No Martin,' I shouted, 'don't kick him in the bollocks.'

Conner, grabbed the sheet off his bed and hid underneath it, shouting 'don't hit me,' several times.

'Martin, you're twice his size, he's not a bad lad, he's just a bit mouthy,' I said.

'You should pick your friends more carefully,' Martin, yelled.

'Well when you're in hospital it's a little difficult. It's not as though you can walk about the wards asking people who you don't know if they would make a good friend or not.' I replied.

'Well look at this' said Casper, 'the infamous blonde wig!'

Conner, had been hiding it all the time under the bed sheets. Martin, pulled the bed sheet off Conner, he was curled up on the floor with his arms covering his face, still shouting, 'don't hit me!'

'I must ask you to leave now,' said Nurse Fisher, 'Security is on its way.'

I quickly put on some clothes and apologised to the nurse. Martin, had calmed down, even though he was now barred from the hospital, Casper, who looked like he was in shock, took the wig and put it in my plastic bag.

He was convinced he could sell it to someone,

Security never turned up, and as we walked down the corridor Conner, had a new lease of life, shouting obscenities at Martin.

'Your right' said Martin, 'I shouldn't have hit him, the little shit, He comes from a bad family they're all rotten, it's not all his fault.'

'Are you all right Martin?' I asked, 'Yes, course I'm alright.'

'Oh, I just wondered. Apart from smacking Conner, on the nose, there seems to be a much gentler side to you today that I've never seen before. What with the flowers, letter and then the tears, have you found God, or joined the Samaritans?'

'What tears?' he asked, angrily.

'Well back in the ward, you seemed to have a few tears in your eyes, not actually sobbing, maybe you have a cold, something like that?' I asked him.

'Listen you two bastards there was no tears, and if you mention anything about that to anyone, I'll rip your   heads off. Understand?'

'Understood,' 'I replied, 'isn't it, Casper?'

'Oh yes,' said Casper, understood.'

'But you are right, I am softening in my old age, I can't go hitting people all my life, there comes a time when it all becomes a bit boring.'

Me and Casper, just looked at each other.

'Ah, toilets' said Martin, 'must go for a leak.'

'He's like a walking time bomb.' Casper, said. 'Did you see the state of that kids nose? I had a job not throwing up.'

'Don't you start,' I said, 'they'll be calling us the throw up cousins.'

Casper, went white.

'I thought his reputation was a bit of an exaggeration but not anymore, you were lucky the other day when he just grabbed you round the neck.'

'You were lucky you didn't shag his daughter, 'I replied. '

'Oh, don't remind me,' said Casper, 'I keep going hot and

cold thinking about it. He just phoned me this morning, and told me he was coming to pick me up, to bring me to the hospital to see you,'

'Change the subject,' I said.

Martin, was coming out of the toilet still doing his flies up. Casper, ran straight past him, white as a sheet with his hand to his mouth.

'What's up with him?' Martin, asked.

'He doesn't like the sight of blood,' I said.

'Well he shouldn't be in the hospital if that's the case.'

Casper, came out of the toilets, still as white as a sheet.

'Have you read the note from Gloria?' asked. Martin,

'Oh no, I forgot about that,'

I opened the letter, it was difficult to read sat in Martins, car swerving left and right, and shouting at the other drivers telling them to fuck off.

'She's gone to live with her sister and I can stay at the house, but we need to sell it as we can't afford to pay off our debts,' I said.

'I'm sorry Robbie.' Said Casper, 'I never thought, for a moment, things were that bad.'

'Yep shit happens, I've been paying off one credit card for another over the last few months, the money just ran out.'

'Don't worry,' said Martin, 'at least you're lucky enough to have good buddies like me and Casper.'

'Yes,' I said. 'It could be lot worse; I could have a broken my leg like poor old Freddie, I do feel bad about that. The doctors think I have some sort of blood disorder, so it's all going great for me at the moment.'

'Don't worry about what the doctors say, they talk a load

of shit,' said Martin, 'one of my old bosses in the car trade was feeling a bit rough. He was a big man with his own little gym, the doctors told him he'd just had a bad cold, and he'd be alright in a couple of days. Twenty-four hours later he was dead in bed.'

'Thanks Martin,' I said, 'that really does make me feel better.'

'Mind you, I suppose the bottle of vodka a day didn't help. His wife was in bits,' said Martin.

'Was she there when he died?' Casper, asked.

'No, that was the problem,' said Martin, 'he died of a heart attack in a bed that he kept in the corner of his gym. The greedy bastard was bonking two women at the same time.'

'Two women in bed at the same time,' repeated Casper. 'That's not fair, how old was your boss?'

'Fifty-eight.'

'Fifty-eight,' said Casper in amazement.'

'Is there an echo in this car?' Martin, asked. 'Will you stop repeating everything I say, its irritating,'

'Sorry Martin, 'Casper replied.

'He was a vain man,' said Martin, 'He always told people he was ten years younger than he really was. He was always doing press-ups in the office, well I say office, it was a converted caravan really. He used to have his nooky in there to start with. You could always tell; the caravan would start rocking.

'It's a wonder it didn't topple over. He'd make Freddie, look like an amateur. He even had a nose job.'

'What, cosmetic surgery?' I asked.

'Yeh, he didn't look any different, I told him I could have done it for nothing. He didn't think that was funny, anyway Robbie boy, here we are at your house safe and sound.'

'Thanks, guys, for the lift and everything,' I held the key that was in the envelope Gloria, had sent me tightly in my hand.

'Thanks, Casper, for looking after me the last few weeks, it's been an experience.'

'Listen Robbie,' said, Casper, 'this is a big house if you have to sell it you'd get a fair amount .Tell you the truth, I'll miss you a bit, even if you didn't pay any rent and never stopped moaning.'

'Don't forget,' Martin, said as he drove off, 'you've got our phone numbers, and keep out of trouble, you ugly bastard.'

It felt strange being back home, Gloria, had left things nice and tidy. I noticed Casper, had left the wig in the plastic bag, I better hide that from Sniffer, just to annoy him.

Gloria, had left a few notes about our financial situation, and how we needed to sell the house quickly. She's always been organised; I do miss her.

I feel a little sleepy, that might be the medication I'm on, it's raining quite heavily now, and the snow has almost disappeared. I'll have a sleep and then get back on the road and earn some money. Fuck, I've just realised, I've left my car at Casper's.

I woke up several hours later there was a knocking on the door, oh shit, I hope it's no debt collector. I looked out the window. Standing at the door was someone dressed as a vicar. Collar on back to front, tweed jacket, he was dressed like Rupert the bear's dad. Debt collectors wouldn't be that devious, would they? He saw me looking out of the window and waved, it's not Sniffer, in disguise is it?

'Hello Robert,' he shouted, 'remember me, Reverent Percy? The last time I saw you, you were half hanging out of your car with that terrible man leaning over you ready to give you a good hiding.

I suddenly remembered him and opened the door.

'Come on in vicar. I'd offer you a drink, but I don't have any milk.'

'That's okay, a glass of water will be fine.'

'Help yourself to a chair, I must thank you for your help that day, I can't remember much but what I can make out, you more or less saved my life.'

'I don't know about that, but that man who attacked you was in a fearful rage, I managed to restrain him a little.'

'Well thanks any way,'

I looked at his small frame as he sat down in Gloria's favourite chair.

'Well I think you were very brave; he was a big man.'

'God was on my side and yours, Robert, it was more than luck that I happened to be walking past when I did. God made it happen, it was like the story of the good Samaritan.'

'Was he a taxi driver?'

'No' said the vicar, half smiling.

'I can see you're not a religious man yourself, Robert.' It was a half question, half statement of fact.

'Not really, and if you don't mind could you call me Robbie, I hate being called Robert.'

'That's fine, you can call me Percy, I only came around to see how you are. Your wife's very worried about you she thinks you're having a breakdown; she loves you very much.'

'Bollocks!' I said, she hates me.'

'Have faith in the Lord,' said Percy, 'and there's no need to swear Robert.'

'Robbie,' I said, 'call me Robbie, I'm sorry, it's good of you to be concerned, and I'm grateful for the help you gave me a few weeks ago, but things aren't good between me and Gloria.'

Suddenly the phone rang, it was Casper,

'Robbie, just to let you know Inspector Snipe, has taken your car, I had to let him have your car keys he was threatening me with all sorts of things, what the hell does he want your car for.'

'I have no idea Casper, he's got a bloody nerve, 'I'll get back to you in a few minutes, I'm having a serious conversation with the local vicar.'

There was a slight pause.

'Are you okay?' asked Casper. 'In my experience, vicars only turn up at births, deaths, and marriages, and I can't see you being involved with any births and marriages at this present moment.'

'Listen Casper, I'm alright, Gloria, asked him to come along and see me, I'll phone you back later.' I put the phone down.

'Have faith in the Lord. I can see you have friends that are concerned about you.'

'Yes, I am lucky, but quite frankly Percy, if your cock doesn't work and there's no money in the bank, I can't see what God can do to reassure my wife how lucky she is,'

Percy coughed.

'You have an earthy way of analysing the situation, Robbie. That man that hit you, he was not a believer, he threatened to shove my bible up my bottom, and to leave immediately. So much anger and bad language is profane, one needs to be at peace with the world.'

The phone rang again, it was Martin,

'What's going on?'

'Nothing,' I said.

'Casper said the vicar's down there, he must be there for a reason and don't kid me you're thinking of joining the church choir. 'Put him on the phone, you're not suicidal, are you?'

'No, I'm not and there's no need for you to speak to him Martin,' I replied.

'I just want to speak to him for my own satisfaction,' said Martin.

'Let me speak to him, he's obviously concerned about you,' said Percy.

'I'd rather you didn't.'

'What's wrong?' asked the vicar.

'It's Martin, he's a fellow taxi driver,' I said with my hand over the phone 'He's just got things all wrong you being here, he thinks I'm suicidal.'

'Let me speak to him. The Lord will give him comfort.'

'If you think I can be a bit earthy, you could be in for a bit of a shock,' I said, as I handed over the phone. it was hopeless trying to persuade him otherwise.

'Hello Martin, Reverend Percy, here. I believe you are a close friend of Robbie's?'

I could only hear the conversation from Percy's side, and I could tell it was quickly going downhill.

'Martin,you must contain this anger,' said Percy. 'Yes, it is obvious you're a non-believer. I beg your pardon, I will do no such thing, apart from the fact that it is a physical impossibility. No, I won't do that you horrible man, how dare you talk about the church and the Christian faith in such an odious manner.

Don't tell me to fuck off, you can fuck off and stick whatever you like up your own arse,'

The vicar slammed down the phone, 'How in God's name

did you ever make friends with a man like that?'

'I don't know really rev, I've known him for years, but lately he just seems to have latched on to me.'

I'd like to say his bark is worse than his bite but in Martin's case that's not true, I thought to myself.

'I think you better leave now vicar; I've got things to do, thanks again for helping me the other week. I do appreciate it. I'm sorry about Martin, he's a little rough around the edges.'

'A little,' said Percy, 'that man is evil, having a friend like that is like sleeping with the devil's disciple,'

'I'm not sleeping with him, I'm not gay, and if I was, I wouldn't choose Martin, as a partner, the thought of that big lump jumping on top of me is revolting.'

There was a knock on the door.

'You better leave, Vicar, that could be Martin, I can't be responsible for his behaviour.'

Are you suggesting this Martin would hit a man of the cloth? The good Lord is with us at all times.'

'Haven't you learnt from your short telephone conversation, this man is mad and twice your size? Please leave by the back door, please leave, unless God is the heavyweight boxing champion of the universe, you will meet him in heaven sooner than you realise.'

There was a knock on the door again.

'Please leave.'

'It may not be him,' said Percy, 'It could be anyone.'

He was right, it was Sniffer, 'You were a long time answering the door Robbie.

'You weren't hiding anything by any chance? Oh, I see you have a guest, Reverend Percy. I haven't interrupted anything

104

by any chance? He gave us a quick look up and down, well it's nice to know you've both got your trousers on,' he said with a smirk on his face.

'Hello inspector,' said Percy, 'I see your still as homophobic as ever.'

'I bet you've come along to save the soul of this poor taxi driver,' said Sniffer.

'That's correct,' said Percy, 'this man has been going through hard times, I've just come along to see with the help of our Lord, if I can help in any way.'

'Oh, I think he's beyond help, you could be at home right now. writing one of your inspiring sermons instead of wasting your time on this twat, with or without the help of the Lord,' said Sniffer. 'Now run along, I need to ask Robbie, a few questions.'

Just as the vicar was about to leave, Sniffer, stopped him.

'By the way you wouldn't have noticed a blonde wig hanging about, you might have both been trying it on?'

'Are you still banging on about this bloody wig?' I said in disbelief.

'Language Robbie. We, are in the company of a man of the cloth,' said Sniffer.

'Don't worry about that, I've heard enough bad language today to last me a lifetime. I'm off now Robbie, if ever you need me, give me a call, and as for you inspector, I think you are extremely childish, good bye.'

'That was pretty frightening, I was quaking in my boots.' Replied Sniffer, have you ever heard one of his sermons? They're so boring, funerals are the worst you feel like getting into the coffin with the corpse.'

'I'll let you know when the next one comes along,' I said.

'If you look outside Robbie, you can see your nice clean car the engine sounds a bit ropey. Not surprised really there's a few miles on the clock.'

'What are you up to, Sniffer?'

'I just want that wig, that's all, it's obvious it's not in your car, but there's a nice pair of ladies sunglasses in the glove compartment. Little things that drunken passengers leave in the car, gloves, mittens, the odd coat, items in the boot you should have reported missing but didn't. I could have confiscated all those, so just tell me where this wig is?'

'So, you've been searching through my car, you arsehole?'

'Careful Robbie, your talking to the law now.'

'I had a couple of porno mags in the boot, what's happened to them?' I asked.

'Oh, they're amongst the football magazines in the police canteen.'

'Did Casper, give you the keys, the gutless bastard?'

'Don't be too hard on Casper,' said Sniffer, 'I just threatened him with tax avoidance and dealing with stolen goods, he gave me the keys straight away, God bless him. 'You're very ungrateful, Robbie, just look how clean your car is.'

'I can't believe you're spending all this time and effort looking for a wig just because your boss goes to the same holiday camp as the licensee's wife,' I said.

'Robbie, Robbie, Robbie,' said Sniffer, 'You would never have made a good detective, you get everything wrong. I said they go to the same lodge in the freemasons and it's not the wife, it's the licensee himself. They don't have women in these sorts of places.'

'Is that why they wear an apron, because they have to wash their own cups and saucers after they've had their tea and cakes?' I asked.

Sniffer stared at me for a moment, 'You know Robbie, I can't make out if your completely dim witted or just a sarcastic little shit, looks like you got another visitor.' Sniffer said as Martin, parked his car on the drive.

'Well' said Sniffer, 'you do have a variety of friends one minute it's the local vicar, next its Mad Martin.'

This could be interesting I thought, I'll try and keep them both out of the house.

'Well this is a surprise, if you're looking for the local vicar, he's just fucked off,' said Sniffer. 'Shame that, he could have given you his blessing, thou shall not brake young men's noses while in hospital that's pretty low, even by your standards,'

Martin just stood by his car, looking surprised.

'Hello Sniffer, long time no see,' Martin looked at me, 'You all right Robbie?'

'Yes', I said, 'I was just hoping for a quiet afternoon.'

'Sorry I couldn't make it to your brother's funeral,' said Sniffer.

'That's all right' said Martin. 'I understand. Mixing with the enemy and all that, five years ago now. The funeral service was one of the most boring I've ever been to.'

'So, you're a taxi driver now, how the fuck did you manage to get a licence with your violent history?' Sniffer, asked.

'A bit of luck and persuasion, knowing the right people. That sort of thing,' replied Martin.

Sniffer, smiled, 'I must say looking at some of those taxi drivers, you fit in very well, they look like a right bunch of crooks.'

'I'm a changed man now,' said Martin.

'Try telling that to young Conner,'

'I've no idea what you're on about.'

'Don't worry,' said Sniffer, it wouldn't have bothered me, if you'd have thrown him out of the window, the little shit.'

'The hospital wants to keep it quiet. It would be bad publicity. The local rag love anything like that, "Man in hospital with broken wrists, leaves with broken nose.' They're still trying to gain public confidence after last month's fiasco, amputating the wrong leg of one of the patience. The nurse on the ward has been officially informed not to mention it. Conner, has been warned, I'll charge him and his drunken cousin for selling stolen phones if he wanted to make an official complaint. The security cameras had all been turned off, that was a bit of luck, so all in all everything is under control, but don't think this is a special favour to you Martin,'

'Why were all the security cameras switched off?' I asked.

'Bit unfortunate really.' said Sniffer, 'couple of security guards; one happened to be a female, switched them off so they wouldn't be seen going into one of the stock rooms together. When somebody called for security, they were seen rushing back out, flush faced, shoving their shirts back in their pants. I'll let you two decide on that one.'

'You see Martin, everything has a knock-on effect, you punch someone on the nose, and two security officers who wanted to fuck each other end up getting the sack. You make sure you don't pull a stunt like this again or you'll end up in court, and never drive a taxi again. Do you understand?'

Martin, just stood there like a little boy; I was amazed.

'Okay,' said Martin. 'But if the cameras weren't switched on, for all you know it could have been Robbie.'

'Just shut it,' said Sniffer, 'I recognise your trade- mark anywhere, in fact I know the dubious habits of most people in this town. You know what I'd love? It is to wake up one morning and meet someone I actually like. My boss said something quite profound the other day.'

'What was that?' I asked.

Sniffer, stared hard at both of us,

'He said, if you walk through a muddy field your bound to get shit on the souls of your shoes.'

Was your boss wearing his apron at the time? I thought to myself. Me and Martin, looked at each other, wondering what the fuck he was on about.

'So how long have you been living here?' Sniffer, asked. 'You do realise that the previous occupiers, the wife murdered her husband in the kitchen. There's no chance that could happen to you is there, Robbie? Life for me would be so much quieter.'

'Was it, food poisoning?' Martin, asked.

'No, she had an accident with a kitchen knife, you, thick twat,' said Sniffer, 'terrible mess,' he paused for effect.

'Well Martin you can take me back to the station now,' he commanded.

'What the train station?' Martin asked.

'No, the police station.'

'But I've come to see how Robbie is,' said Martin.

'Excuse me, is this the guy you've just accused of punching Conner, on the nose?' Sniffer, asked. '

'I'm okay Martin,' I said, 'You take your old buddy back to the police station.'

'We're not old buddies,' said Sniffer, angrily. 'Let's just say our paths have crossed several times over the years, so Martin, get me to the station quick as you can. I've heard enough dribble for one day, and Robbie, get your front tyre changed, it's as bald as a coot and pop into the station tomorrow, or I'll take you off the road.'

Go fuck yourself, I thought. I better get that tyre changed.

Several days have passed, I have a new tyre, and I am reasonably dressed and clean. Gloria, has had left me some clean clothes, I think living with her sister isn't proving to be that good, things are a little frosty between us, but at least we're talking.

Trades been good even though I'm waiting on the rank at the moment. I'm sleeping well, thanks to the tablets I'm taking. They're giving me terrible nightmares usually about killing someone but that's better than the old ones I used to have. At least in these dreams I'm in control.

The house is on the market for a ridiculously good price. I don't feel too bad, and the dent on my forehead is healing well. Freddie, came hobbling passed my car yesterday. He was still in a bad mood,

'I'm still getting aggravation from Sherlock Holmes, about this stupid wig. Have you any idea where it might be?' Freddie, asked me.

I did know where it was, but I'm not telling anybody, just to annoy Sniffer, I thought to myself.

'No idea,' I said, 'How's the leg?'

'Painful,' he said, and hobbled off.

I think it's going to take a while before I get back on his Christmas card list. I popped round to see Casper, the other day, he's still collecting a load of shit from the tip. He seemed particularly happy about an old life-sized stuffed bear he'd acquired.

He's not going to sell it. Once he's dusted it down, and found some new eyes for it, he's having it as an ornament by the front door.

That should entice a few young females to his flat. I did mention to make sure he puts the eyes in the right way, it'll scare everyone to death walking into his room to be confronted by a six-foot, cross-eyed bear. He just 'accused me of being old-fashioned and an interfering old bastard.

'So, what' going on with you and Martin?' I asked.

'I'm not sure,' said Casper. 'He just seems as though he wants someone to talk too without threatening them, perhaps he's found God.'

'I don't think so, you should have heard the way he spoke to the local vicar the other day. see you later, Casper.'

So, I'm sitting on the rank at the moment, looking at all the usual suspects as they walk by with their shopping bags and trolleys. Some speak to you some don't. Some, you just feel like telling them to fuck off, but I usually leave that to Martin, he's much better at it than me.

It's strange and amusing, people watching, as they call it now, ever since the government have tightened up on disability benefits, there's been an incredible deterioration in the health of some members of the public. People who could walk unaided, suddenly are being pushed around in wheel chairs, others who were partially sighted, have overnight become totally blind.

'Itchy Steve,' known by me, and most people around the town, has suddenly started to walk about with a white stick, dark glasses and bumping into things.

'How's your eyesight Steve?' I thought I'd go for the throat.

'Terrible,' he said, as he nervously scratched at his scrotum, hence the name 'Itchy Steve,'

'Woke up one morning just before Christmas, couldn't see a thing, total darkness,' he continued to scratch away. He was better known for this, than this sudden spell of blindness, walking around the town, (not so fast now,) scratching his balls, they must be red raw.

This was very odd I saw him playing on the fruit machine the other day at the penny arcade. He always wore a filthy heavy duty Hi Viz jacket with a big tyre mark up the back. Rumour has it, he acquired the jacket many years ago, before his eye sight started to deteriorate, from some council worker who was run over one dark winter's afternoon while working on road repairs.

This accounted for the tyre mark on the back, and while the paramedics were trying to bring him back to life, the jacket, lying nearby in the gutter was scooped up by old itchy bollocks. Who then ran off into the distance? The authorities knew it was Itchy Steve, but decided it was best not to prosecute, if they'd put him in prison it may have increased the suicide rate, both with prisoners and the officers?

Also, the widow of the council worker, a wealthy, highly religious woman, and slightly un-hinged, felt he wouldn't have stolen it if he didn't need it.

'He must be desperate to wear a dead man's coat,' she claimed, 'and a dirty one at that, let him wear it, it will keep him warm. God would have wanted that, and also it will be a good way for the town to remember my lovely late husband, especially when they see the tyre mark on the back.

'Where's your big mate today?' It was Scottie.

'I suppose you mean Martin?' I replied.

'That's the one, you two seem very friendly lately, you and I have still got a score to settle, and you haven't got your big mate to protect you now.'

'I'm sorry Scottie, if your referring to the punch up at my house I was very upset and run down that day. I've had to get a loan to pay for all the biscuits you shoved down your throat, you greedy bastard.'

'You almost strangled me, you big turd. What on earth Freddie, was doing going out with you the other day when he broke his leg is beyond belief. You're a curse, still he's learnt his lesson that night who he picks as friends.'

'And so, have I,' I said. 'Just fuck off and don't bother to speak to me again you big twat.'

I took a chance there, Scottie's a bit of a mommy's boy and couldn't punch his way out of a paper bag, come to think of it neither could I.

Mavis, wasn't in the best of moods today, swearing over the radio at the taxi drivers and customers, more than usual. Maybe her boyfriend had refused to kiss her with the lights on.

'Is she always like that?' asked one half of Claudia, and Ruby, a couple of regulars sitting in the back seat. They were Colin, and Rupert, during the day, Claudia, and Ruby, at night. I was never too sure at what time of the evening this transformation would take place, and exactly who was who.

Their attire was colourful, bright lipstick and overwhelming perfume that made it difficult to breathe. It was no good opening the car windows, the cold wind blowing up their short skirts was, as they put it, 'non-conducive to the wellbeing of their testicles.' I kept the windows closed, and avoided any further discussion on this matter. Ruby, tapped me on the shoulder.

'You all right driver?'

'Yes' I said.

'You've just taken the wrong turning.'

'Yes, I've just taken my eye off the ball, so to speak. Lack of concentration.'

'Oh, you don't want to do that,' they said in unison.

I realised that using the word ball was probably inappropriate, but it was funny to them,

'Oh, don't worry driver, we're in no rush tonight will do.' she or he said laughing, and tell that bitch on the radio to do one, she's so rude the way she talks to people.'

'I bet she's ugly as well. That's right driver, you're going the right way now, a bit more practice, you'll be all right.'

'She could do with a make-over.' I replied

'Oh, you bitch, driver. Is she really ugly then?' Claudia, said, at least I think it was Claudia, the nine-o' clock shadow tended to be a bit more prominent, particularly against the bright red lipstick.

'Oh bollocks, I've got a ladder in my tights,' Ruby, started to cry, 'I can't get out of the taxi looking like this. Everyone will be laughing at me.'

'I've got news for you dear; they usually do.'

'You can be such a bitch at times,' the tears were running down Ruby's cheeks, smudging his or her eye liner and make-up.

'I can put up with the laughing, that's because they are all ignorant bastards, but a ladder in one's stocking is inexcusable.'

I was glad we were near the end of our journey; this was

all getting a bit tiring. Thankfully, Claudia, had a spare pair of stockings in his handbag. Even though there was also the problem of smudged eye makeup with the help of his partner Ruby, looked magnificent with a new pair of stockings over his muscular calves not that I was looking. A quick repair job on the eye make- up, and Ruby, stepped out of the taxi looking the most handsome man, or woman in town.

I can't imagine what my dad would have thought if he'd have seen this spectacle. I'm not sure what I think about it, but if nothing else this job offers its own entertainment. If I had any sense or money, I'd be at home watching 'Strictly Come Dancing', or 'I'm a knobhead get me out of here,' thinking about it. I'm better off working weekends.

Things were getting better. Mavis, had finished her shift, and Vodka John, had taken over for the nightshift.

He was an ex taxi driver and as long as he had a plastic cup, a bottle of vodka and a magazine of big- breasted women he was fine.

I was given a job in the wealthier part of the district, a nice middle-aged couple. Professional people, polite and well mannered. It was a twenty-mile trip to a private golf club with a return trip later on, a good earner with no hassle. George, and Claire, where dressed correctly for their annual dinner dance. They looked a handsome couple. They introduced themselves to me and asked me my name, George, looked like the sort of man who would never have tattoo's or soil his underpants. Polite and loving to each other they asked me what time I started, what time do I finish, and they weren't taking the piss.

Then they ask the usual question. 'You must get some right nutters in your taxi at night Robbie? 'They actually, didn't say it that way.

'You must have intoxicated people with issues later on in the evening? was how they put it.'

'Most people just want to go home happy.' I replied, trying to convince myself.

'Do you play golf, Robbie?' asked George.

'No, I'm useless, I replied. 'I used to play a lot, but the more I played the worse I became. Football used to be my game, I'm a bit old for that now.'

'Yes, I used to be a good footballer, 'said George. 'I could have turned pro unfortunately I was the victim of a serious knee injury.'

If I could have a penny for every time somebody has told me this story I would be worth a fortune, I thought to myself.

We arrived at the golf club safe and sound.

'Thank you, Robbie, we'll see you later,' said, George.

'Have a good night,' said Clair. 'Watch out for those drunks.'

'Thanks,' I replied. I watched them walk across the car park, shaking hands with other well-dressed couples and kissing each other on the cheek.

The car park was badly lit, apart from the reserved space for the Captain and vice-Captain. I drove slowly up to the exit gate and after several minutes on the security intercom pleading with some pompous prat to lift the barrier, I managed to drive out.

The night went well, and reasonably smooth. One drunk almost threw up in my car, but I managed to stop and get him out of the cab in time. He was very apologetic and gave me a good tip so that was okay.

I thought there was going to be a fight in the car shortly after that. How wrong was I? It was a short journey with a young couple both sitting in the back seat. Dropping off the young lady first, she gave her boyfriend a kiss and told him she didn't want to see him again in a very matter-of-fact sort of way, oh dear, I thought.

'Why not?' he sounded angry.

'I just don't,' she said. 'Bye.'

'Well there must be a reason, I won't let you out of this car until you change your mind. I love you very much,' he said, sounding very aggressive.

'I've told you I don't won't to see you again, so let me go.'

I'm thinking I better ask them to calm down. I'll just give it another minute, there was a quiet pause and then the young lady opened the car door and stepped out.

'Is that it then, you bitch?'

'Yes,' she replied, with no emotion, she closed the door slowly and walked away without looking back.

I gave a little cough.

'Where to now?' I asked. The silence was unsettling, I had visions of him tearing the seat out of the car in anger, or grabbing me by the back of the neck, and strangling me.

'Are you okay in the back there?' I said. No answer.

'I love her to bits,' he started crying.

'I've been ever so good,' he was crying even more. 'I've always loved her.' Now he was crying like a toddler that has had his lollypop snatched from his hands.

I checked to see if all the windows were shut, he was crying that loud it was embarrassing.

'I love her so much, I been ever so good.'

He kept saying this in despair, crying louder than ever.

'I'm sorry about this but where do you want dropping off?'
I asked. I was getting a bit tired of all this crying shit.

No wonder she doesn't want to see him again, he was blubbering even louder.

'I've done everything I can for her,' the tears were still flowing.

I felt like saying, well I heard she was a lousy shag, but thought better of it,

'You'll get over it,' I said.

'What did you say?' He was crying that loud he couldn't hear me,

I shouted. 'I said, you'll get over it.'

'No, I won't, she was the love of my life.' Ten minutes and several tissues later the jabbering wreck had stopped crying and gained a little composure. Apart from just the odd sob now and again. He was, not surprisingly, extremely apologetic and a little embarrassed. However, he gave me a big tip, a huge hug and thanked me for listening. I was tempted to give him the phone number of my sister in law, but that would be too cruel for both of them.

Sounds like an eventful evening,' said Christine'

'There's still more to come,' I said, 'this is the evening everything happens, my life changed completely.'

'You better tell me more. Robbie.'

7

I'm on my way back to the golf club and apart from blub-bering Billy, the evening's been pretty good so far, not too many idiots and a few good tips. The night is clear as I drive through the main entrance, the half-moon shines down on the large Georgian building casting a large shadow on the poorly lit car park. There were several couples leaving the hall. They seemed happy enough, the men looking smart in their suits and dicky bows, the women's jewellery glistened in the moonlight. Their expensive dresses and scarves swayed in the cool breeze. I looked to one side of the car park, at the carefully marked spaces which read: 'Captain', 'Vice-Captain', 'Chairman.' I'm sure in the hallway of the clubhouse, along with other commit-tee members there are framed photographs hanging on the walls, their names and status in bold print.

I glanced to the left and waving from a distance, I could see George, and Claire.'

She was pissed, even from a distance this was obvious. George, was doing his best to hold his wife up, he didn't look amused. Let's hope the chairman, or any of the committee members haven't noticed this disgraceful behaviour. Mind you, they're probably just as drunk inside the building, dicky bows round the back of their necks. One half of their wine stained shirts hanging out of their trousers, trying to stick their hand up the waitress's dresses.

'Hello Robbie,' Claire, slurred. 'Have you had a good night?' she held tightly onto the car door, George, trying his best to push her in the back seat.

'Do you know what women do with their arseholes before they have sex? Robbie Wobbie'

Oh no, I thought, please change the subject.

'They drop him off at the golf course,' she answered

This could be awkward. George, was looking red faced.

'Come on dear, there's no need for this, be a good girl.'

'Don't you think that's funny Robbie,

'The old ones are the best,' I replied. Please, please be quiet, I thought.

'Oh no they're not Robbie, Wobbie.'

By this time, they were both in the back of the car I started driving off slowly narrowly missing somebody pissing in the hedge. Now that would have made a good photograph on the club house wall!

Claire, leaned forward, she hiccupped.

'Darling don't distract the driver. 'The old ones aren't the best Wobbie, give me a bit of young rough any time. All those hard muscles and.'!

'That's enough,' said George.

'Driver, I must apologise for my wife's behaviour.' I'd noticed he wasn't calling me Robbie anymore, just driver. God knows what he'll be calling his wife when they get home. I could sense his suppressed anger and embarrassment. She may have felt suppressed for other reasons. There was an awkward silence for a few minutes as I drove the not so happy couple home as quickly as I could.

'Henry's wife seemed a delightful woman,' said George,

obviously trying to defuse the situation. Claire, burped.

'Delightful. Oh yes, there's you, smiling trying to hold your stomach in pretending to be happy and suave You've had more dances with that tart tonight than you've had with me all the time we've been married, and where on earth did you learn to dance like that. Swaying your hips and running your hands through your hair. Who do think you are? Michel Jackson? You looked a right pratt delightful indeed!'

George, snapped. 'I was just trying to be sociable, Henry, has very influential friends.'

I just kept driving, keeping my head down.

'And she's not a tart.'

'George, you couldn't have made it more obvious if you'd stuck your head up her dress. That's if you can call it a dress and if you're trying to impress Henry, you might as well stick your head down his pants and suffer the awful sight we women have to endure, just to fulfil your sexual desires because you men are too tired to fuck us properly.

My god, it's like looking at a bag of offal that's just fallen off the back of a lorry. You think more of your golf than you ever think of me. I wished you'd all fuck off.'

Then everything went quiet for the rest of the journey.

'Home,' I said loudly, and with a certain amount of relief. I was starting to titter, 'home,' I repeated with difficulty. Please, I thought, don't start laughing.

Claire, shot out of the taxi without saying a word, which was probably just as well. She was heading towards their large house it was one of those fast walks, her head was way in front of the rest of her body. But her legs where desperately trying to catch up before she heads butts the front door.

'My wife's been under a lot of stress lately,' said George.

We both turned our heads simultaneously as we heard the thud on the door, she was lying flat out on the door mat, shouting out,

'Bastard, bastards.'

'Is she alright?'

George, was holding a few notes in his hands.

'She will be fine, just a little knock on the head,' he said with a certain cynicism.

George, stepped out the cab, staring me in the face, his cold blue eyes became a little unnerving, in the background from the doorway came shouts of 'arsehole', and other expletives.

'Listen Roy, it is Roy isn't it?'

'Robbie's the name, Robbie.'

'Arr Robbie, same name as my grandfather, he was a good man, a wise man. Are you a wise man Robbie?'

I looked to the left, where his wife was now trying to get up off the floor. She fell down again, shouting 'Bollocks.'

I'm surprised she didn't shout 'Offal's.'

'Shouldn't we try and help your wife?'

'Fuck my wife, fuck her!' George, had really lost his composure.

He was in a rage, his face and eyes turning bright red.

'Listen,' I said, 'I don't know what sort of relationship you and your wife have but I'm not into that sort of thing. Maybe if I was a bit younger, don't get me wrong your wife's very attractive and smells lovely.'

'What? I don't mean I want you to fuck my missus, I meant don't bother about her. It's her own fault she's pissed, for god's sake,' shouted George, as he grabbed my arm.

'Oh, thank god for that, I've been having terrible erection problems lately.'

'Can't get it up then?' George, asked, with a smirk on his face.'

'That's right.'

'Well Roy,' George, took his hand away, he was a little calmer.

'Robbie.' I replied.

'Oh, sorry Robbie. Personally, I don't have a problem in that department.'

Behind me I heard a door slam. Claire, had managed to get into the house, but not her dress. It was jammed in the door. Through the small door window, you could see the back of her head rapidly going backwards and forwards trying to free herself from the door still shouting, 'Bollocks.'

She was tethered like a mad dog. Either that or somebody was giving her one hell of a knee trembler.

A large man with a booming voice appeared from next door.

'I could hear all the noise and thought you might need a hand.'

'It's all right Granville.'

George, was looking a little embarrassed. Granville, must have been at least seventy. A tall imposing character with a red face, bald on top with thick long white hair hanging over his ears.

He must have been formidable when he was younger. He had a nasty looking dog with him that looked as though it had been crossed with a crocodile. The big man looked at me then glanced over to the door, then looked at me again.

'You been having trouble with this taxi driver, George? They're all the bloody same.' His dog was growling, sniffing around the taxi.

Oh no, I thought, not another posh pratt, probably an ex-army Major, or something like that.

'How come you're not black or Asian? I know, you must be one of those Eastern Europeans, Bosnian. Do you know' he continued, 'I ordered a taxi the other day for a very important meeting and it was ten minutes late, ten minutes! I'd ordered the damn thing the day before the driver gave some excuse about the traffic. He was one of those Eastern Europeans like you.'

'I'm English.'

'What?' Don't interrupt while I'm talking. Well set out ten minutes earlier, I said to him it's obvious, bloody foreigners.'

'Why is your wife banging on the door George?'

'She's a little drunk, well actually she's pissed out of her brain and her dress is caught in the door. I was about to pay the driver and then go to her assistance. Then you came along, everything's alright really.' Granville, didn't say anything he just looked at the door, then at George, and burst out laughing.

It was a big hearty laugh, almost like a lion's roar, he slapped George, hard on the shoulder.

'Well you better pay the foreigner and sort out your good lady. Just rip her dress off and give her what for, that will cheer her up.'

George, gave me a generous tip and advised me not to mention tonight's events to anyone or there will be consequences. He emphasised he had friends who could be rather physical.

I wondered if his wife was aware of these men. I gave him the address of a good handyman to patch up the door and as

I drove out of the gateway, I could hear Granville saying to George.

'Roy, that can't be his real name, Bosnians don't have names like that.'

'No, I shouted, it's Robbie!'

'Don't mention this to anyone,' shouted, George.

You've got to be joking, I thought. Claire's, joke about the arsehole was very funny though.

I better have one of my tablets, I stopped the car just around the corner from George, and his wife. I got out of my cab and had a good stretch, too much excitement in one day. I don't know what's in these tablets but they make me feel relaxed.

Is there such a thing as a normal relationship? I've seen no sign of one tonight. I could hear crocodile dog barking in the distance. I got back in the car and quickly closed the door; I think I'll head home I've had enough for one day.

It had started to rain quite heavy and I was getting tired. Vodka John, was on the radio.

'Got a job Robbie, nearby were you should be. Just take the two ladies into the city centre and then you can go home, you've had a good shift tonight you must be worth a fortune.'

'It's been good and entertaining, thanks John,' I said.

Life's a lot easier without Mavis, I thought to myself. The time was midnight, best to finish after this job he'll be slurring soon. You never know what to expect, the next two customers were a couple of smart middle-aged women moaning about the taxi company. The next-door neighbour their ex-husbands, the window cleaner, and what bastards' men are. I thought I better not say anything, they might drag me out of the car and cut my prick off. The rain was really heavy now, they got out of the cab paid and looked at me as though the rain was my fault. The city centre was busy, I might have had a good night but I realised I couldn't find my phone, bollocks!

I was just about to get out of the cab to see if I had dropped it under the seat. When suddenly from out of nowhere somebody got in the back of my cab.

'Drive driver, and be quick about it, drive to the nearest motorway junction.'

His voice was gruff, and he didn't sound too well.

'I can't give you a lift, I have someone else to pick up.'

'No, you don't here's fifty quid, just drive this bag of nails as quick as you can.'

He started coughing badly. I didn't feel happy about this at all, but fifty quid is fifty quid, great! Especially as I've lost my phone. This guy sounded desperate.

'I can't drive too fast, the rain is pissing down and the traffic is really busy,' I said.

'You're a taxi driver for fucks sake. Just do what taxi drivers do, put your foot down overtake and cut up every bastard on the road.'

I noticed he kept looking out of the rear window, he was coughing badly.

'You don't think too much of the way taxi drivers drive?'

'I don't think much of taxi drivers, full stop. Turn left here,' he said.

'This isn't the way to the motorway,' I replied.

'I know that just turn left.'

'I don't like the way you're talking to me if you continue in this manner, I shall have to ask you to get out of the taxi.'

'I'm sorry,' he said in a sarcastic way, 'So you'd kick a sick man who's just give you fifty quid, out of the car into the pouring rain?'

He started coughing again. He did sound really, ill.

'I just don't think there's any need to be so aggressive, do you want me to take you to the hospital?'

'Just turn left again please.'

'This is a cul-de-sac,' I replied.

'That's okay just turn around at the end, stop and leave the engine running. Let me open my suitcase and give you another fifty pounds. Then you can take me to the nearest motorway junction. Is that okay?'

He sounded short of breath. Another fifty quid, I'll go for it, this is turning out to be a good night.

I'll make sure I'll get this arsehole to his destination before he dies.

'Here you are another fifty quid.'

Just as I went to take the money from his hand, he moved it away and placed something cold on the back of my neck.

'You'd take it wouldn't you? You money grabbing bag of shit. Do you know what this is at the back of your neck?'

I froze for a couple of seconds.

'No,' I said, in a high-pitched voice.

'It's a gun,' he said.

'If you shoot me you won't have a driver and anyway how do I know it's a real gun? It could be a water pistol for all I know.' I said, trying not to shit my myself.

'You really are the dumbest bastard I have ever met,' he turned the window down.

'See that cat walking past?' There was a low thudding sound behind my head and the cat fell to the ground making an awful squealing noise.

'You've shot the cat.'

'That's right, I wouldn't be able to do that with a water pistol. Now it's your choice drive, or I'll scramble what little brain you have all over the window screen.'

He started coughing again.

'Motor way junction it is,' I said. 'My sort of man really,' 'I can't stand cats. They go around killing birds, have you noticed if you go walking around the parks or woodlands you just don't see any?'

I'm in shock and just talking gibberish. This guy is going to kill me whatever I do.

I drove back on the main road; the rain is chucking it down. Perhaps I should stop and drag him out of the car and disarm him, he sounds very weak. I could be a local hero; I can see the headlines in the newspapers. "Brave taxi driver risks his life and tackles notorious gun man."

'I'm not going too slow, am I?' No answer, perhaps the bastard died. I turned into a side road, still silence. I stopped the car and opened my door slowly; I was undecided whether to run away as fast as I could (so much about being a hero.)

The rain had stopped, it was about 1.30 in the morning, I wish I had my phone. I opened the back door slowly and for the first time I could see what Mr Gunman looked like. He was well dressed; his eyes were closed and there was no movement.

I couldn't tell if he was dead or sleeping, he was slumped against the back seat with his gun in his hand. I'm not sure if I wished he was dead or not. His case was on his lap one of those slim type cases that business men often use these days. I felt sick in my stomach, I must get that gun off him before I do anything else. I wish I had Martin's ability to knock him out with one punch. Here goes I grabbed the gun, his eyes opened wide like a man insane.

'What the fuck?' he said. He pulled the gun away from my grip.

I screamed and fell backwards onto the grass verge. He pointed the gun at me. 'Shut the fuck up.'

'If you shoot me, you'll wake up the whole neighbourhood,' I said in desperation.

'If you didn't notice when I shot Mr Pussycat, I had a silencer on my gun. I still have a silencer on my gun the only thing making a noise is you. Shut up or I'll shoot you.'

He started coughing again. He looked around,

'Where are we? I think I'm dying.' His eyes closed again as he slumped back in the car.

It started to rain again I was tempted to run off, but a couple of things had changed my mind. The gun had dropped from his hand, I'd no idea if he was dead or alive. The case on his lap had fallen out of the car it was chained to his wrist and opened up, it was full of money. Fifty, Twenty and Ten-pound notes, it was full to the top. I grabbed the gun, this time there were no surprises.

He just remained still. Some of the wads of money had fallen out of the case onto the pavement.

I picked them up quickly and put them in my pocket.

My mind's racing, I've never seen so much money in my life. What the fuck should I do? I can't remember the proper way to check if someone has a pulse so I just put the gun out of harm's way in the boot of the car. I was about to close the case, but changed my mind. I might not be able to open it again. So many things are racing through my head, who is he and who knows about this man, does this money belong to him or someone else.

I took all the money out and put it in a plastic bag. I started shaking Mr Gunman by the shoulders, asking him several times if he was still alive. Then I remembered the trick with the mirror by his mouth, he was dead. Was there another car following us? I feel sick, he looked as though he'd been shot, there was blood all down his back. Let's get out of here. After making sure he was secured in his seat belt, I tried to make him look as much as possible, as though he was asleep, I even put a pair of sunglasses on the corpse. If I could just get rid of this body. Who's going to know about him and his money? I could be rich for once in my life.

I've got that blonde wig in the boot and a fancy woman's scarf, that's it! If I put that wig on his head and the scarf around his neck and if the police stop me. I'll tell them he's an art director for the B.B.C who's had too much to drink!

I was just about to set off when a police car appeared on the scene. Oh shit, what's that saying? 'They never turn up when you want one and when you don't, hey presto!'

'Everything all right driver?'

What should I say? I feel like I'm going to faint.

'Yes, I'm fine.'

'Is your passenger okay? We had a call from one of the neighbours about somebody screaming, would that be you or your passenger by any chance?'

'Oh dear, was it that loud? He was having an argument with his partner on the phone about being out so late. He got out of the car ranting and raving, he's very dramatic. He's fast asleep now, he's had a long day.' I said.

'He looks dead on his feet,' said the police man. 'When you say he was on the phone speaking to his partner. What sort of partner do you mean?'

'Well you know,' I said. 'Look at the state of him.'

'He looks like a poor man's Andy Warhol,' said the constable. 'I bet he gets paid a fortune for prancing about all day. He hasn't made sexual advances, has he? I can soon drag him out of the car if you want me to. If I had my way, I'd shoot the lot of them.'

'Oh really?' I replied.

'If you're okay, I'll leave you to it.

Best if you get him home in one piece. It's been a busy night tonight, there was a bad accident in the city centre. You didn't happen to witness the incident at all?'

'No, nothing officer.'

'Okay driver, I let you get off. Just be careful, there seems to be a madman shooting cats around the area.'

I'm trembling like hell, and no idea where I'm driving too. It's no good asking the passenger, I'm committed now. I just told the policeman a pack of lies. Where do I dump the body? The whole things giving me a headache, just think of all that money. I better check if there is any I. D. on him. A couple of miles further on, there was a small woodland with a gravel car park. A popular place for couples to have a shag. The ground was uneven with large puddles, but there were a few cars there with all their lights off, and windows steaming up. If I get into the back, nothing will look suspicious. There's a river nearby, that could be useful. I better check all his pockets.

8

I suddenly woke up in bed, was this all a dream? Someone was knocking on the door. I'm lying in bed in my own home. I looked under the sheets, to see a big plastic bag full of money, oh shit this has really happened. I looked at the clock, it was midday. It was Sniffer, oh no, I thought, I opened the door.

'You look a pretty sight, I bet you bought those pants from Primark? You don't exactly look like Bruce Willis, in that white vest. Next time you have a curry try shoving it in your mouth,' said Sniffer.

'The police station has been trying to phone you all morning. You all right, you look as white as a sheet.'

'I had a busy night last night. I should be resting more. I lost my phone and I'm behind on the payment on the landline, so the bastards have cut me off,' I said.

'Oh dear, it just hasn't been your day has it?' Sniffer, said sarcastically.

'Looked like someone's thrown up in the back of your car.'

'Why do you say that?' I asked him.

'When you kindly let me drive your car, the other day from the police station, you had different coloured seat covers.'

Is he playing games with me? He doesn't miss a thing.

'No someone just shit themselves.' I replied.

'That wasn't very nice,' said Sniffer.

'No, it wasn't' I replied, 'it was an off-duty policeman.'

Sniffer, just stared at me, he didn't find that funny.

'Is there any particular reason you're here inspector?'

'I'm here because your one phone is lost, and you can't afford to pay B. T. for the other one.

Your wife heard that there was an accident in the city and was concerned when there was no answer on your mobile. So, she phoned the police station.'

'So, Gloria was concerned?'

'Yes' said, Sniffer. 'She was trying to find your life insurance policy.'

'You take advantage of your rank,' I said.

'No, I don't I'm just fed up of people like you wasting police time.'

'Do you realise your big arsed mate is in hospital with several broken bones and concussion?'

'You mean Martin,' I said.

'That's' right, they thought at first, he was brain damaged, until they realised, he's always like that.

You're lucky you opened the door when you did, P. C, Duffy, my assistant for the day, was ready to bash the door down. It's one of his specialities. I was hoping that maybe you'd been drowned in the bath by your mates Freddie, and Scottie, they're not very fond of you these days.

Anyway, I'll go back to the station to give your wife a call, let her know that you are still alive.'

'Thank you, inspector.'

'Think nothing of it,' said Sniffer. 'Just get your phones sorted out. I'm off now, just get yourself dressed properly; you look like shit.'

Why did he mention murder and body's under water? I keep

having visions of Mr Gunman being pushed in the river and he suddenly comes alive, shouting 'bastard, I'll get you for this.' Then he's floating quickly downstream as the level of the river was very high. I still can't believe what's happened in the last twenty-four hours.

I must get some more sleep and then I'll go and see Martin. I went upstairs and threw all the money on the bed, then I rolled over on it and rubbed the notes all over my face.

It was like having an orgasm, all this money. I'm rich! I put the money back in the bag I still haven't counted it yet but there must be thousands of pounds. Then I fell asleep. I was woken a few hours later. I looked at the time it was three o' clock. I quickly put on a pair of trousers and a clean jumper. It seems impossible to get any sleep in this house, I thought.

I ran downstairs, it was Gloria.

'Hello, Robbie, you look tired,' she said.

'I had a busy shift last night, and then I was woken by Sherlock Holmes. But it's nice to see you Gloria.'

We've hardly had a civil word to say to each other over the last few months and virtually nothing over the last few weeks and now she just appears, well-turned-out with a smile on her face.

'I was worried about you Robbie.'

Can she smell the money? Is it some sort of six sense women have? It's happening already. A bit of money in my pocket, and I don't trust anyone!

'Whose Sherlock Holmes?' asked Gloria.

'Oh, some twat from the police station.'

'I've brought you a phone, it's one of my old ones but it works okay. Would you like me to make you a cup of tea?'

'Thank you, Gloria, that would be very nice.'

She looked around the kitchen.

'My word you have become domesticated, washing machine on, ironing basket full of clean clothes.'

'Yes, it's the new me, if only she knew I spent the early hours of the morning trying to get the mud and the bloodstains off my clothes. I think she would run out of the house screaming.

'I became very afraid last night, I thought I'd lost you,' said Gloria.

'We've lost each other,' I said. 'Don't do this to me Gloria, I've been a mental wreck over the last few months. When I needed help you kicked me out of the house, remember?'

'There's your tea, it was just when I thought you were dead, I realised I do love you. We can sell this house and down- size, as they call it. Most of our problems have been caused through lack of money,' Gloria, said.

'Let me think about this I must go and see Martin, in hospi- tal, he was the one that was in the accident.'

'That big lump, I'm sure there would be quite a few people that would be more than happy if he passed away. What are you bothering with him for? He's nothing but a big thug,' said Gloria.

'Well, at least that big thug came to visit me when I was in hospital' I said.

'Yes, and, broke a patient's nose. That's a good example of bed side manners,' Gloria, added.

'How did you know about that?'

'Freddie, told me.'

'Oh, I see, you've been talking to Freddie. Tell me, did he have his pants off or on at the time?' I asked.

'Don't be ridiculous, I was speaking to him on the phone and anyway you should be grateful to Freddie, fighting off those rugby players, while you and Casper, ran off.'

'Is that what he told you the lying little shit, was he wearing his corset at the time. Thank you for the phone Gloria, I'll let you know how Martin is when I get back.'

'You're the first friend to visit Martin,' said the nurse. 'Apart from the police, they seem very annoyed they can't get any sense out of him. You can see him for a few minutes, but I must warn you, he may not recognise you. He can't remember anything about the crash at all.'

I didn't know what to say, he was asleep and looked awful. Wires and monitors all around him, tubes up his nose. His legs were heavily bandaged, and his face was every colour of the rainbow.

The nurse came up to me,

'He's steady at the moment, does he have any friends or relatives?'

'I just don't know. He wasn't the easiest of men to get on with,' I replied.

'He wasn't the easiest of men to get out of the car,' said the nurse. 'The size of him, the car was wedged upside down against a lorry. It didn't help with the rain pouring down, it took the rescue service ages to get him out.'

'I just don't know anything about the crash,' I said. 'Were there any passengers?'

'Two,' said the nurse. 'One of them died on the way to the hospital, the other one is critically ill and is suffering with concussion.'

'Could I have a drink of water? I don't feel too good. I didn't realise things were as bad as this.'

Martin, grunted and opened his eyes, he looked at me and the nurse with a glazed look on his face. He looked slowly around the ward.

'Do you know where you are Martin?'

'Yes, I'm in fucking bed,' and fell back to sleep.

'Yes, I think I can see what you mean,' said the nurse, 'he doesn't seem the easiest man to get on with.

'Being as you're, the only visitor Martin's had, apart from the police, could I have your address and phone number? We need to be able to contact someone if the situation changes,' said the nurse.

I was a little reluctant, I better hide that money well. Poor Martin, how much things can change in the space of twenty-four hours.

'Robbie, can I have your address please?' the nurse asked again.

'Sorry,' I apologised, 'I was day- dreaming, all this has been really upsetting for me.'

I gave her my address and phone number. 'I suddenly realised, he has a daughter called Martina, I've never met her and have no idea where she lives.'

'Has he a wife?' the nurse asked.

'She died many years ago.'

I sipped at the plastic cup of water the nurse had given me as I walked slowly down the corridor. Fuck it, I thought, I'm never going to drive a taxi again.

I phoned Casper, and told him the news and asked if I could come over.

'Okay,' he said, 'but if you're thinking of drowning your

sorrows, don't forget we're barred from the local pub.'

'That's Okay, I'll buy some on the way. And some decent drinking glasses.'

'Blimey, have you robbed a bank or something like that?' Casper, asked.

'No, financially, I've had a good week. I'm just a bit upset about Martin; do you know where his daughter lives?'

'No, but I still have her phone number. Don't ask me to give her a call, she would never believe me if I told her Daddy was critically ill in hospital. In fact, since our little meeting in the grave yard, Martina, wouldn't believe me about anything.'

'Yes, I can understand that,' I replied. 'You better give me her phone number, the poor wench.'

'I still think you ought to be more careful who you choose as friends,' said Casper.

'Come on Casper, you're not that bad.'

'Bollocks, you old get, I'll see you soon,' said Casper, and turned off his phone.

As Casper, opened the door, I had the fright of my life. I'd forgotten about the life size bear, standing on his back legs.

'Well what do you think?' Casper, asked.

'Very nice,' I said, 'the sun glasses work very well. Do you think it's wise to have it so close to the door? I almost shit myself. If Aunt Mabel, or Aunt Bettie, come to visit you, they'll die of a heart attack,' I said.

'Is it that good?' he asked, 'I tried using ping pong balls for his eyes and panting black spots on them, but it looked a bit scary.'

'Really, you do surprise me.'

'It gives the place that bohemian feel,' said Casper. 'Are you on drugs? It's hideous, have you been talking to some of your old university mates? Bohemian, indeed.' I said.

'See Robbie, you've just put your foot in the door, and you've started moaning already.'

'You're right Casper, it's just very frightening and my nerves are on edge at the moment. That crash of Martin's, it was a really bad night with the weather. The traffic was bad and as taxi drivers we're always rushing about trying to grab every penny we can get our hands on. It could have happened to anyone; it could have happened to me. It could have been me lying in that hospital bed.'

Casper, shoved a can of beer in my hand and a nice clean glass,

'Get this beer down you, and here's me thinking you were upset about Martin.'

'I am upset about him.' I said. 'That phone number you gave me for his daughter is unobtainable.' Casper, took a large gulp of vodka and coke.

'Well it didn't happen to you,' said Casper, 'Martin, has done a lot of bad things in his time, and drives like a maniac, he's a thug. You're alive and kicking and look at you, clean and smartly dressed. Have you robbed a bank or something like that?'

'No, no,' I lied, thinking quickly. 'I'm just wearing my Sunday best.'

'Perhaps Martin's gay and fancies you, he did bring you a bunch of flowers,' said Casper.

'I thought they were from both of you.'

'Not really, Martin, nicked them from the reception area bold as you like,'.

'Oh well, it's the thought that counts and of course he's not gay,' I said.

'You never see him with a girlfriend.' Casper, replied.

'That's because he's ugly and uncouth. In fact, you never see him with any friends,' I replied.

'That's probably because he's killed them all and dumped the bodies in the river,' Casper, said, jokingly.

'Why do you say that?'

'Say what?'

'Throwing bodies in the river, why did you say it?'

'I was just having a little joke,' said Casper. 'Stop being so edgy.' He paused for a moment and sipped his drink.

'He probably buried them in the woods instead, thinking about it, it must be difficult, getting rid of a dead body,' said Casper.

'How did his wife die?'

'Suicide,'

'Suicide?' Casper, asked.

'Yes,' I said. 'She jumped off the top of a multi- storey car park.'

'How long have you known this?'

'Martin told me a few years ago, in strictest confidence, please Casper, don't repeat this to anyone.'

'No wonder Martina, was so annoyed and upset when I told her that story about my parents being dead.'

'No, Casper, that story would have upset any young girl.'

This is really pissing me off, I said. I came here for a drink and you keep talking about death and corpses, will you please just change the subject?'

'Okay,' said Casper, 'I've got a new iron.'

'It's a bit late now,' I replied.

'I was only joking,' said Casper. 'Your phones ringing.'

It was Gloria, 'how's your new boyfriend?' she asked sternly.

'My boyfriend, I don't know what you mean.'

'Martin, he's you're new boyfriend.' 'Don't you start I've got Casper, winding me up about this. Martin, is in a really bad way do you know apart from the police, I'm the only visitor he's had.'

'I wonder why?' she retorted. 'Anyway, Gorse Heath Police Station phoned me and want you to pop round and see them. It's very posh round there.'

Oh no, I thought, calm down, that station's nowhere near the river.

'Robbie, are you still there?'

'Yes, what do they want?'

'You're in luck. They've got your mobile phone; they need you to collect it in person.'

'Thank God for that. Thank you, Gloria, that is good news. I must have dropped it when I got out of the car after I dropped a man and his rather drunk wife off late last night. Is there any chance you could take me there? Me and Casper, have had a few drinks.'

'So is that how you spend your Sunday afternoons these days, getting pissed.'

'Not just Sunday, any afternoon,' I said.

'You realise,' said Gloria, 'that between us, we've hardly got a pot to piss in.'

'That's because we broke them all at that punch up the other week, when you were showing everybody your tits.' She put the phone down.

'She can be so serious at times, the miserable bitch.'

'How can you be so drunk on one can of beer?' Casper, asked.

'It must be the tablets I'm taking.'

'You shouldn't talk to Gloria, like that. she seems a nice woman.'

'I shouldn't really, she was being nice to me earlier on, I just had an argument with her about Freddie the Flirt.' I said.

'You worry too much about Freddie,' said Casper.'

'I just don't trust him, he'd fuck a rabbit if he could stop it jumping, I better call a taxi.'

'My word, you are splashing out,' remarked Casper.

'You just don't realise how much you need your phone till you lose it,' I said. As I was about to walk out the door, I looked at this hideous black bear.

'Were you really going to use ping pong balls for his eyes?' I asked Casper.

'Yes' he said, 'it's so difficult to get a pair of false eyeballs, even on the internet.'

'Have you tried the local abattoir?'

'That's sick, 'said Casper. 'Oh, and by the way that was nonsense about a left eye and a right eye, they're all the same, you just made that that up.'

'You were very lucky,' said the desk sergeant. 'Major Granville-Sharp-Ensill, found your phone this morning while taking his dog for a walk. Well his dog found it really, you were lucky he didn't eat it, the ugly vicious bastard.'

'What the Dog, or Major Sharp's pencil?' I asked facetiously. 'Sharp- Ensill, not Sharp Pencil,' said the sergeant.

'It makes a change for him to do something like that. He's

usually complaining about something. Have you ever met the man? Big fellow with a booming voice.'

'Yes, I think I met him and his dog last night, they make a lovely couple.'

'I dropped off his neighbours.' I said. 'You've had no reports of a murdered wife?'

'We don't have things like that happen round here. Everybody is very civilised and dignified, it's not like the city centre. When the Major came in this morning, I thought here we go again, always threating to complain to his local M.P. 'He thinks he's the sheriff of the county. Always complaining about trivial things, cars driving past with their radio on too loud, the odd empty beer can in the front of his huge garden. The other week all hell was let loose he found a pair of skimpy knickers and a used condom in his garden hedge. He was demanding we should have a sperm check on every male that lived within a twenty-mile radius of his house!'

'It's a shame really,' I said, 'I should imagine most of the time things are pretty quiet around here. Do you think I could have my phone now please?'

After answering a few questions, and giving a couple of signatures, the sergeant gave me my phone.

'It's fully charged, we had to make a few phone calls to track you down.'

'Well thanks anyway,' I said.

'You're, right. Apart from the Major, it's pretty quiet around here,' said the sergeant. 'So, you're a taxi driver? I couldn't do your job,' he added. 'You never know who you're going to get in the back of your car.'

'No, you don't,' I replied.

Is it just a coincidence that he asked that question? He doesn't know I had a dead man in the car. Keep calm.

'That was a bad accident in the city centre last night.' said the sergeant. 'I heard that it was a taxi driver driving like a maniac, is that your taxi out there?'

'Yes, it is,' I replied.

'I can smell alcohol on your breath,' said the sergeant. 'I shall be forced to breathalyse you.'

'No, I don't actually mean this is my own taxi that I will be driving.'

'You just said it was.'

'Yes, I did, but what I meant is, this is the taxi that was for hire. I paid the taxi driver to drive me here, and he will be taking me back.'

'So, where is he?'

'He's probably stretching his legs or popped over the road for a newspaper.'

'Is that him there, with a few cans of beer under his arm? That doesn't look very good, does it?'

'Well, it's not as though he's drinking out of them. When he drops me back home, he will finish his shift and go home and enjoy a few drinks.' I said.

'It still doesn't look good. What's his name?'

'Well, we call him Piddling Pete,' I replied.

'What, does he smell of piss? He doesn't seem to be walking very straight,' said the sergeant.

'He suffers with bad balance; he's been like it for some time. If you stand next to him in the urinals it's best not to have a conversation with him. He'll just piss all over your shoes. Hence the name Piddling Pete.'

The sergeant just looked at me, 'Mm, like I said people round here are very dignified, I can't imagine anyone around here having a nick name like that.'

I could think of several, I thought. After checking Piddling Pete's documentation and general wear and tear of his taxi, he wished us a safe journey back to the evil suburbs of the city.

These guys that work in these posh places suddenly think they're the Duke of Edinburgh, and everybody squeaky clean, get real I thought. So, after getting back to Casper's humble abode, I became really pissed on three cans of lager. These tablets are fantastic, even the grizzly bear is starting to look good.

'I'm thinking of giving up taxi driving,' I said to Casper.

'Oh, that's good timing, you're up to your neck in debt, and you want to stop working that's a brilliant idea,'

'I knew you'd agree,' I replied.

'I didn't say I wanted to give up work, I've just wanted to do something else. Being self-employed really pisses me off.'

'What do you fancy doing?' asked Casper.

'I suppose you could get yourself a job as a male model.'

'I thought I was the sarcastic one of the two of us.'

'Just learning Robbie, just learning. Do you think Martin's wife jumped off the top of the car park because she couldn't find the exit lift?'

'You are joking,' I said.

'Well you know what it's like, if there's a sale on somewhere,' said Casper. 'These women can get into a right frenzy trying to get there before anybody else. Do you think that's sexist?'

'No, it's just sick,' I replied, 'and we're both pissed.'

'Anyway, I think you better get home,' said Casper. I've got an early start in the morning, and you look dead tired.'

'Why did you say dead tired?'

'All right, you look knackered, you, sensitive bitch, just fuck off home.'

It took me several minutes to get the key in my front door, the taxi driver that brought me home seemed very serious.

I think he was worried I'd throw up in his car. I sat down on the settee and fell asleep. I awoke in the middle of the night freezing and then climbed up stairs clutching the bannister. Oh, for a good night's sleep! I'm defiantly not going to work in the morning,

I have a few financial items to sort out and then I'll phone the hospital about Martin. I managed to turn on the bedroom light. Lying in bed was Gloria.'

'Well don't stand there opened mouthed, I know you're drunk but get into bed and keep me warm.'

'Gloria, is that really you?' I asked, totally dumbfounded.

'Of course, it's me, who did you think I was, someone from rent a bonk?'

'I don't know what to say.'

'Well I suggest you have a good shower wash your cock and, in the morning, when you're sober and had a good night's sleep I'll decide whether to give you a mind blasting blow job or a good knobbing. Or, if there is still difficulty in that department we can just roll around and have multiple orgasms in all this money I've found in this plastic bag. Don't worry, I'm not going to tell anybody about this, it's our little secret. All of a sudden you've become so much more attractive.'

After a few minutes in the shower, I realised it was best if I took my clothes off. Gloria, must be one of the shallowest bitches I've ever met, but who cares. It's lovely to feel the warmth and smell of a female body, if I'm lucky in the morning I will have skinned the cat.

'Would you like two eggs with you fry up?' Gloria, asked.

'Well I'm trying to cut down.'

'Don't be silly, you burnt up a lot of energy this morning, if you'd carried on for much longer, I would have had to put a plaster on my fanny.'

Where's all this dirty talk come from, she would never use a word like 'fanny', especially her own. She would use words like, 'vagina', 'penis' and 'intercourse', all that sort of stuff.

'Robbie,' said Gloria, 'there's two ugly oversized men looking at my car.'

'Not only that, my taxi is missing, phone the police. I'm not going out to confront those two, they look evil. I suppose they could be debt collectors; they've taken my vehicle and now it looks like they're going to take yours,' I said.

'Robbie, you came home in a taxi last night,' said Gloria.

'Did I, I can't remember? 'Was your car there?' 'Yes, you, drunken fool.'

The police answered the phone, and Gloria, explained the situation.

'We'll get someone round as quick as we can. Make sure all the doors are locked, don't answer the door or pull funny faces out of the window, just pretend you're not in.'

The big fellows started knocking on the door.

'It's about time you got that doorbell fixed,' said Gloria, as we hid behind the settee.

'Have they come looking for the money?' she asked.

'They wouldn't know about that.'

'How can you be so sure?'

'I'll explain later.' I replied.

'The skirting boards need cleaning,' said, Gloria. 'Silly me, I forgot to pick up a duster before we got on our hands and knees. Gloria we're in fear of our lives and all you can think about is cleaning.'

'Any reason, you two are hiding behind the settee?' said the big fellow, as he looked down on me and Gloria.

'How did you get in here?' I asked with a mixture of anger and embarrassment.

'The garage and back door were unlocked.'

'Well, you have no reason to be in here. You realise you are trespassing, and the police are on their way,'

'We are the police, do you think you could stop this game of hide and seek and let my colleague in?'

He put his hand in his inside pocket. Oh no he's going to pull out a gun and shoot us, I thought to myself.

'This is my I.D, Inspector Wyatt, I have reason to believe your life could be in danger.'

'Why, is my sister in law coming around?' I asked. Gloria, looked at me in disgust,

'I'll go and let your colleague in,' she said.

'Don't do that Gloria, we don't know if this is a genuine I.D.'

'Have you been approached by anybody? You seem very nervous,' said the inspector.

'Of course, I'm nervous, two men come around my house, built like giant brick shit houses claiming to be police. I've never seen a police I.D. before. How the fuck do I know if these guys are genuine? You look more like the Kray twins, than the police, so just fuck off out of my house.'

'Calm down Robbie,' said Gloria, 'the uniformed police have just turned up.'

This is the one time I do wish Sniffer, was here, at least I would believe him. I don't know if these guys are genuine or not. There seemed to be a bit of an argument going on between the uniformed officers and the two big fellows, Gloria, put her arm around my shoulder.

'You were very brave. Robbie, 'she said, even though I think the joke about my sister was a little unnecessary.'

It turned out these big fellows were real police. Special Branch from the city, but it seems that this isn't their patch. They should have informed the local police first about paying me a visit.

'They need to speak to you about Martin Carr,' said one of the uniformed officers, 'it's pretty important.'

'Martin's car, it's a write off, I should imagine.'

'I didn't say Martin's car, I said Martin Carr, – that's his full name and they need to know what your relationship is with him.'

'What do you mean, relationship?'

'These two detectives will explain,'

The uniformed police officer got back in his car and as he drove off, he said to his fellow officer,

'the last time I was here there was a big punch up.'

'Oh, was this the place she'd had her tit's hanging out?'

'The very same.'

Me and Gloria, sat at the dining room table, with the big officers facing us.

'So, Inspector Wyatt, why do you think my life could be in danger?'

'Mr Carr, Martin to you, doesn't seem to have many friends and we think he could be involved in some serious criminal activity. The fact is that you and his housekeeper are the only visitors to see him, we need to know how well you know Martin?'

'I don't understand, he's just been involved in a serious car crash. I know he was involved with some dodgy characters years ago.'

'I must stress this is not a formal interview, it's just that Martin, is still unable to give us an account of what happened that night, one of the passengers is dead, the other is in a coma. Eye witnesses say he was driving like a maniac.'

'Martin, always drive like a maniac,' I replied.

'It's seems he may have driven into the lorry on purpose. Even stranger there was no type of identification on either of the passengers. No credit cards they had pay as you go mobile phones with just each other's phone numbers on them. They both had another number which seems to be unobtainable. Between them they had five hundred pounds in cash and two hand guns with silencers,'

'Two guns, was Martin, shot?' I asked.

'No, but both guns had been used,' said Inspector Wyatt.

His colleague, didn't say a word, he was just looking round the room.

'So why should I be in danger?' I asked.

'We don't know until the passenger comes out of a coma, or Martin, gains full consciousness. There are so many possible scenarios. Was he being held at gun point and chasing another car, or were they being chased? There was an empty suitcase in the car. Was there some sort of exchange going on that went horribly wrong? Even though we don't know who these people are, we're convinced they're big-time gangsters.'

'I know him as a taxi driver, that's all. As I say he always drives like a maniac, to tell the truth he seems to have latched onto me lately. He scares me to death.'

'He might not survive all this,' said Wyatt.'

'He has a daughter, Martina,' I said.

I explained, I've never met her, but Casper, might be able to give some more information about her. (That'll get Casper, worried, if these fellows come knocking on his door asking about his relationship with Martina,) Let's hope the big black bear will scare the shit out of them.

'It was a bad crash, and of course there's the other problem,' Inspector Wyatt, said.

'What other problem?' I asked.

'Didn't you know he's got cancer?'

'Bollocks,' I said'

'I don't know if it's testicular cancer, but it's quite advanced,' said Wyatt.

'Poor Martin, I can't believe that, he's so big and strong. Have you spoke to DCI Sniffer, sorry I mean, Snipe? He seems to know Martin, from a few years back.'

'Snipe, I haven't seen that old shit kicker for years, is he still wearing that old mac?' asked Inspector Wyatt.

'Does the inspector know you well?'

'You could say we've bumped into each other on the odd occasion,' I said.

'Eighteen months, that's what we use to call him.' 'Eighteen months?' I asked.

'Yes, he's got half an ear missing. One and a half ears, rhymes with one and a half years, equals eighteen months,' said the inspector.

'Yes, it's quit a subtle sense of humour you have at special branch. Don't you think Sniffer's a little less complicated?' I asked. 'How did he loose part of his ear?'

'God knows, he reckons he lost it in a knife fight, just him against four young yobbos. But I heard some big slapper with a tattoo on her forehead bit it off. Any- way, the guy's a twat,' said Wyatt. 'But I'll pay him a little visit, he might be able to give me some useful information about Martin. What about yourself, are you going to see him again at the hospital?'

'I was thinking of going to see him this afternoon,' 'I said.

'That's fine, if he does come around and tells you anything let me know straight away. It could be very useful. Here's my card and thanks for your time.'

'I'm sorry if we scared the shit out of you earlier on.'

'That's okay' I said, 'I think I over reacted.'

'I see your selling your house.'

'Yes, we're struggling financially, so we decided to downsize, as they say these days.'

'Best of luck, and don't forget to contact me if Martin, mentions anything to you about Saturday night.' They closed the door behind them.

Gloria, put her hand on mine, 'Robbie, has this got anything to do with all that money upstairs?'

'I don't know, Gloria, but I think we better hide it safely and not be too extravagant with our spending at the moment.'

'I know I didn't won't to know how you managed to get your hands on this money, replied Gloria. Obviously, it wasn't a gift from the bank manager. But maybe it's best if I do know, so we can cover each other's backs.'

'Do you really want to know?' I asked. 'You might not like what you hear.'

'Try me, big boy.'

So, I explained about Mr Gunman dying in the car and taking all his clothes off in the back seat in the lover's car park. It was very dark and raining heavily. One or two cars drove in. One or two drove out, but they didn't take any notice.

Seeing two people in the back of the car wouldn't seem unusual it just happened to be my partner was dead. He was a small bald man so it wasn't that difficult to get his clothes off. I then drove off to the nearby bridge, it was raining harder than ever. It took all my strength but I managed to get him out of the back seat and dumped Mr gunman in the river as naked as the day he was born.'

Gloria, looked at me in disbelief.

'It was a fast-flowing current, the river was starting to break its banks. He disappeared downstream almost immediately.'

'How could you manage that,' Gloria, asked me.

'One big bag of money. That's how I managed that. I have never seen so much money in my life, I'm fed up of being broke. There was no way I would have seen any of that money again if I'd have handed in to the police. Anybody who says money doesn't make you happy, is talking utter shit.

They ought to be broke for a while, trying to keep a roof over your head trying to keep your wife happy, trying not to go insane. This gift has come my way and I'm grabbing it with both hands. Fuck what the law says.'

Then I broke down in tears.

Gloria, put her arms round me,

'It's all right Robbie, I admire you for being so strong, all that stress and emotion. One minute you could have been shot dead the next minute you're worth a fortune. To make all these decisions is incredible. Did he have any identification on him?'

'None, he was carrying a wallet with about two hundred pounds in it. Oh, and one of those hotel key cards, a gun, and of course, the suitcase that was attached with a chain to his wrist. But I managed to cut that off.'

'What his wrist?', Gloria, squealed.

'No, the chain,' I said, 'he didn't even have a mobile phone.'

'Okay, is there anything in this house or garden that belonged to the dead man? If there is, I'll get rid of it now. Apart from the money of course,' said Gloria. What about the clothes you were wearing?'

'I washed them all, ready to throw them away.'

Just then, the phone rang. It was the nurse from the hospital. 'Martin's just regained conciseness. He's a bit confused and bad tempered but he has asked for you.'

'Must you go and see him? You could do with the rest,' said Gloria.

'I need to know if his car crash was anything to do with the gunman that was in my car.'

'Don't tell him, or anyone about the money, no one.' she insisted.

'I won't,' I replied.

'Let's make sure there is nothing that belongs to him in this house,' said Gloria. 'My brave little honey bun.'

I don't trust her one bit, I thought to myself.

9

Christine, stopped typing and just stared at me.

'Surely you don't expect me to print all this.'

'No I don't but you did say, warts and all, the part about the body and the money all came out at the trail, you asked for a story, and that's what I'm giving you, I hope what I've told you about Casper, hasn't upset you.'

'Of course not,' said Christine, 'Casper, was just naïve, he knew nothing about the dead body, not to start with. I'm just finding it difficult being face to face with someone who dumped a dead body in the river. It's just a bit scary.'

'I didn't kill him, he just died in my taxi, with a suit case full of money"

'Do you want me to stop telling you the story.'

Neither Christine, or myself spoke for a minute.

Then she took a deep breath,

'No, lets carry on.

So, you went back to the hospital to see Martin.'

I was surprised to see a plain clothes policeman sitting outside the ward. A young man with polite manners, must be new at the job. I'd never seen him before but he recognised me straight away. He showed me his I.D. then apologised that he needed to be with me in the ward and he had to take note of anything Martin, might have to say. I looked around the ward. Martin, didn't look any better since the last time I saw him.

'Is this all necessary?' I asked.

'Well we hope not,' said the inspector, 'but we can't be certain how safe Martin, is. It's not every day a taxi driver has two gunmen in his car.'

'Or even one,' I replied. Oops, I shouldn't have said that, I thought to myself.

'Has he ever mentioned recently about any of his relatives or friends? We know he has a daughter; does he have any hobbies?' the inspector asked.

'I think his only hobbies are eating and working. I don't even know where he lives.'

'Does he have any sexual relationships?' The inspector continued.

'Not with me he doesn't.' I said angrily.

'I didn't mean with you, I just meant with anybody,' I started to laugh. 'What's so funny?' asked Martin.

His eyes where wide open.

'Martin, you're awake, thank god,'

'Thank god! Have you been talking to that vicar again? I'm thirsty and feel like shit.'

'Martin, this is Inspector Mullion, from special branch.' Martin's, one eye was badly blood shot and made him look more sinister than ever.

The nurse came into the ward and told us both to step back from his bed. She checked his blood pressure and one or two other things and gave us two minutes to speak to Martin, and not a second longer.

It was no use, as far as the inspector was concerned, Martin, couldn't remember anything about the crash.

He said he could remember vaguely having an argument

with two customers, and telling them to fuck off, but as I explained to the inspector that was nothing unusual, Martin, recognised me, and asked if I had a good night, and starred at me in a way that made me feel uncomfortable.

The nurse more or less pushed us out of the ward insisting he needed his rest.

'He doesn't look too good,' said the inspector. We could do with the passenger gaining consciousness just to find out what really happened in the car that night.' The nurse looked at me.

'You can sit by his bed side if you wish but I can't have him being harassed.' As she spoke, she looked at the inspector sternly.

'I understand,' said the inspector, 'but don't forget Robbie, I need to know anything he tells you. It doesn't matter how trivial it may seem.'

'Is that including the bad language?' I asked.

'Even that,' said the inspector, 'I'll be sitting outside in the corridor, good luck.'

What a pleasant young man, I thought, unlike that bastard Sniffer. I sat by Martin, for about half an hour. His eyes opened now and again there was the odd grunt and twitch. I asked how he felt, but there was no response.

I wondered why he had asked for me, I left the hospital with such a mixture of feelings.

My wife is back with me. Even though she says she loves me, I don't believe her. If it wasn't for that big bag of money, she'd drop me quicker than it took me to drop Mr gunman in the river.

I know Martin's, done a lot of bad things in his time but to be stuck in that hospital all broken up, advanced cancer and no friends or relatives to visit him just seems to be so cruel.

For a few moments I couldn't find my car, in the hospital car park then I remembered I was in Gloria's, car. She was busy cleaning mine inside and out, getting rid of any evidence, even though I cleaned it myself shortly after the incident. But she always cleans the car better than me, even though she was probably looking to see if there was the odd wad of notes.

I drove out of the car park, on the passenger seat there were a dozen holiday brochures. I turned on the car radio, no report of a naked dead body, so that's good. Maybe we should have a holiday, nothing too extravagant.

We don't want to draw too much attention to ourselves.

Gloria, opened the front door as I drove on to the drive.

'How was your boyfriend?' she asked.

'Will you stop saying that? But being as you've asked, Martin, is in a bad way, it's impossible to get any sense out of him.'

'No change there then,' said Gloria. Why don't we catch a taxi and drive down to the city centre and buy some new clothes, have a nice meal at some posh restaurant? have a nice chat about how we spend all this money.'

You mean how you spend all this money, I thought to myself.

'Do you love me Gloria? It's not just the money is it?'

'Of course, I love you Robbie, the fact that you have dumped a dead body in the river doesn't repulse me in the slightest. We're rich and in love.' She gave me a kiss on my forehead.

I didn't believe a word she said the lying bitch.

'Thank you, Gloria, I'll get myself scrubbed up and we'll hit the town.'

I felt really happy actually spending money and not worrying about it, Gloria, was ecstatic.

We sat in some Italian restaurant eating a nice meal, drinking a bottle of wine and telling each other how good we looked in our new clothes. It was agreed that I should join the local gym as my waist was looking as though it might explode and go to a good hair dressers and have a professional haircut. I did suggest that I could have some cosmetic surgery on my neck and eyes. But Gloria, said I was being silly, who cares, I feel good.

The next few days we managed to keep our debt collectors happy either by paying them a large percentage of what we owe. Or convincing them we had a buyer for our house and that there should be some ready cash soon.

We could pay the lot off in one go, but that would look suspicious. I had a call from the police. It was Sniffer, he said he'd send a car round to take me to the hospital, he'd explain things when I got there.

'Is this about Martin? I said, 'I thought special branch was dealing with this.'

'Let's just say they need my expertise,' said Sniffer. 'Just make sure you're ready.'

While I was waiting for the car, I turned on the news, still no report of a dead body.

Sniffer, met me at the hospital entrance and told me we needed to find out what happened that night. Special branch feels because he knows us, he might be more forthcoming with anything he can remember. Sniffer, didn't hang about.

'Martin, special branch thinks this loss of memory is a load of bollocks. You remember me. You remember Robbie, so how come you don't remember anything about the crash?'

Martin, stared at us for a moment,

'I just don't,' he replied.

'Okay let's just stick to the facts. On Saturday night you drove like a mad man into a big lorry killing one passenger and who knows what will happen to the other fellow? We can make up lots of stories that because there were two guns in the car, you were being held at gun point by hardened criminals, but we can't prove that. We don't even know who these men are. If we can't get any information off you and the other fellow dies. You could be charged with dangerous driving and end up in prison with one leg and dying of cancer.'

'Fuck off Sniffer, you bastard, you wouldn't talk to me like that if I was well and standing on my own two feet.'

'Well, that could be the problem. You may not have two feet to stand on. Everyone will be calling you Hoppy,' shouted, Sniffer.

'What's the matter Martin? For once in your life, are you scared? Just tell me what happened in the car before the crash,'

'I don't agree with the way you're talking to Martin; this is way out of order,' I said. 'He is very ill and what you have just said is very insensitive.'

'Well you talk to him Robbie, because this thing could involve you,' said Sniffer.

'What do you mean, why should it involve me?'

'Well again, it's only guess work. But if these guys belong to a syndicate and let's just say someone out there is walking about with a case full of money, drugs, or jewellery that doesn't belong to them. They'll come looking for Martin, and any of his friends to see if they can get any information out of them.

Maybe Martin, had a gun to his head and was told to follow a car. They might think you're the driver of that car with all the goods, see what I'm trying to say?

It's all guess work at the moment.' said Sniffer.

'Come to think of it, you look very smart today, new haircut too, you usually look like a bag of shit,' said Sniffer. 'You could do with a sun tan though, you look as white as a sheet.'

'That's not funny.' I said.

'No. I know it's not funny it's deadly serious and it's about time everyone in this room realised this,' Sniffer, shouted.

'That's enough,' said the nurse, as she came rushing into the ward. 'This man is lucky to be alive; you must leave him to rest now.'

'But we need information now,' said Sniffer.

'I don't care,' said the nurse.

'I can't allow you to talk to my patient in this manner. I will have to report you to your superiors.'

'Silver Vauxhall Vectra,' said Martin.

We all turned to look at Martin.

'I'm sorry but you must leave now' repeated the nurse.

'Silver Vauxhall Vectra,' said Martin. 'They told me to follow it.' His eyes closed and opened again. 'They held a gun to the back of my head,' His eyes closed again.

'He's not dead, is he?' Sniffer, asked, with urgency.

'No just exhausted, so please leave the ward.'

'Do you think you really needed me? I don't think I was a great help; we know it was a Vauxhall but that's not much to go on,' I said.

'Listen Robbie, it's great news, not necessarily that he just remembers the car, but the fact he was told to follow it. When he comes round again we should find out a lot more, I almost feel happy.'

'Was that true about the cancer and his leg?' I asked.

'I may have laid it on a bit thick, but it's not good,' said Sniffer.

'I better phone up Wyatt Earp, and give him the latest news. That should cheer the big ape up a bit, fancy a drink?'

'No thanks, I need to get back home. Gloria, will be waiting for me,' I said rather proudly.

'So, you and Gloria, are defiantly back together? I heard not so long ago she never wanted to see you again, so what's happened?' asked Sniffer.

He just always seems to know what's going on. Is he playing games with me? Saying I might be driving the car that Martin, was chasing and mentioning my new clothes and haircut.

He said it in a sarcastic joking kind of way but did he mean it? Thank God, I don't drive a Vauxhall, he'd have me in hand-cuffs by now. Perhaps I should have a drink with him? See if I can tell what he's really thinking?

'Tell you what, I will have a drink, but only if you tell me your first name?'

'Fuck off, you'll be wanting to kiss me next. Just call me Sniffer. I'll get the first round. You better phone your wife,' he said.

'It's very sad, the only two friends you have is a thug and an evil detective,' said Gloria. 'Is this wise having a social drink with that arsehole?'

'It's okay, Martin's, been able to give us some useful information. He was chasing someone in a Vauxhall,' I said.

'Well that's good news,' said Gloria.

'I won't be long,'

'Okay, don't be, I've got some good news too, about the house,' said Gloria. 'Someone has put in a very good offer.'

'Great,' I replied.

'What did Gloria, say why are you drinking with that arse-hole?' said Sniffer.

'Word perfect that's exactly what she said.'

'And then she said don't be too long,' said Sniffer.

'Right again,' I replied.'

'Is that what you want?'

'Yes, that is what I want,' I said,

'You realise she'll leave you again.'

'What makes you think that?' I asked.

'They do it once, they'll do it again,' said Sniffer.

'They may stay a bit longer if you're worth a fortune, or you have a cock extension, but in the end, they'll fuck off with some good time Charlie.'

'Oh, you're a real bag of laughs to have a drink with,'

'Luckily for you Robbie, I'm in a good mood today.'

The police car dropped us off just around the corner from the boozer.

'Don't want to cause any alarm by parking a police car directly outside the pub,' said Sniffer.

'So were looking for someone who drives a silver Vectra. Oh, and by the way address me as Mr Snipe, while we're in the pub.'

The bar was fairly busy with one or two characters, it was obvious most of the locals knew he was a copper. I've no idea what they thought of me.

'Do you think Martin, was telling the truth?' I asked.

'Don't know, but special branch will be seeing him in the next half hour to try and extract some more information out of him.' Mr Snipe, replied.

'And if they can't, they'll probably ask me back.'

He took a sip of his vodka and coke,

'I used to drink whisky, but it was giving me a red nose. How's your lager?'

'It's fine,' I replied. Whatever I might feel about Sniffer, he was good at his job. In the twenty minutes or so we were in that bar he had managed to find out everything about me. Well, almost everything from what school I went to what jobs I had before I became a taxi driver, what Gloria, did for a living even what was wrong with her sister. But trying to get to know anything about him was almost impossible.

'Have you managed to get in touch with Martin's daughter?' I asked.

'Don't know, I've left that up to the big boys, have you met the housekeeper yet?' asked Sniffer, as he took a gulp of his drink.

'No'

'Doreen, that's a real rave from the grave, up until yesterday I hadn't seen her for years. Housekeeper, that's a load of bollocks, bookkeeper more likely.'

I asked him about Martin's brother and how long he had known him but no luck there either.

'Another time Robbie, ask me another time.'

'I still think the way you spoke to Martin, was wrong.'

'Listen Robbie, there's old ladies out there being assaulted and robbed in their own homes. young girls being raped and groomed for prostitution, all that sort of stuff. These are the cases I should be dealing with. I don't care about big-time gangsters getting themselves killed, nobody's reported anything or anyone missing. Okay, Martin, was unlucky, but I know he's done some terrible things in the past.'

'If that's true.' I said, 'how come he's never served a long prison sentence? And if you're so keen on prioritising your work, what was all that nonsense a few weeks ago about that landlady's blonde wig?'

'Oh well that was just my boss, trying to impress his apron wearing twats at the lodge, we never did find that wig. Apparently, it cost a lot of money she thought it enhanced her beauty, she'd be better off wearing a gas mask, the ugly cow.' Sniffer's phone rang.

'Well that's interesting, our mystery gun man who was in a coma has suddenly woken up. It's all happening today Robbie. Let's get back at the hospital, I can't wait to have a go at this gun slinging bastard,' said Sniffer.

'Let's get back in the car. Once I'm dropped off at the hospital, the officer will take you back home to your loving wife. I'll tell him to put the siren on and flashing lights, you'll enjoy that.'

He's a sarcastic arsehole, I thought to myself. I thought Martin, was a mad driver this copper was frightening, I think he was driving at warp speed ten.

I thanked him for the experience and was quite surprised I didn't shit myself. Gloria, greeted me with a kiss.

'You look very pale, Robbie, I think a holiday would do you good.'

The holiday brochures were spread across the table.

'I think you're right Gloria, what did you have in mind, four nights at a holiday camp in Bognor Regis?' 'I replied.

'You're teasing me now Robbie, we need to get away from all this rain and snow.'

'We've been very lucky round here, down south they've had

loads of the stuff,' I said.

'Exactly, that's why we're not going to Bognor Regis, we need to go abroad, get some sun. I thought a cruise would be very nice,' said Gloria.

'Listen Gloria, let's just take it easy. Both Martin, and the passenger of his car have gained conciseness. Who knows what they've got to say? Don't you think it's a bit of a coincidence, that on the same night a man gets into my car with a gun and a suitcase full of money? And seems convinced he's being followed by someone?

At the same time Martin, not too far away is possibly being held at gunpoint by two men. And told to chase after a car that might have something they desperately want.'

'Not really,' said Gloria. 'That's all guess work.'

'Guesswork! What if Martin's passenger says he was chasing my car? Let's just say he has my registration and full description of the car. That crushes the theory of any Fucking guess work,' I said, exasperated.

'Robbie,' said Gloria, 'I wish you wouldn't swear so much, your always like this when you get nervous.'

'Gloria, I'm more than a little nervous I'm worried to death, I'm terrified.'

'Robbie, just hold your nerve, the police don't know who they're looking for. He could be dead or alive. If they were to find the body tomorrow, they wouldn't necessarily link it up with this incident. Trust me once we've sold the house which could be soon, we'll rent a flat for a few months and that'll explain the excess money, just stay calm,' said Gloria.

'Just think of all that lovely money.'

'Your right, Gloria, just think of all that lovely money.'

The next day, after a good night's sleep and a visit to the doctor, I went to visit Martin, again. I felt better and more relaxed. The doctor said my health and state of mind had improved. He told me that if I keep taking the tablets, get plenty of sleep and have another week off work, I should be fine.

I think it helped last night, me and Gloria, played a little game in bed. We stuffed our underpants and knickers with loads of money and rummaged around to see how the stock market was performing. Whether we need to invest or withdraw depending on the market growth, generally speaking things were performing very well.

There was still a policeman sitting outside the ward. I'd not seen this one before, he looked very tired.

'Who are you?' He asked.

'A friend of Martin,' I explained.

'I need to see some sort of identification.'

I showed him my driving license.

'Are you a taxi driver?'

This guy could do with a personality transplant, I thought to myself.

'Yes' I replied.

'What sort of car do you drive?' I told him.

'Do you know any taxi drivers that drive a silver Vauxhall Vectra?'

'Yes Martin, for a start, it's a pretty popular car with taxi drivers. Can I go in and see Martin, now?'

'Okay,' said the policeman, 'I think he's awake.' Martin, looked at me with a glazed look, he lifted his hand slightly to acknowledge me. He looked a sorry sight.

'Hello Robbie,' he said, almost in a whisper. He seemed very weak.

'Thanks for coming to see me, I've had the police questioning me all day. Same questions all the time,' he paused. 'I've heard you're back with Gloria?'

'That's right,' I replied.

'Well, you look a lot better than I've seen you look for a long time,' he said. 'It's times like this when I wish I had a bit of crumpet to look after me, it can get very lonely sometimes. It's not going to happen now.'

Martin, stared at me for a moment.

'I crashed the car on purpose you know, I didn't mean it to be as bad as it was.'

'Do the police know this?' I asked.

'Oh no,' replied Martin.

'Those bastards in the car would have killed me. One of the them was sitting behind me with a gun pointed at my head, the other shithead was telling me who to follow. He was in a right state of panic. It was difficult with the traffic and bad weather, in fact I'm not even sure if we were following the same car just before the crash. I'm not even sure which one of the gunmen is still alive.'

'Has he told the police anything,' I asked.

'Fuck all,' said Martin. 'That's really pissed the police off. They were so excited when he woke up. But he can't remember his name or anything, or so he says.'

'I think you better leave now,' said the nurse, 'he still needs to rest.'

Martin's eyes started to close.

'Yes nurse,' I said. 'Will he get over this?'

'We honestly don't know,' she replied. Martin's eyes opened again.

'Nurse, I need to speak to my friend,' then he fell asleep again.

When I arrived home, I explained to Gloria, what Martin, had to say.

'See Robbie, we have nothing to worry about. I've seen some nice properties for rent in the paper. We could go and have a look at them and then go and have a meal somewhere. Are you all right, Robbie?'

'Yes,' I replied, 'fate is a strange thing.'

'What do you mean?' Gloria, asked.

'It could have been me driving those two gangsters and Martin, could have been the driver that picked up the dying man with the suitcase.'

'Oh Robbie, get a grip,' said Gloria. 'If my auntie had bollocks, she'd be my uncle! Now put your coat on we're bloody rich for God's sake cheer up.'

'It's just that it seemed he wanted to tell me something important.' I said.

While we were busy looking at flats, or apartments, things became quite exciting down at the hospital.

The detectives who were questioning the gunman were becoming pissed off with his so-called loss of memory. They knew he was lying and that he was probably scared that if he gave them any information he might get bumped off.

So, they tried a little trick. They pretended someone with a gun had come looking for him in the hospital, they even staged an arrest outside the ward.

The gun was loaded with blanks and the person carrying the

gun was a plain clothes policeman. One of the officers acquired a sachet of red sauce from the canteen for special effects.

The man with the memory loss looked on in disbelief as four officers apprehended a man rushing towards the ward with a gun in his hand.

It was so realistic the officer pretending to be shot, fell and banged his head on the floor and had to spend the night in a hospital bed with concussion. One of the other officers slipped on the opened sachet of sauce which had accidently been dropped on the floor and broke his ankle.

Nothing changed for the gangster with the lost memory, he just insisted on being moved to another hospital where there were fewer maniacs.

At more or less, the same time, Sniffer, had decided to see how Martin, was shaping up. Martin, who was still angry with him, managed to punch him in the face and broke his cheek bone, knocking him senseless. Even at deaths door, and wired up, he was still dangerous, I'm sorry I missed it all.

Gloria, was really enjoying herself, looking at different properties. It's amazing some of the descriptions these estate agents use. 'Garden; for someone with imagination, was the best! It was like a jungle; However, we did see a couple of apartments for rent that we liked and told the agent we could leave a deposit, that cheered up the estate agent.

We found a nice restaurant nearby and relaxed with a couple of drinks, then had a nice meal, even though I thought it was a little expensive.

My phone rang. It was Inspector Wyatt.

'Hello Robbie, how are you?'

'I'm fine, you've just caught me halfway through my meal.

'I replied.

'I'm sorry, but I need to speak to you, either at the station or at the hospital.'

'Is Martin, okay?' I asked.

'Martin's, fighting fit, but eighteen months' isn't too well.'

'Eighteen months? 'Oh, you mean Sniffer?' I asked.

Then the inspector explained the details about Sniffer.

'He's in the same ward as two of my other officers, just for observation. Hoping to see if they've got a brain cell between the three of them.'

The inspector started to laugh, 'I'll explain the rest at the hospital in an hours' time, see you then.'

'Why didn't you tell him to piss off? Gloria, asked, in a vexed tone.

'We were having such a nice time.'

'Gloria, where's all this bad language coming from?'

'I just get so frustrated with all these visits and phone calls from the police. 'I just want to be with my darling Robbie.'

She soon cheered up when I told her about the incident with Sniffer.

Inspector Wyatt, met me and Gloria, at the hospital main entrance, he looked as big as ever. 'We're doing a check on all the taxi drivers who were out that night and near the vicinity where Martin, picked up these two men. Did anybody see them get into his taxi? Or pick up someone suspicious?'

'What do you mean by suspicious? we can pick up some strange people, especially on a Saturday night,' I said.

'Well anybody, did you pick up anybody that was especially nervous or edgy. Looking out of the back window maybe there might have been more than one passenger, possibly carrying a suitcase?'

'No, I didn't pick up anybody like that. Is this the reason you wanted to see me? Couldn't this have waited till tomorrow?' I asked, angrily.

'Yes, it could,' said the inspector, 'but time's running out. The boys in forensic managed to clean up a piece of paper that was in Martin's, car at the time of the crash. At first, we thought it might be someone's initials, but it's possible it might be the first two letters of a car registration plate. The same two letters as your car.'

'Me and Gloria, looked at each other.'

'I'm not certain what you're getting at,' I replied.

'We know you were stopped by uniform police shortly after the incident and you had a male passenger in your car. We think that he might have been the man that was being chased.'

I started to laugh. 'I'm sorry inspector,

I know I haven't much experience of picking up hardened criminals, but if you want to go along with this line of inquiry carry on.'

'Don't take this personally, Robbie.'

'Well it's hard not to ever since this crash or incident, as you call it. I've been told my life is in danger because I happen to know Martin. Now you reckon I was driving the car that was being chased because of a couple of letters on a piece of paper.'

'Martin's, already told Sniffer that he was following a car that is totally different to mine,' I said in frustration.   'We're just trying to eliminate this man from our inquiry. If you could tell us where you picked him up and were you dropped him off? It's a shame Martin, couldn't remember the registration number.'

'My car isn't even silver,'

I better start thinking where I dropped him off, I thought to myself. I know it was in the river, but I don't think I better tell him that.

'I picked him up by the town hall.'

'The Town hall? queried the inspector, sounding slightly surprised.

'Was that after you dropped off two ladies near the theatre?'

'That's right,' I replied, 'I was on my way home.'

'When you dropped these ladies off, did you notice Martin's car at all?'

'No,' I replied.

'Is this really necessary?' Gloria, asked, all this has been very distressing for my Robbie,'

'That may be true, Gloria,' the inspector said, 'but I'm sure your Robbie, is well enough to answer a few more questions so, where did you drop this man off?'

I explained I dropped him off at the lover's car park near the river the other side of the city. There was a car waiting there for him I also said that he was polite, and that he was in no particular hurry and gave me a five-pound tip. Inspector Wyatt, stared at me for a while. Then I explained the car looked like a black Mercedes, but it was so dark and pissing down with rain, it was difficult to tell.

'Did he have a suitcase?'

'No, I replied he had a 'man bag that he held above his head, to stop his lovely blonde hair getting wet. He was very effeminate; he was jumping over the puddles like a ballet dancer in Swan Lake.'

'Is that what they do in Swan Lake, jump over puddles?' asked the inspector.'

'No, he was very dramatic,' I said.

'You don't look like the sort that would go to watch a ballet performance.'

'Robbie, took me to see the show last year for my birthday.' said Gloria. 'All those young muscular men, they were so athletic.'

The inspector gave me a hard stare, 'Do you enjoy that sort of thing?' he asked. 'Don't you think that's a little unhealthy? You should be going to rugby matches, events like that.'

'I tried that, I found it violent and boring,' I said. 'I can never understand all that business with the scrums. Sticking their heads up each other's arses and the ref blowing his whistle all the time, telling the players they're not doing it properly.'

'It's a great game you just don't understand the rules. I could have been a professional if I hadn't suffered a bad back injury,' said the inspector.

Oh, dear here we go again, another injured star, I thought to myself.

'Is that all inspector? We seemed to have drifted away from the main point,' I said.

'I was very fast for a big man,' said the inspector.

'I had very strong thighs, I looked very imposing in my shorts and fitted shirt.'

'Sounds to me like you should have been in Swan Lake,' I said.

'I'll have you know; I could have played for England. Excuse me my phone's ringing,' said the inspector.

'You can go now but I may need to speak to you in the near future,' he said, as he walked off.

'Perhaps, next time we meet he might have a couple of spare

tickets for the next England international.' said Gloria.

'I was very impressed with you, Robbie, you've become so good at telling lies.'

'Self-preservation, fear, and practise.' I replied

Gloria, gave me a kiss on the forehead.

'If I remember rightly, I saw Swan Lake with my sister.'

'That's right, you did, and you never stopped banging on about it for weeks, I'm quite angry about this,' I said.

'What, me going on about Swan Lake?' Gloria, asked.

'No, I'm on about this overgrown inspector asking about these two letters on a piece of paper, the big twat.'

'I've told you Robbie, they're just grasping at straws,' said Gloria.

'Hello, Robbie, Gloria.' It was Casper. 'I've just been to see Martin; he might not have forgiven me if I hadn't.

It was a bit awkward really, Martina, was there with Martin's housekeeper.'

'How is Martina?' I asked.

'She found it odd that I was visiting Martin, he seems a bit down at the moment, he was asking about you.

There seems to be a lot of men running about the hospital,' said Casper. Martin, hasn't hit someone else has he?' I asked.

'No, they're looking for the number one suspect, he's disappeared.'

'Who's number one suspect.' I asked. 'The guy with the lost memory that was in Martin's car.'

'How can that happen? there was always a policeman sitting outside the ward,' I said.

'Not this time, the security cameras caught the suspect running out of the ward with not a stitch on.' Casper, replied.

Someone came rushing towards us with a mask that looked like something out of the *Phantom of the Opera*. It was Sniffer, with his broken cheek bone.

'You lot haven't seen a naked man running past, have you?'

'No,' we all said.

'I'll get the bastard,' and then he rushed off.

'I'll just go and see Martin, while I'm here,' I said to Gloria.

'Don't be long Robbie,' said Gloria.

'Give me the car keys,' I said, 'Casper, can take you home, if that's all right, I won't be long.'

As I stepped into the main entrance, a uniformed policeman stopped me.

'Sorry sir we're not letting anybody in or out at the moment'

'But I've just come to visit a friend.'

'Sorry can't do it.'

Suddenly there was a message on his radio. 'Naked man seen running out of rear entrance, all officers assist.'

He paused for a moment,

'How can we be sure this is the same naked man we're looking for?'

'How can I be sure you're the right man for the job. Just move to the rear entrance now, you big twat.' Came the reply.

I walked quickly down to the ward that Martin, was in.

'Hello Robbie,' said Martin,' bit of excitement going on out there at the moment.' He stopped to gain breath. 'Seems they lost a patient. This is my daughter, Martina, and my house-keeper, Doreen,'

All very civilised for Martin, he doesn't usually introduce anybody.

'Hi,' I said to both of them. They're all rushing about outside looking for a naked man.' I said.

'Bunch of wankers, all of them,' said Martin. 'So how are you Robbie? you've just missed your mate, Casper.'

'Yes, I've just seen him.'

'I've seen the damage you've done to Sniffers face, that wasn't a wise thing to do' I said.

'Fuck him, fuck the lot of them. They're just a bunch of idiots.' Said Martin. 'I feel like shit, but that cheered me up a bit, Sniffer, was rolling around the floor like a wounded pig. when I hit him.'

The two women looked at me as though I shouldn't be there.

'We'll just go and have a coffee, while you and Robbie, have a little chat,' said Doreen. 'We'll be back soon.'

'I feel like I've interrupted something,' I said to Martin.

'You have, they're concerned who's going to look after me, when I get home, the pair of blood suckers.'

'Sniffer, showed me no respect, talking to me the way he does.' He paused for a moment. 'Robbie, I know I probably scare the shit out of you but I just need someone I can talk to. This thing about having my leg off, frightens me to death.'

Suddenly Inspector Wyatt, came running past. Stopped and walked back.

'You're not supposed to have a conversation with anyone unless there is an officer present,' he said angrily. Another officer came running past, well almost. Inspector Wyatt, grabbed him by the collar almost choking him to death. I'm surprised he didn't give him a rugby tackle.

'Perkins.' he said, 'Stay in this room and make a note of anything they say.'

'Well I'm not sitting to close to the big fellow in the bed. I've seen what he done to eighteen months earlier on.'

'Well that's okay,' said the inspector. 'Just make sure you don't leave this room. Any problems Perkins, just use your radio, you do know how to use your radio?'

'Yes Boss.'

Wyatt, ran off, Perkins, sat in his chair as far away as possible from Martin.

'I hate this job, under-staffed and low on resources. My mum went crazy when I came home with blood on my collar the other day it took me ages to convince her it was a nose bleed. She was going to write to the chief inspector. I haven't had a day off for weeks, it's all too much,' he said.

'What happened to the officer that was supposed to be guarding the criminal with no memory?' I asked.

Perkins, looked around.

'Well between you and me, we are severely under-staffed, even worse after that mock arrest in the corridor with those two officers getting injured.'

'So, are you saying they just didn't have someone watching over this criminal?' Martin, asked.

'Well we can only assume he is a criminal,' said Perkins.

'Well I was the one in the car being held at gunpoint by this criminal and his mate. You, dozy bastard!'

'Take it easy Martin.' I said. Perkins, looked terrified.

'They did have an officer keeping an eye on the criminal,' Perkins, replied with the emphasis on criminal.

'But the officer needed to go to the toilet, he was virtually shitting himself. He'd had a vindaloo the night before, that didn't agree with him. Nobody would cover for him, that's why he made the patient take off his gown and underpants. leaving

178

him with no clothes on at all.'

'Sorry I don't follow.' I said.

'Well the officer thought if he used the toilet next to the criminal's bed, with the door wedged open. He wouldn't run off with no clothes on. His timing was perfect as soon as the officer dropped his bags and started to open his bowels, as they say in hospital.

The suspect pulled back the sheets and ran out of the ward and down the corridor, like his arse was on fire. The officer whose arse felt like it was on fire, instinctively stood up to run and fell flat on his face, forgetting his trousers were still round his ankles. The shit didn't exactly hit the fan, but it did almost everywhere else. Some of these officers are very sensitive about losing face, he's probably being hosed down in the staff car park as we speak.'

10

Christine, started to laugh.

'This is the craziest story I've ever heard,' she put a hankie to her face and wiped away the tears,

'If you don't believe me just ask Casper,'

'Robbie, I believe you, just give me a minute to gain my composure. Okay let's get back to Martin, laughing in the hospital.'

'I had never seen Martin,' laugh so much in my life, even Perkins, was chuckling.'

'Don't tell anyone I told you,' he said. Martin, was uncontrollable with laughter.'

'Perkins,' he said, 'You've made my day; you're in the wrong job you should have been a comedian.'

'Apart from the uniform what's the difference?' now all three of us are in fits of laughter. Suddenly, Sniffer, with his new face mask covering his right cheek, walked into the ward.

'What's so funny?'

'I'm sorry Mr Snipe, but we've had strict instructions not to allow you in this ward,' said Perkins, still chuckling. 'Sniffer, pointed at Martin. 'You're going to pay for this, you, big fat bastard.' Martin was still laughing.

'Oh, come on Sniffer, you must learn to turn the other cheek.'

Sniffer, looked round the ward and grabbed a bed pan, jumped on the bed and started to hit Martin, over the head with it. But Perkins, surprised us all, he grabbed Sniffer, by the hair, pulled him off the bed and poked his fingers in both his eyes.

'You've blinded me,' yelled Sniffer, and ran straight into the wall almost knocking himself out.

'Are you all right Martin?' said Perkins. 'That was all a bit unorthodox, but it did the trick.'

Sniffer, wandered out of the ward.

'I'll have you!' he yelled.

'Perkins,' said Martin, 'you've gone up in my estimation.'

'Well, I thought when he hit you over the head with a bed pan, he was taking the piss,' said Perkins. We all started laughing again.

'Please don't make me laugh any more it hurts too much,' said Martin.

The hospital staff thought the police we're a bunch of maniacs. The naked man had disappeared out of site.

As for Mr Vindaloo Man, he was reprimanded and was ordered never to eat a curry again and always carry a toilet roll with him! Perkins, was recommended for a commendation. But they thought they'd better wait to see if he had blinded Sniffer, first.

'Thanks for coming Robbie. This has all been hilarious,' said Martin, he looked at Perkins and said, 'Inspector Perkins, you are my new hero. All for some and some for others', as the saying goes.'

Perkins, looked confused, but thought it best not to say anything.

'Is it possible I could speak to Robbie, without anyone listening? Martin, asked.

'Not really,' he said, 'but I'm having a little trouble with my radio I'll just stand by the door for a couple of minutes, but no longer,' said Perkins.

'What is it Martin?'

'I'm not certain, but let's just say, hypocritically speaking.'

'Do you mean hypothetically speaking?' I asked him.

'Yes, that as well,' said Martin, 'let's just pretend you come into some money for whatever reason, and you didn't want people to know.'

'Inspector Wyatt's, coming back.' said Perkins, 'End of private conversation.'

Martin, grabbed my arm and whispered in my ear.

'It, was your car, I was told to follow that night.'

My heart sank. That's it now, no secrets.

'The big boss is coming through the door any second now,' said Perkins.

'Well, we look like we've lost our prime suspect,' said Inspector Wyatt.

'That's impossible, how can a naked man escape, it's freezing out there?' I said. Then I suddenly thought.

'You've let him escape on purpose,' I said. 'You've fitted him with a tracking device, hoping he'll take you to his hideout.'

Martin, looked at me,

Where the fuck would you stick a tracking device on a naked man,' he said.

'In his neck or wrist, or even up his arse,' I replied.

'It's a lovely theory Robbie, I wish it was true,' said Inspector Wyatt. 'But don't you think it's a little elaborate to make the

182

officer who was guarding him shit up all four toilet walls? Still we've got his D.N.A. fingerprints and a mug shot.'

'Mug shot?' I asked

'photograph of his face.'

'Are you talking about the officer that shit himself?', 'I asked in reply.

'No, you idiot I'm on about the naked man.' said Inspector Wyatt.

'We know his height and distinguishing marks; we just don't know who he is. If only you could give us some more information about that night. You do realise your life could be in danger?' He said to Martin. 'Possibly yours as well Robbie.'

'Inspector, we've been through all this before,' I said.

He looked back at Martin,

'You do realise I could put you on a charge for assaulting a police officer?'

'Sniffer, was way out of order,' Martin, replied.

'I know that,' said the inspector, his style is a little old-fashioned and inappropriate.'

'Inappropriate!' Martin, said sarcastically. 'Is that a posh word for arse hole?'

'Yes, it is, and your yesterday's hard case who I believe isn't telling me everything that happened that night.'

Martin, glanced at me. Please Martin, don't tell the inspector you were following me, I thought to myself, please, please don't.

'I've told you everything I can remember,' said Martin.

'Okay,' said the inspector, 'but just remember if things go wrong you could be charged with dangerous driving, assaulting a police officer despite being in fear of your life. Because someone from the criminal underworld needed to extract some information from you. I can assure you their methods will make Sniffer, seem like Snow White. It seems to me the only real friends you have are Robbie, and your housekeeper.'

'So, what's that got to do with me?' Martin, asked.'

'Come on Martin, you know the score' said the inspector. 'You get home one night and all the furniture in the dining room has been carefully rearranged. The phone rings, and a sinister voice tells you they're sorry they missed you, but they have a good friend of yours in their 'care,' You can hear scream-ing in the background because they've just cut off one of your friend's fingers, and send it back to you through the post.'

I went into a hot sweat, my brain was swirling the room was fading, I could feel myself falling to the ground as I fainted.

Where am I? It's raining hard, very hard, it's dark, I'm in a small boat trying to row upstream. There are loads of human skeleton's wearing blonde wigs and dark glasses, trying to get on board, I keep trying to beat them off with my oars but they keep coming back. Their bones clattering. I'm getting exhausted, the more I beat them off the more blood appears on my hands.

I can see, Gloria, sitting on a bridge, urging me to row, as fast as possible. She was a mermaid. Suddenly, out of the river appears a thirty-foot-high Sniffer, with his dirty mac on, with sharks' teeth and empty sockets were his eyes should be. He was snapping at my legs; the skeletons were trying to take my clothes off. The giant Sniffer, was chewing at my legs. Gloria, was now swimming round the boat, telling me to try harder. Her hair was perfect. I was lashing out at the skeletons and shouting.

I was trying to kick Sniffer, away, but my legs were chewed to my knees.

I woke up shouting and screaming, lashing out at Inspector

Wyatt, and Perkins.

'Calm down Robbie, calm down,' said Inspector Wyatt, 'You're hallucinating.'

'I need to get to the toilet, I feel sick,' I felt awful. I was as sick as a dog; my head was in the toilet bowel. I felt breathless, my heart was pounding, please stop, I can't stand feeling like this.

'I think you better stop taking those tablets,' shouted Martin.

'Every time I come into this ward there's always some sort of disruption,' said the nurse, angrily.

'I'm sorry.' said Inspector Wyatt, 'but this man fainted.'

'Well get his head out of toilet and put it between his legs.'

'What?' Perkins, asked. 'Put the toilet between his legs.'

'No' said the nurse, put his head between his legs. Have you no sense at all? Don't you men think it would be better if you were outside looking for this naked man. Instead of causing trouble in here? off you go,'

The nurse gave me a cup of water. 'I'm sorry nurse, I thought I was getting better.'

'Let me see these tablets your taking?'

I looked up and I could see inspector Wyatt, and Perkins, standing outside the ward.

'Keep your head down and take deep breaths,' said the nurse.'

'Is Robbie, okay?' Martin, demanded.

'It would help if he had a little less excitement in his life, you're all like a bunch of children.'

'Well, nurse I can't thank you enough for looking after me,' said Martin. But I didn't choose to come here unlike those two arseholes standing out there.' Martin, gave them the 'V' sign as he spoke.

'Martin, I've told you about your behaviour and bad language.'

'Sorry nurse,' he replied sheepishly.

I gave the nurse my little jar of tablets.

'I suggest you take half the dosage, and no more,' she paused for a moment, 'how long have you been taking these?'

'About four weeks,' I said.

'For Christ sake, it's a wonder you haven't tried to commit suicide, or kill someone,' said the nurse. 'These doctors haven't got a clue, pompous twats.'

'Language, Nurse,' said Martin, looking rather smug. 'That's very improper.'

'Have you driven here?' She asked. 'I think you better stay here for about twenty minutes before you go home, just sit here and relax.' Inspector Wyatt, was insisting that there should a police officer present in the ward, but the nurse would have none of it.

'You can sit outside and that's it, you are too much of a disruptive influence.'

'That was the worst nightmare I've had for a long time,' I said to Martin.

'Don't worry Robbie, 'I won't tell anybody our little secret,' said Martin.

The Nurse had left the ward, telling us she'd be back shortly.

'You need to toughen up.'

'What do you mean?'

'That wasn't the tablets, that made you faint, it was Inspector Wyatt's, horror story. He's just frightened the shit out of you. You'll give the game away if you're not careful.'

'How can you call this a game. There's been a big car crash

and one death could have been two more, guns being pointed at people's heads, death threats. That's not exactly my idea of snakes and ladders,' I said.

'Keep it calm Robbie, we don't want to draw attention to ourselves, do we?'

'I'm sorry Martin, but if you tell the police you were following my car, I'm in deep shit.'

'How deep?' He asked.

'Tons of the stuff,' I replied.

'You mean way above your head?'

'Yes.'

'Listen Robbie, I don't want to know what went on in that car, but I defiantly know it was your car I was following.'

'So why didn't you tell the police?' I asked him.

'Instinct, I suppose. Don't worry Robbie, as long as you don't change your story, I'm not going to change mine, but it looks a little suspicious you turning up with new haircut and brand-new clothes, your wife comes running back to you. Does she know what happened that night?'

'Yes, she does.' I replied.

'Oh Fuck,' replied Martin. 'You better tell her Wyatt's horror story and curb her spending. I reckoned this guy that was in your car gave you a backhander to keep your mouth shut. I just wondered where did you drop him off, was it at the airport, something like that?'

'No, I dropped him off in the river.'

Martin, looked round the ward and swallowed hard.

'Don't you mean you dropped him off by the river?'

'No, I dropped him off in the river, he was already dead.'

'Fuck off,' said Martin. You couldn't pick up a dead cat off the road without throwing up. Are you saying you dropped a corpse off in the river? Does Gloria, know?'

'Yes,' I replied.

'Of all the taxi drivers, in all the hospitals, in all the world, I happen to be talking to a murderer.' Martin, was shaking his head. 'It's, like being told Thora Herd, was head of the S.A.S.'

'I, didn't say I murdered him, he was already dead when I dropped him in the river'

'Oh, that's not so bad, is there anything else I should' know he said in uncontrollable laughter. 'Did you take his clothes off and chop him up into little pieces?'

'No. I just took his clothes off.'

'Oh, stop it Robbie, it hurts when I laugh, I'll have a heart attack. All this talk about feeling tired run-down fainting and spewing everywhere and as cool as you like, you dropped some corpse in the river. Please tell me Robbie, is this a joke?' The nurse returned.

'You seem a little happier Martin, and how do you feel Robbie?' you seem to have a little colour back in in your face.'

'Yes, he's fine,' said Martin. 'Robbie could kill for something to eat; we've had a nice little chat.'

'Yes, I feel fine to drive home,' I said. 'See you, Martin.'

'See you, Robbie. Remember what the nurse said, cut down on those tablets it's making you see things,' he said, still laughing.

'You were having a good chat in there,' said Inspector Wyatt, as I walked out of the ward.

'What were you talking about?' He asked.

'Have you ever had a conversation with Martin, inspector? It's not one of the easiest things. It was just light-hearted stuff, trying to cheer him up.

Good night, inspector.'

I drove home that night wondering whether it was the right thing to have told Martin. He didn't believe a word of it anyway. But the truth is, I trust him more than I would ever trust Gloria.

I shall tell her Martin, lied to the police about the car he was following, and that he mentioned it had been noticed we seemed to be spending a lot of money. But I won't mention to her that I told Martin, about the dead body. Martin, phoned up just as I got home.

'They've found the naked man from the hospital halfway up a tree in a nearby woodlands. He's still alive, freezing to death, lucky he didn't bump into you first Robbie.'

'What do you mean by that?' I asked him.

'We probably wouldn't have seen him again, there was a vicious dog trying to bite his dick off. The owner of the dog, an old widow said she's never had so much fun taking pictures with her new phone.

She'd outlived three of her husbands and reckons the three of them, put together, wouldn't have as much meat and veg between their legs as this bastard. The police have taken him some were a little more secure. It's all been happening today,' said Martin, with a loud laugh.

'Inspector Wyatt, seems a lot happier too.'

'Thanks Martin, that's good news, I'll pop round and see you tomorrow,' I said.

'No rush,' said Martin. 'I feel exhausted after everything that's gone on today, I need a good night's sleep.'

'You look very pale,' said Gloria.

'Yes, I wasn't very well at the hospital, by the way Martin, told me it was my car he was told to follow.'

'Oh shit.' Gloria, said,

'But don't worry, as long as we stick to our story, we'll be fine. 'He's not going to tell the police that, as far as they're concerned, Martin, was told to follow a silver Vauxhall.'

Gloria, looked confused.

'I'm grateful he lied, but why?'

'Instinct, and his mistrust of the police,' I said to her, 'let's go to bed, I'm knackered.' I woke up in the morning to find Gloria, looking at the holiday brochures, again.

'There some good last-minute deals on the I pad,' she said.

'Gloria, let's just have a quiet day at home. I'm fed up of looking at holidays brochure visiting hospitals, and being questioned by the police.'

'Don't worry, I'll cook you a nice breakfast, and then you can repair the doorbell.'

'What's the point? The house is almost sold,'

'Well we don't want the place to go to rack and ruin, do we?'

'I'm sure a broken doorbell wouldn't stop any one from buying the place.' I replied.

'Your phones ringing,' said Gloria.

'Fuck off.'

'What?'

'Not you. Whoever's on the phone, tell them to fuck off. I just want a quiet day.'

'It might be someone inquiring about the house, and there's no need to swear so much.' Gloria, said, as she answered the phone.

'It's Mavis, for you. Do you want me to tell her to fuck off?

Or shall I go, and cook the breakfast?'

'I'll have two eggs with my bacon, please darling. With a bit of luck, I might enjoy this conversation.'

'Hello Robbie,' said Mavis. 'Any chance you're coming back to work one day? I know you said you wanted some time off but this is ridiculous.'

'Is it really?' I asked sarcastically.

'Yes, it is, you need to pay your rent, or we'll have to dismiss you. You know you can't afford to be without a job.'

'Is your dad there?' I asked her.'

'No,' said Mavis, 'he's had to do some taxi work himself today, because bastards like you don't turn up for work. All of them using silly excuses like being involved in a pub brawl or getting knocked out by a man in a wheelchair. I suggest you get in your taxi now and do some work, you idle get. Anyway, why did you want to know if my dad was here?'

'It would have been nice,' I replied, 'to speak to you together, and tell you and Daddy to stick the job up your arses, and go and fuck yourselves. You ugly cow, goodbye!'.

'I gather you've, tendered your, resignation,' said Gloria.

'Yes,' I said, 'That's really made my day, I think I made myself clear enough.'

'Very clear,' said Gloria.

I had a really nice breakfast and, even though I was interrupted on the phone by Mavis's Dad, I had just as much enjoyment repeating my thoughts to the big twat.

'I love it when you're so strong Robbie,' said Gloria. 'Do you think we can trust Martin?' she asked.

'Martin, might have many faults, but I trust him,' I said, 'he's more concerned about losing his leg. They did take the wrong leg off some poor bloke the other month, maybe that's playing on his mind?'

My phone rang again, so much for a quiet day.

Gloria, answered,

'It's Inspector Wyatt,' she turned pale and struggled to speak. 'You okay Gloria?'

'I'm not sure. Martin, won't have to worry about his leg anymore,' said Gloria. 'He died in the early hours of this morning. They think it was a massive heart attack.'

'Martin's dead?' I don't know what to say. I don't know what to think. 'He risked his life for me, I've only just thought about it that way,' I said to Gloria. She put her arm round me.

'Well he was trying to save his own life as well,' said Gloria. I looked at my wife.

'I was, so concerned about myself, I never gave it a thought, no other driver would have done what Martin, did, driving into that lorry on purpose not telling the police he was told to follow my car.'

'Robbie,' said Gloria, 'Perhaps Martin, wanted it this way, he didn't want to die slowly of cancer, hobbling about on one leg.'

'You sound like Sniffer.' I said. I've never seen Martin, laugh so much as he did yesterday, for the rest of the day a black cloud hung over me.

I had a phone call from his housekeeper, asking if we could meet up somewhere. She wanted to discuss details of Martin's funeral with me. She gave me the address of Martin's house and we met each other the following day.

I was amazed how organised Doreen, was, she had been Martin's housekeeper for several years. She stood upright, and was smartly dressed, albeit in an old-fashioned way. The house was surprisingly clean and tidy.

After the death of his brother and the chaos it caused, Martin, wanted everything, financially and legally, to be sorted out properly before he died.

'He's left everything to me and Martina,' said Doreen. As I am sure you are aware, Martin, didn't have many friends or relatives.

'Doreen,' I said, 'why are you telling me this?'

'Because, like Martin, I have very few friends or relatives. Until such time when the funeral is over, I need someone to assist me and run me about, are you still working as a taxi driver?'

'Strange you mentioned that, I told my boss only yesterday to stick his job.' I paused for a second.

'Up his arse,' said Doreen.

'That's right,' I replied.

'So, you still have a car?'

'Oh yes, I still own my own taxi.'

'Good.' she said, she was very assertive and spoke with a loud, clear voice.

'Inside this envelope there is two thousand pounds, take it. In effect I'm hiring you to be my chauffer and odd job man. Do you think you can do that for me and for Martin?'

'Excuse me Doreen, but you don't even know me and I certainly don't know you.'

'Let me explain,' said Doreen.

This is Martin's money. He knew he was dying, and he could trust me to carry out his wishes and that I would need someone to assist me in carrying out my duties.'

'I didn't think he liked me that much,' I said.

'He didn't like most people. You were lucky. I will need receipts for everything. Fuel, hotel bills, meals, and you will be reimbursed weekly.'

'Why would I need to stay in hotels?' I asked.

'Because, Martin, had a small property down south. Are you married?' she asked.

'Yes'

'Good, if you have to go down there take your wife. Men go silly with alcohol and prostitutes if they go to hotels on their own. You don't seem certain about all this Robbie,' she said.

'What about his daughter, Martina, can't she help you?'

'No. this has all been too upsetting for her.'

'It's all a bit of a shock for me,' I replied, 'first Martin, dying so suddenly, then to find out he seemed relatively well off and organised. Please don't take this the wrong way, but you seem more like a personal assistant than a house- keeper.'

'What were you expecting, someone with jet black hair, excessive eye makeup and an artificial tan?'

'I think what I'm trying to say is, Martin, and you seem so wrong for each other.'

'Robbie, I'm offering you a good deal, all I ask is apart from your wife no one else needs to know about this.'

'Okay,' I said, 'when do I start?'

'I'll give you a call tomorrow.

I'm sorry if my manner makes you feel a little uneasy. Martin, in his own way was very good to me, but at the moment I have little time for sentiment. I thank you and will speak to you soon. Your help will be greatly appreciated, good afternoon.'

That was all a bit scary. I can't imagine Martin, with his farting and bad language getting on with Doreen. If she wanted a job as housekeeper, I'm sure she could have found someone better than Martin, and she's not an easy person to get on with.

Doreen, seemed very precise cold and middle class. Still she's done all right if Martin's, left her and Martina, two houses, and who knows what else? She's probably been waiting years for Martin, to die.'

'Is Doreen, good looking,' asked Christine.

'No, I replied, 'why do you ask.'

'Oh, I can't imagine Gloria, being too pleased about this woman appearing on the scene.'

'Your right she wasn't too happy.'   'Do you want a break Robbie, a drink or something like that?'

'No thanks, have you ever been married Christine,'

'I wondered when you were going to ask me that question. It seems to cause a certain amount of interest and confusion to a of lot of people that a person my age is still single.'

'Well you are a very attractive woman.'

I felt tempted to ask if she had ever been in love. I'm sure she's broken a few hearts.

'Thank you, Robbie, that's very kind of you, let's just say I enjoy my independents and thanks for not asking my age.'

'I wouldn't dream of it; shall we carry on with the book.'

'Okay, said Christine, you had just left Martins house after talking to Doreen.'

I called in at Casper's, flat on the way home.'

'For fucks sake Casper, this bear looks scarier than ever.' I said as I walked through the door.

'Where did you get those eyes?'

'Egg shells' he said proudly. 'I cut two eggs in half and then painted eyeballs on them.'

'I must have missed that episode of Blue Peter. Mind you, I suppose if you took it down to the Tate Gallery, you could be awarded artist of the year. You'd probably cause a few accidents on the way down to London if you put him in the passenger seat.'

'What's Blue Peter?' Casper, asked?

'Never mind,'

'Bit of a shock about Martin,' said Casper.

'Yes' I replied.

'Will you be going to the funeral? I can't imagine there'll be many there.' said Casper.

Then I explained my meeting with Martin's house- keeper. I didn't mention about the property down south, or her generous pay packet. Casper, can talk too much and Doreen, did ask me to keep quiet.

'Have you seen Freddie, lately?' I asked.

'I spoke to him this morning on the phone. He's forgiven us Robbie, he was in a good mood, he must have given someone a good knobbing.' said Casper.

'Hope it wasn't Belinda,' I said. 'I must go home now.'

'Well that was a quick visit,' said Casper. 'Still you don't want Gloria, to think you've been kidnapped.' 'Kidnapped, why do you say that?'

'Calm down Robbie, it was just a joke,' said Casper. 'Oh yes, very funny.

I'll see myself out. Bye' Casper, bye Mr Bear.'

To say Gloria, was angry was putting it mildly,

'Why did you agree to do this for this woman? You don't

need the money, have you taken leave of your senses?'

'I'm doing it for Martin, it's the least I can do.'

'You and Martin, what is it with you two?'

'Listen Gloria,' I said angrily, 'if it wasn't for him, we probably wouldn't have this money.'

'Robbie, it was you that had a gun pointed to the back of your head.'

'So did Martin.'

'If Martin, had done his job properly he would have made sure he killed both those gangsters,' said Gloria. 'Then we wouldn't have to worry about the only survivor giving the police so-called useful information.'

'That's a bit harsh, poor Martin's dead.'

'Yes, and you could have been, but you made decisions, strong decisions,' said Gloria. 'Not many people would have had the nerve and composure to do what you did, using a wig and sunglasses pretending to the police he was a sleeping passenger. Do you think Martin, would have been that smart?'

'Well no,' I replied.

'Do you think Martin, would have thought to drive to a lovers car park and get into the back seat and take all the dead man's clothes off without raising suspicion?'

'I've been thinking about that' I said. 'Martin, at that stage, would probably have dropped him off at the car park and driven over his head to destroy any dental evidence.'

'That's rather barbaric,' said Gloria.

'I think that might have caught the attention of the other couples.'

'Possibly,' I said.

'Robbie, you were the true professional, you dumped the

corpse in the river with no form of identification on him at all. You don't have Martin, to thank for that, now tell this woman you've declined her offer.'

'No.' I replied. 'This property, down south, might be just the place to stay for a few months, somewhere to relax for a short while.'

'You don't know anything about the place,' said Gloria.

'Exactly, this gives me a chance to have a look at it. Come on Gloria, let me do this and I promise we'll go on a cruise after all Martin's stuff is sorted out.'

'You promise,' said Gloria, giving me one of her frightening stares.

'I promise.'

'Okay, I'll go and check things out on the internet.'

I decided to give Sniffer, a call, just to see if he knew much about Martin's housekeeper.

'They go back a long way,' Sniffer, said, 'I wish I did know a lot more about Deadly Doreen.'

'Deadly Doreen,' I said. 'Why is she called that?'

'Because years ago, like Martin, she used to rub shoulders with some of the biggest villains in the Midlands. But unlike Martin, she had brains. That was in the bad old days or good old days, depending on your point of view.'

'It's not that important, I said, 'she just doesn't seem the sort of woman Martin, could tolerate and she certainly doesn't seem the sort that would tolerate Martin.'

'It takes all sorts, Robbie she's a hard woman, I'm sorry about Martin, but he's rode his luck over the years. I'd come around to see you but I'm suffering with blurred vision at the moment after that bastard young Perkins, poked his fingers in my eyes.

I'll have him. I must say Robbie, you seem to be attracted to the criminal element, first Martin, and now deadly Doreen.'

'How's the broken cheek bone?'

'Still broken, even in his dying days Martin, managed to leave his trademark. He could throw a punch.' Sniffer, said, with a grudging sense of admiration.

I told Sniffer, about the phone call from Doreen, and how surprised I was to see what a decent home Martin, had. I was uncertain if it was actually his home.

'I can't see what you're worried about,' said Sniffer. Martin, obviously told her you were an okay sort of guy. Someone she could trust who would be able to do a few errands for her. If you don't feel easy about her just refuse the offer, have you heard any more about our mystery gun man with no memory?' he asked.

'No' I said.

'They're closing the case,' said Sniffer. There's nothing to go on it's just become a complete waste of police time. The big problem is, what to do with Donkey Man?

'Who's, Donkey Man?' I asked.

'The naked gunman, that's his new name,' said Sniffer. They're not certain whether to send him to a care home an asylum or the local freak show.

'Do you think he's really lost his memory?' I asked

'I don't think so, but he's putting up a pretty good show. Nobody seems to know anything at all. I know there's been all this talk about your life could be in danger but I think that's all bollocks now. If I was you Robbie, I would just go home and relax and tell Doreen, to fuck off.

I must go Robbie. I need to put some drops in my eyes, only

phone me if someone has killed young Perkins.'

Doreen, phoned me the next day.

'It will take some time before the funeral takes place,' She said. 'The hospital has yet to decide what Martin, died of. I have phoned the funeral director informing them about the size of Martin, and the delay with the hospital.

I need you to take me to check on the state of this property down south. I know there's been a lot of snow and flooding down that part of the country but I believe it's clearing up quite nicely. All things being well we should get back about ten tonight. Bring your wife if you wish.'

Gloria, asked how old this woman was and whether she was attractive, after I told her the truth, she paused for a moment.

'I still think this is stupid Robbie, but you carry on being the good Samaritan. I'll find something to do around here. I don't fancy the journey in this weather.'

11

I picked Doreen, up at Martin's house. She had several bags with her. That gave me the impression she was staying the week. Gloria, was probably right, the further south we went the worse the weather became.

'I daresay your wondering why the rush?' Doreen, asked me. 'There's a part time gardener, come general handy man that we employed. But I've not been able to contact him, he hasn't answered his phone and he hasn't bothered to phone me.'

'Has he worked for you a long time?' I asked.

'About twenty years,' replied Doreen. 'His wife died about twelve months ago, and he's never been the same since drinking whisky all day and not eating. You know how weak men are in a crisis? They always turn to the bottle; they always need a woman to look after them. It's all right when they're young attractive full of fun. But it's different when they're old single and smell of urine and moan all the time. Women have got more sense these days. Do you get on with your wife?' Doreen, asked.

'Yes, I do and I bathe on a regular basis,' I replied. 'how did you get on with Martin?

I could feel Doreen, staring at me.

'Let me make this clear, this was a business arrangement. Martin, was loyal. Yes, he was uncouth but between us we managed to survive some difficult times. But to answer your question I got on with Martin, very well, so let's leave it at that.'

'Does this handyman live far from the property? 'I asked, feeling it was wise to change the subject.

'Fergal? No, he lives in a caravan about a mile away from West Farm cottage. He has a small piece of land by the river where he keeps a few pigs and horses. The trouble is any bad weather, the land gets flooded. He used to be reliable but not since his wife died.'

'So, it's a cottage?'

'Yes Robbie.'

'Nice name, West Farm.'

It took a couple of hours to get there, the snow had turned to rain, but the last couple of miles where a little tricky. The cottage stood amongst two big fields, very few trees, and you could see further on where the river had broken its banks. The tarmac road came to an end at the cottage and continued as a dirt track.

'Fergal, lives just over there.' As Doreen, pointed to the river. 'The floods are worse than I thought they would be. Let's go inside the cottage and check it out.' she said.

The cottage was cold and damp with very little furniture and no ornaments.

'At least no one has broken in,' said Doreen.

'Does that happen often?' I asked.

'No, but normally Fergal, keeps an eye on the place,' replied Doreen. 'I think he's just given up and died. I'll phone the local police, there's no way to get access to his caravan. Hopefully he moved out before the floods started. Do you know how to start a log fire?' she asked.

'Course I do, I used to be in the Boy Scouts,' I said.

'Good get cracking,' said Doreen, and when you've done that, get those bags out of your car.'

'You sure you were in the Boy Scouts? You don't seem to be having much luck starting that fire. Give me those matches, you go and get those bags out the car, she said,

'What did the police say about Fergal' I asked her.

'Nobody's heard from him, the police managed to get to the caravan yesterday, in their police dingy but the caravan was locked and there was no livestock about. They banged on the door, but there was no answer.'

'Why didn't they brake in?' I asked.

'Because they'd dropped their specialist equipment in the water and couldn't find it again,' said Doreen. 'They flew over today in their helicopter and could see no sign of life, so they'll try again with their dinghy tomorrow and see if he's popped his clogs,' she added, in a 'matter-of-fact' manner.

'I need to employ someone pretty quick. Come on Robbie, get those bags out the car I think I've got the fire started. We'd have been all day waiting for you I don't think you were in the Boy Scouts at all.'

She's a bossy old cow, I thought to myself as I brought the last bag into the cottage.

'You've got company, Doreen,' I said, as I could see a police car coming down the road.

'Don't worry, Robbie, every time I come here, they always give me a visit, looking to see if I'm hiding some known criminal or a body perhaps? They'll be really interested in you just be ready for twenty questions. Let me see how mentally tough you are.'

Mabey Sniffer, was right, I shouldn't have got involved

helping this woman.

'Hello' said the plain clothes officer, 'my name is Inspector Todd, I assume you are, Doreen McCluskey?'

'You assume correctly,' said Doreen, 'I'm sure the sergeant standing behind you can vouch for that, we have met on one or two occasions.'

'That's correct, Doreen, where's the big man today?' asked the sergeant.

'Martin, he's resting quietly in hospital,' said Doreen, 'he's dead.'

She looked at me. 'This is Robbie, he brought me down here and is going to help me tidy the place up, and to see what's happened to Fergal.'

'Martin's dead, is he? How did that happen?' asked Inspector Todd.

'He was in a bad traffic accident,' Doreen replied.

'Well, that should make my life easier, the locals will be glad to see the back of Martin.' He looked at me.

'You don't look like a hard man Robbie, does he to you, Sergeant?'

'No Chief.'

'Anyway, you're still barred from the local boozer, Martin or no Martin.'

'What, me as well?' I asked, 'I've never been here before.'

'Even more reason to bar you. I know nothing about you. Tell him Doreen, what happened on that first visit to the pub, you were there with the big man.'

'That was almost twenty years ago,' said Doreen. 'My memory fails me. What's happened to Inspector Rashford? He usually visits me on these welcoming parties.'

'Early retirement,' said the sergeant.

'Oh, so he was found guilty on those corruption charges?'

'Like the sergeant says, early retirement,' replied the inspector.

'And a big fat pay cheque,' said Doreen.

'I would suggest you put this place on the market.' said the inspector. 'If Fergal, has disappeared, or died. You are vulnerable to break-ins and the police don't have the financial resources like they use to have in Inspector Rashford's days. We can't keep checking on isolated buildings, we are not security guards.'

'You don't seem to say much, Robbie.'

'No, I'm a quiet sort of guy. Did you want to check my driver's license, and taxi badge?'

'Sergeant, just take his details. So, are you two staying the night?'

'Yes, we are,' said Doreen, 'and we're not sleeping together or having sex. Is that okay inspector?'

'Oh yes,' said the inspector, looking all embarrassed.

So was I.

Thanks for letting me know, I thought. Gloria's, not going to be too pleased about this. Doreen, might be dominant and scary. But this was not the agreement when we set out this morning, I will have to put my foot down.

'Well your documents seem to be in order,' said the sergeant, and gave them back to me.

We'll leave you now,' said the inspector. 'I will let you know if we hear anything about Fergal.

'Bye inspector,' said Doreen.

When was it decided we were staying the night? I asked Doreen, my wife is going to go ballistic.'

'It's amazing,' said Doreen, 'how some wives think their

husbands, who they usually can't stand the sight of, are irresistible to other women. You're not exactly Brad Pitt.'

'Well there's no need to be personal and whether or not I look like Brad Pitt, that's not the point, you said we should be back by ten.'

'Relax Robbie, do you want me to phone her?'

'For Christ sake, don't do that, she'll hit the roof.'

'Robbie, I need to find out what's happened to Fergal. Now, if you would rather stay overnight at a nearby hotel or boarding house, that's fine by me but I will need your assistance first thing in the morning. I am staying here all night, and I will tidy the place up and keep the fire going.'

'I can't leave you on your own.'

'Don't be silly I can manage, but thanks you for your concern. You better decide what you're going to do and phone your wife,' Doreen, said.

'I've tried several times, but there was no answer, I've left a message on her phone.' I told Doreen.

'I hope she's all right,' I added.

'I'm sure Gloria, can look after herself after all she is a woman.' She was looking out the window watching the police car drive out of site. 'I don't trust him,' said Doreen.

'Is that because he's a man, or a police inspector?

'I don't dislike men Robbie, it just irritates me when they think women can't look after themselves, so just keep your sarcastic comments to yourself.'

'Excuse me for breathing,' I replied.

It was getting dark, Doreen, kept looking out the window.

'Turn the lights off, quick,' Doreen, hissed. 'What's wrong?' I asked her.

'Two ramblers,' replied Doreen, walking down the road. No one would be walking around here this time of night. Put your coat on Robbie, were sneaking out the back, follow me and don't make a sound.'

Oh no, I thought, I'm defiantly staying somewhere else tonight. We kneeled behind the hedgerow at the side of the cottage.

Doreen, held a big garden spade in her hand, somehow, I didn't think it was for gardening. With the aid of the small light over the cottage door it was easy to see that these two guys were carrying guns instead of walking sticks. As one rambler knocked on the door, the other walked around the back.

'Robbie, we know you're in there, we have your wife.' Doreen, looked at me and put her fingers to her lips, as a gesture to keep quiet.

Oh no, they've kidnapped Gloria, Inspector Wyatt, was right, the bastards have probably got her little finger with them.

'The backdoor is unlocked,' said one gunman.

'Just be careful!' Shouted the guy at the front door,

'Tell Robbie, were armed and we don't want to.' 'BANG'

The Spade vibrated round the back of his head as he fell to the ground unconscious. Doreen, shouted, as she threw the bloodied spade on the garden,

'I don't know who Robbie, is and I have no money to speak of, so just fuck off now or your mate's going to die.' she shouted.

'Can't do that, lady I have a job to do. I need Robbie. alive,' he shouted back.

'And what about me?' Doreen, asked. She pulled a gun out of her pocket and kicked the other one that was on the ground towards me.

'I've no interest in you lady one way or the other,' said the guy at the back door.

'I'll give myself, up' I said, 'all this is freaking me out.'

'Robbie, he's going to kill us both,' Doreen, said in despair.

'Just stand back twenty feet from that door and if anybody comes rushing through the door or looks through the window just hold the gun with both hands and shoot It's all, ready to use, just pick it up.'

It was too late.

'Stick your hands on your head and move away from Robbie,' said the gunman who was standing ten feet behind Doreen.

'That was a nasty little lie you told about Robbie, not being here, and what about my mate, he doesn't look too well move away from Robbie.' Said the gunman.

'He's going to kill me now, and you later,' said Doreen. She turned quickly, and dived to the ground, firing a shot at the gunman but not quickly or accurate enough, the gunman shot, and Doreen, yelled out in pain.

Then there was a huge loud bang from behind the gunman, blood spurted from his torso as he hit the ground. There was a big hole in his back and smoke everywhere. I was paralysed with fear I tried to speak but there was no sound as the smoke cleared through the haze an old man appeared with a shotgun, I looked down at Doreen, she was still alive.

'Fergal,' she said, 'how nice to see you.' Doreen, looked at me.

'You'll never make a gangster; Robbie, and you don't seem to have very nice friends.'

'How can you joke about all this?' I asked. 'This is all my fault,' I said. 'Where did you get shot?'

'Just get me a blanket so I can keep warm 'she said.

'Tell Fergal, not to shoot me first.' as Fergal, walked towards me and Doreen, he was looking round as though he wanted someone else to shoot at.

'You okay Miss, you look very pale.' he said.

'It's okay,' said Doreen, 'Robbie's my chauffer.' She started to wince with the pain.

'Bit different from Martin,' he replied.

Fergal, reloaded his shotgun.

'There must be a car nearby these guys wouldn't be here in the middle of nowhere without a lift,' I said as I walked around the two bodies to the cottage. I tried my best not to look at them, I came back with a couple of blankets. Fergal, was leaning over the fellow that Doreen, hit with a spade. There was blood dripping out of his ear, but he was still alive It didn't seem bother Fergal, at all; I wrapped the blankets as best as I could around Doreen.

'It wasn't your fault Robbie,' said Doreen. 'I should have shot them dead as soon as they came to the door I hesitated, I wasn't sure whether they were after me or after you.' Fergal turned off all the lights.

'We don't won't to be sitting targets,' he said.

'Well that's all very well, I can't see a thing.'

'Your eyes will adjust to the darkness,' said Doreen.

'It's not my eyes I'm worried about, it's just the general fear of being shot dead. Doreen, shouldn't we be phoning the police you need an ambulance, what exactly are we waiting for?'

'Not sure,' said Doreen, 'could be no one, but it could be somebody in a car waiting for a signal from these two guys. Make no mistake if Fergal, hadn't appeared when he did you and I would have been shot dead,'

'So, where's he been all this time?' I asked.

'I've no idea', Doreen, replied. 'Robbie, we'll hide by that bush, by the telegraph pole.'

'Are you okay to move?' I asked her.

'We're like sitting ducks, if we stay here,' she said.

'Are you all right Robbie?' Doreen, asked.

'Course I'm not all right, I never expected an evening like this. It's like the gunfight at the O.K. Corral.'

'That's good Robbie, you can be Wyatt Earp, and I'll be Doc Holliday.'

'Please Doreen, please phone the police all this killing stuff is too much for me, and you're badly injured they've probably got Gloria, tied up somewhere, minus one finger.'

'Robbie, if they had your wife as a hostage, do you think they would have gone to all this trouble tonight? They would have just phoned you up and made her speak to you and arranged a rendezvous. Then if all goes well, you exchange the cash for your wife if not, they'll just kill you both.'

I stared at Doreen, 'What money?'

'Oh, don't sound so surprised, Martin told me all about your little adventure Just think, down there is probably the same river you dumped the body in.'

'That was supposed to be a secret.' I said.

'Don't worry Robbie, your secret is safe with me, we'll get through this together.'

I've heard that before I thought, a phone started to ring and we could see a faint light coming from the jacket pocket of the unconscious gunman.

'Just let it ring.' Doreen, shouted to Fergal.

'Me and Robbie, are going to hide on the other side of the road. You go and turn the lights on, lock the back door and hide in the hedgerow.' Then she phoned the police.

The gunman's phone stopped ringing but Doreen, seemed to be having difficulty convincing the police what was happening in this quiet part of the country.

'They're only used to rustling and sheep shagging, round here,' said Doreen, 'they'll send someone round when they can.'

'Well thank God it's nothing serious,' I said.

'I'll phone Sniffer, He might be able to understand the situation, and pull a few strings.'

'Eighteen months, I can't see what he can do, we must be about a hundred miles away from his patch my knee hurts like hell.' said Doreen.

'Is that where he shot you?'

'No, I just twisted it badly, when I dived to the ground, I'm not as young as I used to be,'

'So, where did you get shot?' I asked.

'Oh, I didn't, he missed me completely.'

'For fucks sake! There's me, thinking you're dying.'

'Sssh, can you hear something? It's a car.' said Doreen.

He, or she, was driving very slowly down the road, headlights on full.

'Keep your heads down,' said Doreen. The car stopped about a hundred yards away from the cottage, headlights still on engine still running. I could hear the sound of a car door opening but it was impossible to see what was happening. The headlights were blinding, my heart was pounding.

'Any one there?' Shouted a man's voice. Nobody answered. He shouted again, 'Anyone there?'

'What do you want?' I shouted. Doreen looked at me, 'idiot, what did you answer him for?'

'Is that you Robbie? You owe my boss some money.'

'Tell your boss to fuck himself. I've seen enough death over the last few weeks because of your boss. You want this money? Well, you're going to have to fight me for it, you, faceless prick.'

'You're gambling Robbie. I could shoot you down easy.'

'Just like the advance party. They thought it was going to be easy,' I said.

'Listen Robbie, this has all got out of hand, just give yourself up and show me were the money is, and we won't tell the police about Dennis.'

'Who's Dennis?' I asked.

'The poor bastard you dumped in the river.'

'No deal,' I said.

'Have you gone mad?' Doreen, asked.

'Yes, I have, mad as hell. I've had enough of all this intimidation shit. My clothes are all muddy. Gloria, will go mad when she sees all this mud on my Sunday best. Doreen, is this gun ready to use?'

'Yes, you don't need to do this.'

'Yes, I do, I'm Wyatt Earp, and you're Doc Holliday, remember just cover my back, Doc.'

I stood up, and looked at Doreen,

'Robbie there's blood on your coat, you sure you haven't been shot?

'I was so full of anger; it was almost orgasmic.

'Where are you Robbie. shouted the man in the headlights.

'Doreen, I'm going to run like the clappers till I'm on the

other side of his main beam.'

'Robbie, don't do this, we can sit this one out, you've been overcome by some form of madness.' Just as I was about to run, my phone started to ring. It was Gloria.

'Get down Robbie,' said Doreen. She fired a shot at the car.

'Get down, and just be careful were your pointing your weapon.' she yelled.

'Gloria, are you, all right? I've been worried sick about you, I'm in the middle of a gun fight at the moment.'

'Oh, really is that Doreen, I can hear?' she sounded a little out of breath. If I was you, I'd point your weapon back down your underpants and come straight home. Do you think I'm stupid? In the middle of a gunfight, indeed,' then she switched off her phone. 'Stupid cow,' I said.

'What's he doing Doreen? I asked.

'He's turning the car around, he's not taking any chances, I think he's stuck on the grass verge,' said Doreen, 'We either let him go or let him have it. Too late, he's got back on the road.'

'Hang on he's reversing back towards the cottage,' I said. 'I've just realised he probably thinks there's just the two of us, he doesn't know about Fergal. What's that noise?'

'It's a helicopter, and your phones ringing again,' said Doreen.

'Is it the police? I asked, as I answered the phone.

'I'm. not certain, but that's, some, fancy looking 'chopper' replied Doreen.

'What did she say?' A voice said over the phone. It was Tessa, the sister in law, 'you have a fancy looking chopper. You ought to be shot, you sex maniac.'

'I might well be shot if I carry on talking to you. Now just fuck off.' I turned the phone off.

'Doreen, are you saying these things on purpose?' The noise of the helicopter was becoming louder as it flew nearer, a huge spotlight beamed down upon us. 'That's the police,' said Doreen. 'Look he's circling the area.'

'This is the police, don't move and drop, your weapons,' boomed a voice on a loudspeaker.

A spotlight was beaming directly on the gunman. The silhouette clearly showed he had a gun in his hand. He pointed it up at the helicopter, and dropped to the ground like a heavy stone.

'He's been shot,' I said. At more or less the same time three nasty looking hooded men with nasty looking guns, dressed in black, suddenly appeared behind us from nowhere.

'Put your hands in the air, and move. Now! As fast as you can.'

'Doreen's, injured,' I said.

'Move now,' shouted the hooded men I was told to lay down flat on my stomach, legs apart and arms stretched. My clothes are really dirty now, I hope Gloria, is all right.

After I was frisked and handcuffed behind my back, I was shoved in the back of a police car.

'Let's go,' said the hooded policeman, well I hoped he was a policeman. The car sped off from the scene.

'Is my wife, all right?'

'Why shouldn't she be?' asked the driver.

'One of the gunmen said they have her as a hostage.'

'They'll let you know at the station,' said the other policeman as he pulled off his hood.

'Is the station far?'

'Not far, now shut the fuck up.' I feel like I'm going to faint,

I always do that in a crisis, I'm going to be strong, just like Wyatt Earp. It seemed like hours before we arrived at the police station, they literally dragged me out of the car. 'What's that blood on his shirt?' The desk sergeant asked.

'Oh, that's just mud, he smells like shit.'

'I think I am bleeding. I was when I got in the car, I feel ill,' I said.

'Take his coat off,' said the desk sergeant.

'He's as white as a sheet, you pair of twats, can't you see he's been shot?'

'Well, he didn't tell us he'd been shot.'

'That's why you're supposed to check him all over before you move him from the scene of the crime. Lay him down in cell one, and I'll phone the paramedics and if I was you, I'd check to see if he's carrying any hand grenades. You may have missed that as well, you, dozy pair of bastards.'

'I didn't know I'd been shot sergeant is it bad? I can't feel any pain I just feel cold.' Then unlike Wyatt Earp, I fainted. It all felt a bit of a haze after that.

I can remember an oxygen mask over my face, people shouting at each other, but I couldn't distinguish what was being said. I kept drifting in and out of conciseness. When I came around, I thought I was in hell and the devil with his evil looking face was leaning over me.

'How do you manage it Robbie?' It was Sniffer, wearing his mask.

'Sniffer is that you? I didn't know if I was dead, or, Gloria, had taken me to see *Phantom of the Opera*!'

'Very funny, Inspector Wyatt, just left you've been shouting out his name a few times, what was that all about?'

'I don't know.' Oh, was I shouting out Wyatt Earp?'

'That's right are you two having a relationship, are you into big men with strong thighs?' Sniffer, asked me.

'Fuck off,' I replied. Sniffer, pulled out a piece of paper from his coat.

'See this Robbie? It's a search warrant for Doreen's, nice little cottage, and we're going to search your house from top to bottom.' Then Sniffer, was interrupted by the nurse she quickly asked one of the other nurses to fetch the consultant and she ushered Sniffer, out of the ward. Oh shit, they're going to search the house.

'How long have I been unconscious, nurse?'

'Just a few hours, you've been very lucky but the consultant will explain about all that.' Have I been lucky? my life just seems to be a constant stream of arguments interrogation, fist fights, gun fights and visits to the hospital, either as a patient, or a visitor. I'm truly fucked if they find that money.

'Robbie,' it was the consultant,

'How do you feel?'

'Tired and confused.'

'Well, call me Aubrey. You've been very lucky.'

'Lucky or not, Aubrey, am I going to live?'

'Oh yes, the bullet entered the top of your chest, bounced around a few bones, missed all your vital organs and came out through your lower back. A similar thing happened to Ronald Reagan, with his attempted assassination. He was as right as rain a few days after.'

'I'm not sure all Americans would agree with that,' I said.

'Listen Robbie, we do have to be careful no infection sets in. You need to stay in hospital for a while so you can regain

216

your strength, no gunfights, nothing like that! Do you like my new dicky bow?'

'Pardon.'

'My new dicky bow, do you like it?'

'It's wonderful' I replied, surprised that he should ask such a question.

'Around Christmas time I usually wear one that lights up, and twirls round that's a real hoot for the patients.'

'Is it? I must make sure I become inflicted with some serious injury next Christmas, just to see this spectacle.' Aubrey, laughed.

'That's the spirit,' he said. 'There's a couple of detectives who wish to speak to you now, how exciting!' Then he put his hand inside his coat and pulled it out quickly with his thumb sticking up and two fingers sticking out straight as though it was a gun. 'Give 'em the facts, just the facts.'

Neither Sniffer, nor Inspector Wyatt, looked very impressed when Aubrey introduced them as Butch Cassidy, and the Sundance Kid.

'Stupid cunt,' said Sniffer.'

'My thoughts exactly.' Inspector Wyatt, said.

'Where's Gloria, is she, all right?' I asked them.

'She's fine,' said Sniffer, 'she's staying at her sister's.'

'Has she got all her fingers and thumbs?'

'Yes, she's okay.'

DI Wyatt, spoke, 'Robbie, we need to search your home, is there anything you're not telling us?'

'Is Doreen, all right?'

'Apart from a badly twisted knee, she's fine. Which is more than we can say for the other visitors at West Cottage. One's got a fractured skull seems he had an accident with a garden spade, then there's his mate who's spread all over the crazy paving. And of course, we had the idiot shooting at the helicopter, he's still alive which is very useful, he's got a lot of form.'

'So why do you want to search my home?'

'Money, lots of it,' said Sniffer, 'We've had a tip off that Martin, was following your car the night of the crash and you had a passenger with a suitcase full of money. You shot him dead and dumped him in the river.'

'That's ridiculous.'

'You know Gloria's, been seeing Freddie the flirt?' Sniffer, said.

'You bastard, you're just trying to wind me up.'

'I'm not saying he's inserted his overused knob up her furry burger, they might just be having meaningful conversation at his house. It's quite convenient his place is not too far from Gloria's, sisters house.'

'You have a way with words,' I said to Sniffer. 'Have you been reading a lot of Shakespeare lately? Where is Gloria, now?' I asked him, indignantly.

'She's at your house. Hopefully assisting my officers with their search.'

I just needed to keep my composure, Sniffer, was probably lying through his teeth, the sneaky little shit. After realising I was in a hospital mile away from home, I asked if I could speak to Gloria, on the phone.

'Go ahead,' said DI Wyatt.

'Privately.'

'No chance.' Sniffer, replied.

'Robbie, are you okay? I'll come down to see you once these

bastards have finished turning the house upside down.' she said.

'Don't worry Gloria, I'm okay.' I said trying to calm her down.

'Someone's told the police we've got a load of stolen money stashed away in the house.' she said.

That's its Gloria, keep calm, I thought to myself.

'They've even started to look around the garden. 'she added.

'Oh fuck.' I swallowed hard, 'ask if they can dig out a few weeds while they're at it,' I said, trying to lighten the conversation.

'I'm sorry I shouted at you on the phone last night I couldn't believe it, you being in a gun fight and being shot,' said Gloria.

'I do love you; I'll speak to you later.' Gloria turned off her phone.

'It seems your boys are doing a good job up there,' I said.

Please, please, I thought to myself, don't go lifting any paving slabs.

'I'm going down to the cottage,' said DI Wyatt, to Sniffer, 'you stay here with Robbie.'

I'm starting to sweat, everything's going wrong. I've been shot, and now it looks like the police are going to find the money any second. Bollocks. I'll try and keep calm.

'So, who's been spreading these rumours about me?' I asked Sniffer.

'Who do you think?'

'I've no idea.' I replied.

'Well, if we don't find any money at your house and none at Martin's old bungalow, you've got nothing to worry about, have you? but, if we do find some money, you're in the shit. Inspector Wyatt, thinks you could be 'Mr Big,' said Sniffer, and started to laugh.

'Mr Big!' I replied, 'What do you mean by that?'

'He thinks you organised the whole thing. He finds it hard to believe how anybody who is so stupid can still be alive. He reckons it's just an act, that underneath this guise lies a sophisticated criminal mind. I told him your just stupid and had a fiver bet that there was no money at the house, or the cottage.'

'I suppose I should be grateful you think so highly of me' I said sarcastically.

'Think nothing of it, Robbie.' he replied in the same vein.

'So, Robbie, could you explain to me why three gunmen, decide to visit you and Doreen, at a nice little country cottage. I'm sure it wasn't to have a cup of tea and some scones.'

Just then my phone rang, thank god, it was Casper.

'Robbie you're still alive,'

'Is that Casper?' Sniffer asked. 'Give me that phone now.' 'Casper,' said Sniffer. 'That printer you sold me doesn't work,' there was a slight pause, 'I don't care how cheap it was if it doesn't work it's no good to anyone, you big prat. You better get me another one quickly or I'll find an excuse to arrest you for something. Having sex with a stuffed bear something like that.' Another pause ensued. 'Don't get technical with me,' he shouted, 'just get me another printer, and no you can't talk to Robbie.' Then he switched off my phone.

'I shouldn't get angry, it makes my eyes water, and my cheek bone ache, and this support mask, or whatever you call it, has started to smell.'

'You know what Sniffer? It's so good to have a little chat with you, Inspector Wyatt, can be so bland.' I said.

'Shut it Robbie, you're supposed to be in shock.' Sniffers,

phone rang.

'Well Robbie, this could be the big moment when you usually shit yourself or faint, this is a call from the boys at your house.'

He started to laugh before he answered the phone, 'Mr Big, I don't think so.'

Sniffer, seemed to be ages on his phone and for some strange reason I felt reasonably relaxed. If they find the money there's nothing, I can do about it, apart from deny all knowledge of it, I hope Gloria, does the same.

'Well Robbie. They've found the money, loads of it,' said Sniffer. He's bluffing, I thought to myself.

'I don't believe you.'

'Suit yourself,' said Sniffer. 'Are you saying there is no money to be found? Or my boys are incapable of finding it?'

'There is no money, full stop.'

'Robbie, you know me too well, still that's a fiver Wyatt, owes me. I'll be back later, give you time to think about last night's visitors. You better tell me what's going on, next time you might not be so lucky. See you later Robbie'

I don't trust anybody at the moment, I thought to myself.

Half hour later Doreen turned up, she looked round the ward, as she usually does and sat down by my bed.

'Well they gave the cottage a good search this morning, they found an old bullet proof vest, a rifle and an old revolver. They even searched your car, apart from that everything is fine.

Fergal, had been hiding from a family of hairy travellers. The brothers had found out that their only sister had been going down to Fergal's caravan and taking her clothes off for a bottle of sherry, every Friday night.'

'Is she under age?' I asked.

'Oh no, she's about twenty-six, and needs to shave every day.'

'When you say she has a shave every day, do you mean on her chin?' I asked.

'That's right,' said Doreen.

'Let's change the subject,' I suggested.

'Doreen, did anybody else visit Martin, on his last night in hospital, after I spoke to him?' I asked.

'No, apart from eighteen months.'

'How can you be so sure?' I asked.

'I know one of the security guards and he checked it out for me on the security cameras.'

'So apart from the nursing staff, the only people Martin could have told about the body in the river is Sniffer, Martina, Casper and you, Doreen.'

'That's exactly right, but there's one other person.'

'Who?'

'Your wife,' replied Doreen, 'you definitely haven't told anyone else?'

'No Doreen, have you?'

'That gunman at the cottage, shooting at the helicopter, even knew the name of the man you dumped in the river he called him Dennis.'

'Robbie, if you have this money, I don't want to know, tell no one, and stick to your story that you haven't robbed anybody.'

'I think you'd better leave, Doreen, I need time to think, and I'm getting tired.'

Who do I trust? I should have phoned the police the minute that man died in my car. Too many injury's too many deaths, I thought.

I looked at Christine,

'I know Martin, or Gloria, must have told someone; they were the only two that knew I had disposed of the body in the river. I realised more than ever I was playing with fire; I was getting scared and felt I could trust no one. I curse the day I put my hands on that money.'

'You paid the price in the end.' said Christine. 'Four years in Jail.'

'You're making it sound like I deserved it.'

'Do you think you deserved it.' said Christine,

'You should try being depressed and financially broke, it's no fucking fun. Seeing that money was like a lifeline.'

'Robbie, I'm sorry, I was clumsy with my choice of words. I didn't mean to upset you. Do you need a break'?

'It's okay Christine, I didn't mean to be aggressive, every night I go to bed I tear myself apart wondering if it was all my fault.'

'Do you mean when you were in prison.'

I paused. 'No, I mean every night, let's get on with the book.'

As I lay in the hospital I was awoken by Gloria, and Inspector Wyatt.

'Gloria, it's good to see you. I said. She gave me a kiss on my cheek.

'Are you all right Robbie? You should see the mess those police have left the house in.' she said angrily. 'It's outrageous.'

'It had to be done Gloria,' said the inspector.

'No, it didn't, just because some mad gunman, who shoots at my husband and helicopters, makes up some tale about my husband killing someone and dumping them in the river for a suitcase full of money. My Robbie, should be given a medal. Not only have they made a mess of the house; they've been questioning me all morning.'

I bet they did well to get a word in, thank god they didn't find the money, I thought to myself. The incompetent arse-holes. She's putting on a great show.

'Robbie, we will be formally questioning you in the morning, we know you've been in shock, but the consultant said you will be able to answer a few questions after a night's rest.' said the inspector.

'Do you think I could have ten minutes with my husband alone? We've both been through a lot of trauma in the last twenty-four hours.' Gloria, asked.

'Yes, that'll be okay,' said the inspector.

We both watched the inspector as he walked out of the ward.

'When did you do it Robbie?'

'Do what Gloria?'

'Move the money. I was shitting myself when they started to move the paving slabs, I couldn't believe it, no money in sight. Where's the money now Robbie? are you, all right? You've gone white, say something.' she said anxiously.

'Let me get this straight, the police lifted the paving slabs where the money should be, but there was no money. Gloria, I haven't moved any money. Please, tell me you're joking, please?' Gloria, stared at me in amazement.

'Robbie, please tell me your joking?'

Gloria, began to cry.

'Okay, let's look at this logically,' I said, 'at least the police haven't found any money, so that's gets us off the hook, we're innocent.'

'So, who's the bastard that's got this money? Only you and I knew where it was hidden,' said Gloria.

Has she moved the money herself and is she pretending to be all innocent? Was Sniffer, telling me the truth about Gloria, and Freddie? I feel sick in the stomach, all that money has disappeared, just like that!

'Is everything all right?' Inspector Wyatt, asked as he walked back into the ward.

'Yes, inspector, we are both emotionally upset and tired, I just need some sleep.'

'I'll see you in the morning Robbie,' said Gloria, and gave me a kiss.

'You're my hero,' she whispered in my ear, 'I always thought that was a stupid place to hide it.'

The next day, I was taken to my local hospital by ambulance. I said goodbye to Aubrey, who was still pratting around.

'Give 'em the facts Robbie, just the facts,' he said, waving his arms about as though he'd had a gun in each hand.

'If nothing else Robbie, you should be thankful we've taken you away from that maniac,' said Sniffer.

For some strange reason I felt very relaxed, loosing that money, it was like having a noose taken from around my neck. I'm not sure if Gloria, feels the same. I don't really care who's got the money, as long as I can stay alive.

later on, in the day, unbeknown to me, a smart bald-headed man with a moustache and a well-used looking brief case, walked into the hospital and headed straight to ward fourteen. The ward I was in.

'We've just had a phone call from a Mr Bellow,' said Inspector Wyatt, 'do you know this man Robbie?'

'Never heard of him' I said.

'The cheeky bastard has asked us to delay this meeting till he turns up,' said Wyatt.

'Who is he not another gunman?' I asked.

'So, you've had no contact with this man at all?' Sniffer, asked me in response.

'None whatsoever,' I told him.

'Well, I suggest we start this interview, straight away,' said Inspector Wyatt. 'We've had a bit of luck since the gunfight at the cottage. Both the gunman shooting at the helicopter and the other fellow in the hospital with no memory, have started to talk. They both suggest that you must have some money hidden away somewhere. Quite a coincidence, considering they haven't had the opportunity to speak to each other isn't it?'

'Don't answer any questions Robbie,' said the man with a briefcase as he came rushing through the door.

'My name is Bellow. I am your legal representative.'

'Robbie, hasn't asked for one,' said D. I. Wyatt.

'Have you given him his options?' asked Bellow.

'I can't afford a solicitor,' I said,

'I know you can't. But I have a friend who likes to see justice done and is willing to pay the cost. This is due to the fact that my client has recently been shot and was handcuffed and literally dragged to the local police station before anyone noticed.

He was then left in a cell for over an hour before he received any expert medical attention. Also, he has a history of medical depression. I suggest you terminate this meeting until Robbie, is examined and assessed by a qualified psychiatrist.' Bellow, demanded.

'Bullshit,' said Sniffer.

'Oh, Mr Snipe, I didn't recognise you with your mask, I thought you were auditioning for *Phantom of the Opera*,' said Mr Bellow.

'Very funny, if anyone else cracks that joke again,' replied Sniffer. 'I'll kick them in the balls, how come your friend employed you to represent Robbie, you must be the most expensive lawyer in the county?'

'And the best, unlike you with your poor record of police harassment and brutality. You do realise the newspapers would have a field day with this story.? Have you hit anyone over the head with a bed pan lately? Robbie, should be treated like a hero, warding off three armed robbers. It's a disgrace.'

He's very good, I thought to myself. I could do with him the next time I have an argument with Gloria.

'So, who is paying for your services?' Inspector Wyatt, asked.

'They wish to remain anonymous, so if you don't mind, I would like some time with my client, alone.' said Bellow.

'You're sure Robbie, can stand the stress?' Sniffer quipped.

'Well at least he can have the comfort that no one is going to kick him in the bollocks,' replied Mr Bellow.

'This was only an informal chat,' said Inspector Wyatt.' We were just trying to get a better picture of what happened that night of the shooting, and why'

'Silly me, I thought this was official. I'll let you know soon how Robbie, is.'

'I think you should realise,' said Sniffer, 'that every second counts, there are some big-time gangsters that are convinced Robbie, has stolen some money that belongs to them, his life is in danger.'

Sniffer looked at me. 'Robbie if you have this money, tell

me where it is hidden and I will guarantee that you and Gloria will get police protection,'

'Don't answer any questions Robbie,' said Mr Bellow, as he opened his brief case. The two detectives started to leave the ward, 'Don't forget what I said Robbie.'

'Is Doreen, paying for this?' I asked.

'Deadly Doreen, not a chance. She has her own solicitor, pays her a retainer, employed her for years, I wouldn't trust her to look after my cat.'

'Who Doreen?' I asked.

'No, her solicitor.' Bellow, replied. 'Now Robbie, I want you to tell me all about yourself.'

Luckily for us, when it comes to knowing the law, those two, who have just left the ward, are as thick as shit.'

The next few days consisted of medical assessments, and a couple of visits from Doreen. Her attitude towards me was a mixture of concern and annoyance because she didn't have me to drive her around.

Also, there was a few meetings with the police, formal and informal, all with my solicitor present of course. Gloria, met Doreen, and took an instant dislike to her. But the biggest problem between me and Gloria, was the missing money.

She told me what a stupid place it was to hide the money, yet again. The truth is, neither one of us is sure whether the other one is lying and has hidden it somewhere else.

Then came the real blow.

'Robbie, if you don't tell me where the money is, I will tell the police everything.'

'Go ahead,' I said. 'I will refer it to my solicitor.'

'Don't you care?' she asked.

'Yes, I care but there's nothing I can do about it.'

'You haven't given it to that Doreen, to look after?'

'No, I haven't. Have you given the cash to Freddie the flirt?' I replied, with equal irritation.

'Why do you say that?' Gloria asked. 'And his name is just Freddie.'

'You and Freddie, have been seen together,' I said.

'And you were going to spend the night with Doreen,' she replied. 'Before you were interrupted by those gunmen. One of them was probably her jealous boyfriend who was going to shoot your balls off.'

'Well this is a right lover's tiff,' it was Sniffer. 'Gloria, don't get arguing with Robbie, he's officially under mental stress. You can't talk to him unless his solicitor is holding his hand.'

'I think you ought to know, Robbie, dumped a dead body in the river and had a case full of stolen money,' said Gloria.

'That's sounds very good Gloria. Why didn't you tell me this, when it first happened? So, where is this money now and the dead body?' Sniffer, asked. Gloria, paused.

'The money was in the back garden, but someone has taken it away,' she said.

'And I suppose the dead body is still floating down the river?' said Sniffer, incredulously.

'No chance you took any photographs of the money or the corpse?' he added.

'Of course, I didn't,' said Gloria.

Sniffer, looked at me, as though he wasn't the slightest bit interested.

'Tell me 'Mr Big, is any of this true?' he asked.

'No comment, you'll have to speak to my solicitor,'

'I thought you might say that, but basically you do disagree with Gloria. Have you met Robbie's solicitor? If Robbie, farts he has to inform Mr Bellow,' Sniffer, said to Gloria.

'If you wish, we could take a statement back at the station. But if you've had a big emotional bust up with your husband, you're wasting your time, and ours.'

'Gloria, I can't believe what you've just said, I think you better leave.' I told her.

'Well, if that's the way you feel, fuck the lot of you, you'll come crawling back to me, Robbie.'

'No Gloria, I've had enough of you. You're such a shallow bitch, you go off with your old lover boy Freddie. Do you need some change for his condom machine?' I asked.

'What are you on about?' Gloria, asked.

'He has a condom machine next to his bed.' I said.

'I think you should know,' said Sniffer. 'We searched Freddie's house this morning.'

'Why did you do that?' Gloria, replied

'Well, we thought if you're having an affair with Freddie, he might be looking after some money for you,'

'We're not having an affair,' said Gloria, 'we just see each other from time to time.' Sniffer, looked at his watch.

'We're searching Casper's place at the moment, that might take weeks, all the shit he keeps in there.'

'What are you doing, searching every house in the county?' I asked.

'No, just people that are connected to you and Gloria.'

'Well have you found any money?'

'Fuck all, it's just a wild goose chase, no one has seen this money. No one knows who this man is with a suitcase full of money. There is no sign of a body all we do know is that hard-ened criminals are either trying to kill or kidnap you, Robbie.'

'Then I need police protection' I said.

'Surely, you need to discuss that with your solicitor!' Sniffer, replied sarcastically.

'I've already told you, show me were the money is, and I'll give you Police protection.'

'I need a change of identity.' I said.

'Well, I've always thought that,' said Sniffer. 'You ugly bastard,'

By this time Gloria, had started to leave the ward with one of those angry walks.

'I'm going home Robbie, the house still needs cleaning up, after the police have made such a mess,' she said.

'It should only be a couple of days Robbie, and you should be okay to go home, and with a bit of luck, I should be able to take this mask off,' said Sniffer.

'Am I really in danger?' I asked.

'As long as they think you've got the money, yes.'

'How about Doreen, is she in danger?' I asked him.

'I'm not sure about Doreen, I don't know who's side she's on she still uses the same solicitor that she used years ago so she could still be rubbing shoulders with the criminal fraternity.' he added.

'Do you know who's paying for my solicitor?' I asked him.

'No, I don't, but I don't think its Doreen,'

Talk of the Devil, hello Doreen,' said Sniffer.

'Hello Claude,' she replied.

Claude, Sniffers, first name is Claude! I thought; that's a

'turn up for the books!' Hello Robbie, how are feeling?' Doreen, asked. 'I hope the inspector isn't bothering you too much?'

'No, me and Claude, have been having a nice little chat. How's the knee?'

'A little stiff, but improving by the hour.' She said in a pained voice.

'If you ask Claude, nicely he might massage it for you,' I said, sarcastically.

'Stop tacking the piss, that's what happens when you get to friendly with people. The name's Mr Snipe, or Sniffer, to you two, and don't you pair forget it. You're lucky to be alive. I will see you pair of shits later on.' Sniffer, adjusted his cheek mask and promptly walked out of the ward.

'That always upsets him, calling him Claude.' She looked around the ward and then sat down.

'It's Martin's funeral next week, they've decided it was a heart attack,'.

'Everyone I know, is either a gangster, solicitor or works for the police force, you can't trust any of them. That's why I got on so well with Martin, he was uncouth, but he was loyal, he could be trusted. He was so strong and physical, I'll always remember that night he got barred at the local pub, by the cottage.'

'What happened there, did he complain about the beer? It generally tastes like donkey piss down that neck of the woods,' I said.

'No, that was the night before, on this particular evening, the hairy travellers were in the pub, I think it was the dad and uncles of the ones that where after Fergal. They made a joke about city folk all being Nancy boys and Martin, replied.

'The only virgins nearby are those that can run faster than

their fathers.'

'So, I imagine that's when the fight started?' I asked her.

'No,' said Doreen, 'I'm not sure if they didn't understand it, or thought it was acceptable. Then Martin, said, 'you country folk all fuck pigs.'

'That's when the fight started. Martin, was majestic. He knocked out one of the hairy beast's straight away and grabbed the other two by their hair. Twirled them round and threw them out of the window one by one, he had a bit of trouble with their dog. He wouldn't let go of his leg at first, but he grabbed a pepper pot and threw it all over the dog's face, as he sneezed, it let go of Martin's leg and he booted it out of the window.

You could hear the dog running down the road yelping and sneezing at the same time. It ran straight past its owners, two of them, with big clumps of hair missing off the top of their heads, they were trying their best to carry the fellow Martin, knocked out. They kept looking behind with fear on their faces, making sure Martin, wasn't chasing after them.' Doreen, told a good tale!

'Well it's understandable, you were barred from the pub,' I said. 'If by any chance we get through all this and we end up having a drink together, I hope you won't be expecting the same sort of entertainment.'

Doreen, looked at me and smiled,

'Martin, was a one off,' she said. 'He's had a few blows to his head over the years, and the odd beating. He was a lot brighter years ago.'

'Doreen, I don't know who to trust, but I've got to tell someone.'

'Are you sure? is it about the money?'

'Yes,' 'I said. 'It's gone missing, Gloria, thinks I've hidden it somewhere and I think she's hidden it somewhere. We were the only two that knew where it was hidden, then she told Sniffer, but thankfully he didn't seem interested,'

'Perhaps Sniffer's taken it!' Doreen, suggested. 'Were did you hide the money?'

'Under some slabs in the back garden,' I said. Doreen, looked at me in amazement.

'Well, everyone always hides stuff at the back of the wardrobe or under the bed,' I said. 'You have to go through the garage to get to the back garden. I thought that made it pretty safe. I'm stuffed Doreen, I've lost this money and I can't report it to anyone. You can't be serious about Sniffer?' I asked her.

'Why not. They don't call him Sniffer, for nothing. As I see it, your biggest problem Robbie, is convincing these gangsters you haven't got the money. Even if you could, they would still kill you, they've lost a lot of face on this one, It's bad for their reputation.'

'Well that's really cheered me up you talk as though you know these people.'

'I know what makes them tick,' said Doreen. She paused for a while.

'The gunman that was shooting at the helicopter, I know him, not well but I do know him. I didn't realise at first who it was but the next day the police showed me photographs of the villains.

Robbie, they're just as likely to kill me as they are to kill you. I'll sort something out.'

Doreen, stood up from her chair. 'Keep smiling Robbie, if

any of your friends suddenly start buying expensive clothes let me know.'

'Doreen, I'm sorry, this is all my fault.'

'We are where we are Robbie.

We can tough it out, I'll see you later.'

12

Two days later Sniffer, took me home in his car, he was wearing a smaller face mask.

'The bastards told me the mask was coming off today, they didn't say they would replace it with a smaller one,' he said, 'at least this one doesn't smell.'

'I think it makes you look like a man of mystery,'

'I think that bullet must have travelled through to your brain, man of mystery indeed!'

'Mind you Robbie, it's very strange where these bullets end up sometimes. I knew a police inspector up north who got shot in the back, and like yourself the bullet bounced about all over his body and ended up lodged at the back of his scrotum.'

'Did they manage to remove it?' I asked.

'Not exactly,' said Sniffer.

'They decided to leave it for a while, his poor wife decided to give him a blow job one night and he blew her brains out.' It's not often I have seen Sniffer, laugh, but this was making his cheek ache.

'I don't think that's very funny,' I said.

'Oh, relax Robbie, it was just a bit of fun. I can't talk to you about your recent escapades, that lawyer of yours will have me locked up in the tower of London. I'm only bringing you home because your wife's fallen out with you again, and if you want a few words of advice.' he offered.

'Go on try me,' I said.

'These men that are after you are big-time gangsters.'

'Well that's pretty obvious, it's not rocket science after that gunfight at the cottage,' I replied. 'Is that a new coat your wearing?'

'Robbie, this is getting really serious, I haven't got time to talk about my new coat. We've uncovered a load of new information about these people, it's a huge syndicate that involves a lot of so-called well-respected people.'

'Well what can I do about it?'

Sniffer looked at me, 'staying alive would be a good tip,' he said. 'Listen Robbie, we need to round these bastards up for your own safety. Sniffer, parked his car on the drive, well your house is still here.'

'No broken windows,' he said.

'Are you all right Robbie?'

'Yes,' I replied, 'I've just become very tired.'

'Give me your house keys, I'll give you a hand,' said Sniffer.

'Thank you, Sniffer, is this the new you?'

'Man, of mystery, those were your words, remember?' He opened the front door, and, walked in before me.

He looked around the room as he always does anywhere, he goes. He looked down on the floor.

'There's a few letters for you Robbie, I didn't realise you were that popular, where is Gloria?'

'She might still be at her sister's house.' Sniffer, gave me one of those knowing looks.

'Oh yes,' he said. I picked up the morning post and started to open the envelopes.

'Gloria's done a lovely job of tidying up the lounge,' he said.

'Yes,' I replied, but for some reason, she's put all the furniture in a different place, do you think this is some form of protest?'

As I opened one of the letters, Sniffer, could tell straight away that something wasn't right.

'What's wrong bad news?' he asked.

He could see that there was no writing on the outside of the envelope.

'Nothing wrong,' I paused.

'Oh my God,'

'Give me that letter,' shouted Sniffer.

'No, it's okay,' I said, 'it's nothing.

"Bollocks!' Sniffer, snatched the envelope from my hand and pushed me down on the armchair. He read the contents of the letter and looked at the photograph. He turned the envelope upside down, and a finger dropped onto the carpet.

'You've Fucked it all up now,' I said to Sniffer if I contact the police, they'll kill Gloria,'

'Robbie, for some reason these criminal think you have a load of money you owe them .Was it true what Gloria, said the other day about the dead body in the river and the money hidden in the garden, you better tell me truth,' he said angrily.

You better phone up your solicitor, you're coming straight down to the station, and I want the truth. What happened that night of the crash? Stop crying, that's not going to solve anything.' We need to sort this out for Gloria's, sake, you big fucking idiot.'

Later on, at the police station I told them everything that happened that night of the crash, and everything that had happened after that. Mr Bellow, did his best to convince the detectives I was insane.

Some agreed, some thought I was just a greedy bastard. Freddie, the flirt, Doreen, Martina, and the sister in law where all brought in for questioning. For some reason, they didn't bother with Casper.

'So, we need to capture these guys quick or Gloria's not going to be able to play the piano anymore,'

said Inspector Wyatt.

'Is that because she'll have no fingers left?' Perkins, asked, innocently.

'No, she'll be dead,' replied Wyatt, they are demanding a shitload of money that nobody seems to have. These criminals seem convinced Robbie, has this money and they want it at 1600 hrs tomorrow, at a rendezvous that is still to be confirmed. And not to inform the police, or Gloria, dies.'

'I just hope these villains don't know; the police already know about this' said Sniffer.

His phone rang.

'Don't mention my name, said Doreen are you amongst company? If so, I'll phone you back in fifteen minutes, I have some important news for you, but no one must know about this phone call.'

'I'm at a meeting at the moment, I'll speak to you later' said Sniffer.

Later on, in the day I am sitting at home with a couple of plain clothed policemen, the one policeman is watching out of the bedroom window. The other policeman is keeping an eye on me and generally walking about the rooms and checking all the windows and doors downstairs waiting for a phone call from these gangsters.

Back at the police station, Sniffer's phone rang. It was Doreen.

'Write down this postcode, this is where Gloria, is being held hostage and don't mention were you got this information from.'

That was the end of the phone call. For fucks sake, thought Sniffer, I could do with some more information; how many thugs are holding Gloria, hostage?

Well with the aid of Google and drones, we should be able to get plenty of information about the property. If this information is genuine and I don't see why not, me and the boys could be on a winner. The problem is keeping Gloria, alive.

'This informant of yours is he reliable?' asked Inspector Wyatt,

'Good as Gold,' said Sniffer.

'Right let's find out who owns this property, where it is, and who lives there, A.S.A.P. Well done Sniffer, and by the way, love the new coat,' said the inspector.

Back at the house I checked upstairs to see if my police body guard was okay, he was fast asleep on a chair by the window. He apologised and insisted he'd just nodded off, by the look of the bags under his eyes I think he'd been asleep for hours. He was a big fat man.

'Sorry Robbie, it won't happen again, I've hardly had any sleep over the last two days. Any chance of a cup of tea?'

I didn't mind making him one, as long as he stays awake, it makes me feel a little safer, I think the next several hours are going to be the longest of my life.

I've really screwed things up. Who stole the money? Who's paying for my solicitor? Gloria, didn't deserve to have her finger cut off. It's a shame it wasn't Freddie's dick, mind you what I've heard they would have needed a bigger envelope. The two-faced arsehole.

Back at police H, Q. things were starting to warm up.

'Sniffer, you and Perkins, go down to this address as the advance party, be discreet, said Wyatt, just see if anything is happening there. It's a town house and the next-door neighbour is an old security guard that worked shifts, he's a nosey sod so that should be useful.

'Well young Perkins,' said Sniffer, 'let's see if we can sort out this security guard. You know the address, so let's see what a good driver you are and don't forget to release the hand break, we need to get there as quick as we can.'

The security guard looked tired as Sniffer, started to ask him about his neighbour.

'Now and again he would bring friends around.' said the security guard. 'A right dodgy looking bunch,' was his way of describing them.

'I haven't seen him or his mates for a few weeks but I noticed someone came around a couple of days ago. The walls are like tissue paper; someone only has to fart and you can hear them.' he said.

'Is any one in there at the moment?' asked Sniffer.'

'I doubt it, you can always hear if someone turns the tap on or flushes the toilet,'

Fuck it, Sniffer, thought, has Doreen, sent me on a wild goose chase?

'Do you know his name? said Sniffer,

Dennis, He was a bit aggressive and hated it when I used to call him Dennis the Menace.

He was a short little fucker, and used to threaten me now and again, no sense of humour at all. I had a cat that suddenly disappeared, I often wondered if he'd killed it.'

'Okay, let's get back to the last time you saw Dennis,' said Sniffer.

'I can remember exactly it was the evening of one of the big rugby games. Italy were being thrashed by England, and he came around to tell me to keep the noise down, miserable get.'

'And that was the last time you saw him?' Sniffer, asked.

'No, that was the last time I spoke to him, I saw him later on getting into a taxi. I haven't seen him since.'

Sniffer, thanked the security guard for all his help and walked to the car which was discreetly parked around the corner with young Perkins, in the driving seat.

'That was interesting', said Sniffer. the security guard said the last time he saw his neighbour, he was all dressed up, getting into a taxi with a suitcase in his hand on the same evening that Martin, had his fatal car crash.'

'So, what's your point?' Perkins, asked.

'This is the where the mysterious gunman Robbie, dumped in the river was living.'

'I thought we were looking for Gloria,' said Perkins.'

'We are, but at least we know this person existed, you thick prat, I'm just going to make a phone call. Hello Doreen,' said Sniffer,' Gloria, isn't here, there's no one in the house'

'I'll phone you back in ten minutes,' said Doreen.

'Perkins, I'm going around the back of the house, if anyone appears on foot, or by car, phone me straight away.

'Make sure you don't get that new coat dirty,' replied Perkins.

'Listen, don't fuck about on this one, if anyone appears you phone me straight away and drive the car well out off site,'

'What, now?'

'No, after you phoned me, you idiot. I'm going to see if I can get into the house.'

'Shouldn't we, be getting back up, first?' Perkins,asked.

'I can't keep an eye on the front of the house and the back entrance at the same time, it's impossible'

'I need to get in the house,' said Sniffer. 'There could be some vital information in there.' He took off his support mask.

'What are you doing? 'asked Perkins.

'I don't need to wear this mask anymore every time I look in the mirror it reminds me of Martin.'

Sniffer, walked down the narrow alleyway that lead to Dennis's house and opened the back gate, he moved slowly.

'Everything all right?' shouted the security guard as he poked his head through his back-bedroom window.

'Shisssh,' said Sniffer, as he put his finger to his lips. 'Just shut the fuck up. You haven't seen me, I don't exist.'

'Of course, you exist, I've just been talking to you. I know working shifts can make people disorientated and you've taken off your little mask, but I can still recognise you.'

'Just shut up.' Sniffer, hissed back.'

Suit yourself you moody bastard thought the security guard, let him find out the hard way. I was just going to tell him that three men had walked in through the front door.

Sniffer, was surprised to find the back door unlocked. He opened it slowly and entered the kitchen, he was too late to prevent a large saucepan crashing down on his head. He fell to his hands and knees, rolled over on his back and passed out.

Back at home I managed to sleep a little, but not much.

Where is Gloria? I thought then the phone rang. I tried to remain calm then I answered.

'Hello Robbie, change of plan, be ready at midday tomorrow, with the money of course, and make sure there's plenty of fuel in your car, and remember don't tell the police.'

That was the end of the conversation, the policeman came running down the stairs, with his thumb up.

'Got that Robbie, whoops!' He shouted, as he missed his footing and dived head-first into the lounge cabinet sending all the contents flying in the air and knocking himself unconscious. It's a good job Gloria's not here to see this, we've only just restocked the cabinet with new ornaments since the last punch up with Scottie, and Freddie the Flirt.

Inspector Wyatt, was furious when the other policeman phoned and explained the situation.

'How on earth are we going to get this big idiot out of the house without causing attention to ourselves?

With a bit of luck, he might die in the next few minutes and we can tuck him in the corner of the room for twenty-four hours.'

The injured Policeman was in a bad way. There were bits a porcelain stuck in his forehead and halfway up his nose. He did look a sorry sight. The paramedics arrived in no time, making as much noise as possible, with their sirens and warning lights flashing away.

'The whole operation has been compromised,' said Inspector Wyatt, who had just arrived at the house with W.P.C. Lipinski, and Inspector Black,

'It's paramount we find Gloria, as quick as possible, any news from Sniffer?'   'Not yet,' replied, W.P.C. Lipinski.

'Inspector Black; said Wyatt, give Perkins, a phone, and see what's going on.'

Perkins, phone rang.

'Hallo Perkins, my name is inspector Black. I've been drafted in to help sort out all this shit. What's going on out there?'

'Nothing,' said Perkins, 'I'll phone you back in a few minutes.'

Nobody told me anything about an Inspector Black, thought Perkins, I'll just phone Sniffer. No answer he's been gone a long time. I better phone Wyatt, and see what's to do next and check to see if this Inspector Black is genuine.

'Okay, Perkins' said Inspector Wyatt, 'stay where you are, we'll get the heavy mob round, and yes Inspector Black, is genuine.'

Why does Sniffer have to be so Cavalier thought Wyatt, this whole thing has gone from bad to worse.

'Excuse me sir,' said inspector Black, 'We may be able to play this situation to our advantage, buy us some time at least.'

'I'm listening,' said Wyatt, as he watched the paramedics take the policeman out on a stretcher,

'Will he be all right? 'he asked.

'It's difficult to say,' replied one of the paramedics.

'He's had a bump on the head but he'll probably be okay, it looks worse than it is.'

Inspector Wyatt, looked at me.

'I'm sorry about all this Robbie.'

'I should never have stolen that money in the first place, I need a drink.'

'Robbie,' said Inspector Black, 'what you did that night was wrong but so many people would have done the same. you possibly don't appreciate this but in your own way you have brought so many crooks to the surface. Yes, you and your wife are in danger but I think even at this late hour I'm sure we can sort things out. You get yourself a drink and I'll explain what I think we should do.'

'Inspector Black. Let me remind you I am in charge of this case,' said Inspector Wyatt.

'And let me remind you, you've fucked up at every stage. It's a miracle none of our officers have lost their lives,' Inspector Black replied.

'Okay wise guy let's hear this plan and it had better be good,' replied Inspector Wyatt.

'Take Robbie, out of the house in handcuffs surrounded by uniformed police in a marked car. Make it as obvious as possible,' said Inspector Black.

'Inform the local press that Robbie, seriously injured a police officer and he has been arrested for attempted murder, make it known he has a history of depression.'

'Why don't you add that I'm a rapist, and shag dead people, while you're at it?'

'Don't tempt me, Robbie,' said Inspector Wyatt.

'We could hide Robbie in a safe house. These crooks won't know what to do for a while if they think Robbie's is in police custody,' said Inspector Black.

'But what about Gloria? She might have lost a whole arm by now,' I said in despair.

'Don't worry Robbie', said Inspector Wyatt, with his fingers crossed behind his back, 'We think we know where she's being held hostage. Now put these handcuffs on.'

'Is this really necessary?' I asked.

'We need to make this as convincing as possible,' said Wyatt. 'Look really angry when we're taking you down to the police station.'

'Do you want me to shout obscenities and struggle as you push me into the police car?'

'Yes, that'll be good, there's quite a crowd out there at the moment,' said Inspector Black. 'But be careful, the officers who are picking you up believe you really are a mad man that tried to murder a police man in the course of his duty.' A few minutes later two big policemen both bigger than Inspector Wyatt, entered the room.

'It's all getting exciting now Robbie,' said Christine,'

'That's on way of putting it,' I replied 'Do you think I could have a drink, we should be getting to the end of the story soon,'

'Did you ever find out who was paying Mr Bellow, for his services,' asked Christine,

'No, never whoever it was I was grateful, Mr Bellow, was brilliant in court. How do you think the book is shaping up?'

Christine, poured me a whisky.

'It'll need a bit of trimming here and there, but I think it will be all right, of course I need to hear the end of the story.'

'I better carry on, where was I.'

'Two big policemen came to take you away,' said Christine.

'Hi Boss, we heard one of our boys is in a bad way,'

They looked at my hand cuffs.

'They say, you couldn't recognise the officer, he was that badly cut up it seems the town has its own version of Hannibal.'

'For fucks sake, he dived head-first into the lounge cabinet, my wife will go crazy when she sees this mess. That's if she's still alive.'

Before we even got to the door one of them had punched me in the nose the other kneed me in the balls. I don't know if I looked angry but I was certainly in pain, this seems the most stupid plan I'd ever heard.

Back at the house with thin walls, an ageing security guard was being untied from a kitchen chair. He was shaken but tougher than he looked. He took a deep breath as the sticky tape was pulled from

his face.

'Will someone tell me what's going on?' he asked.

'We were hoping you could tell us,' said the policeman who was leaning over him. We seemed to have lost two of our officers, Snipe, and Perkins, do you know what's happened to them? We've searched the house next door and had a good look around the garden, no sign of them at all.' One of the policemen gave the guard a drink of water.

'You haven't got anything stronger? I need a proper drink.'

'Who wants to phone Wyatt, and tell him all about this?'

'We'll, leave that to you, Boss,' said the other armed officers.

'Thanks, this will really piss him off,' he was right.

'So, according to this security guard,' said Wyatt, 'three armed men drove to the house tied him to a chair and kidnapped Sniffer, and Perkins. Who the fuck do they think they are? This is England, you can't go around kidnapping policeman. How dare they. Is Perkins, car still there?' 'Yes.'

'Okay, I'll send the forensic boy's round, they might find something that will help us. See if you can find out anything more from the security guard.'

'Okay inspector.'

'I can't believe this,' said Inspector Wyatt, 'surely these gangsters can't possibly think they can get away with this?'

Wyatt's phone rang, it was Sniffers, number.

'Inspector Wyatt, there seems to be some confusion about who has this money. So, I think its best you and your officers find out, and during that time I am sure you and her Majesty's government can rustle up enough money. Then we will let you have your officers back.' The phone was turned off.

'Who the fuck is this guy? He's been watching too many James Bond films.'

Wyatt's, phone, rang again, this time it was Perkins, phone number but it was a different voice.

'By the way my assistant forgot to mention if this money isn't ready by twelve o' clock, midday tomorrow. The hostages will die.'

Wyatt, sat down with his forehead in his hands,

'All right, Boss?' asked W.P.C Lipinski.

'No, I'm not everything seems to be going from bad, to worse,' said Wyatt. 'If it hadn't been for a bad injury, I could have been a professional rugby player. Have I ever mentioned that to you?'

'Once or twice, Boss.'

'I was very fast for a big man.'

'Yes, you mentioned that as well. 'If you don't mind me asking boss what are we going to do about this present situation?'

'We'll have to call the big boys in from London. They'll take over in the office and start showing off, you don't want to be bending down when that lots about. Bunch of big heads. Let's get out of Robbie's house and back to the station, just post a couple of officers on the front door.'

I had the impression no one had a clue what was going on, as I sat in the back of the police car. These big fellows were taking me back to the police station, with big snarls on their big faces.

'It was a sad day when they abolished hanging,' said the guy that was driving. His mate looked at me with contempt.

'It's ridiculous, with all this Human Rights shit you can't give anyone a good slapping or shove their heads down the toilets it's no wonder it's not safe to walk the streets anymore.'

I'm sure it isn't when you two go out on the town I thought to myself.

'When I get to the station, I shall phone my solicitor,' I said.

'Oh, you have a solicitor, how very cosy. And what might his name be?'

'Bellow.'

'Bellow, fuck off, you couldn't afford someone like him. Are you related to the Queen, or someone like that?'

'No, but I have a guardian angel who is watching over me. I think maybe ten minutes ago he must have been on his tea break, hence the pain in my nose and groin, which of course I'll have to report to Mr Bellow.'

'Just give the bastard a slap,' said the driver.

'No, that Mr Bellow, can cause us a lot of trouble.' said his mate. 'Especially if Robbie, really is mad. There you go Robbie; I'll just pull the arm rest down for you that should make you more comfortable.'

The driver shook his head.

'Why don't you two have a game of charades, just before we get to the station?'

'That would be quite impossible while I'm handcuffed,' I replied.

The driver, slammed on his brakes, and jumped out the car.

'You piece of shit, you're just taking the piss, let me get at him he'll need more than a guardian angel to look after him when I'm finished with him.'

'Don't hit him Frank,' said his mate, 'he's just not worth it, he's mad.'

'He might be mad. I'm furious, let me get at him, the bastard.'

They started fighting each other in the middle of a busy street it was just ridiculous.

I managed to get out of the car and started to run down the road. Cars where swerving and sounding their horns, trying to avoid the wrestling match. As I was passing pedestrians, I was saying 'God be with you,' hoping they wouldn't notice my handcuffs as I put my hands to my face, as though I was praying. Then a car slowed down by my side

'Robbie, get in the car now,' it was Doreen.

'Thank God you were coming along when you did. Those policemen are insane.'

'Keep your head down Robbie,' said Doreen, 'we need to get away from here as quick as we can. I've been following you since you were escorted out of your house. I was just about to pop in and see you, when the ambulance arrived. You better tell me what's been going on,' said Doreen.'

'Okay.' I said, 'but you're going to find it hard to believe.'

'Robbie, with you anything is possible. That's the first time I've ever seen two policemen fighting in the middle of the road.'

So, I told Doreen, about the two detectives being kidnapped

and all the details about what had happened over the last twenty-four hours.

'That's unbelievable,' said Doreen. She stopped the car, 'Are you sure you've got that right about Perkins, and Sniffer?'

'Sure, I'm sure,' I replied.

'Stay where you are Robbie.' Doreen, stopped the car by a phone box, 'I need to make a phone call, just keep your head down.'

'Have you heard anything about Gloria?' I asked.

'Not exactly,' said Doreen, 'But there seems to be a lot of unrest with these guys, they've made a lot of enemies, with other gangs.'

'Do you know who they are,' I asked.

'I know a man who knows a man, if you understand me? The trouble is Robbie, I think I've rustled a few feathers by asking too many questions. I'm convinced my life is in danger.'

'Who do you think is paying for my solicitor, and why?' I asked her.

'I have no idea' said Doreen.

A few miles away, Inspector Wyatt, was about to hear some more bad news.

Inspector Black, answered his phone.

'Who is it?' asked Inspector Wyatt.

'It's the station they've asked if we can sort out a punch up in the middle of City Street, being as we're driving near bye.'

'Can't they get uniform to sort that out?' Wyatt, asked clearly irritated. Inspector Black, paused for a moment.

'I'm afraid it's two uniformed police officers who are fighting with each other.'

'When we sort all this out, I'll get you to phone the local

circus,' said Wyatt, angrily, 'I might be able to help them out if they're short of clowns.'

When they arrived at the scene of the crime the policemen had just stopped fighting, too exhausted to carry on. 'He started it, Boss!'

'No, I didn't,' said the other officer.

Inspector Wyatt, looked at the pair of them in disbelief, then he looked inside their car.

'So, where's Robbie, then? Is there the slightest chance that you've put him in the boot? Or maybe he's just popped down the road to get you some sweeties? You get back in your car and drive straight back to the station, now! I'll deal with you there.'

'Should we go looking for Robbie?' Inspector Black, asked.

'Oh, don't worry about him if he's run off that's up to him, he's not the sort that can look after himself, he'll come running back asking for protection.'

13

Ten minutes later Doreen, had reached our destination, a reasonable size detached house with plenty of room to park at the front. The front door opened immediately.

'Put these sunglasses on,' said the man that came to the car and put a patterned blanket across my shoulders.

'Let's make sure no one sees those handcuffs quickly let's get in the house.' There was a large hallway, with doors left and right, the house must have been divided into apartments. Frenchie, that was the man's name, unlocked the first door on our right and pushed me in quickly. Doreen, who was behind me closed the door.

'Sit down, Robbie, so you're the little fucker that's caused so much trouble,'

He looked at Doreen, then looked back at me and gave me a mighty punch in the stomach grabbed my hair pulled me up off my seat threw me on the floor and kicked me in the ribs. 'Where's this money?'

'Please stop. I won't be able to take much more of this I was shot only last week, please no more,' I cried. Frenchie, kicked me again,

'Where's the money?'

'I don't know, if I did, I would tell you, I'm a physical coward, please, no more.'

'Listen Robbie,' said Frenchie, 'I'll

do a deal with you, we'll share the money between the three of us'

'I don't know,' I squawked.

'That's enough Frenchie,' said Doreen, 'let's get him back on the settee, here take a drink Robbie, sip it slowly you poor soul.'

'Doreen, why are you doing this?' it was hard to talk, my ribs feel so painful.

I thought you and I where on the same side if it hadn't been for you and Fergal, I would have been shot dead at the cottage and now you allow this to happen.'

I started to cough, the pain in my ribs hurt even more.

'Let's see if we can get those handcuffs off,' said Frenchie.

'Robbie, this is your last chance, we could share the money between the three of us. I have contacts where I can launder money into saving accounts, bonds, gold, euros. It is my speciality

'Where is Gloria, now?' I asked.

'We don't know, exactly,' said Doreen.

'We think she is being driven around in a multi seater. The truth is these criminals have no were to hide her that the police don't already know about.'

'If you tell us where the money is, we

can phone the police and give them the registration number it shouldn't take them long to find them if they're still out on the road.' said Frenchie.

'I told you,' I replied, 'I don't know where the money is. Could someone tell me what's going on with you two? I gasped for air as it became more difficult to speak. The bastard had broken some ribs.

'It's not for you to ask the questions.' said Frenchie.

'Maybe we should tell Robbie, what's going on,' said Doreen. 'Things might make more sense to him. Me and Frenchie, go back a long way, out of the blue he phoned me two days ago. I didn't know he was working for this syndicate that has been after your blood.'

'I wasn't involved at all,' said Frenchie. 'I would have stopped the whole operation. It's been one big cock up.' Our boss was killed a few days ago, and his son has taken over he's a complete fucking idiot. Since his dad died, he bought a big white cat, and a big chair that looks like a throne, and he wants to conquer the world,' said Frenchie.

He showed me a couple of sheets of paper.

'On here are the names of most of the people who are on the syndicate's payroll, secret bank accounts, all that shit. We want you to personally deliver this to a police officer, who we will name later on. It is important when and where you deliver this, understand?'

'Yes, but what about Gloria?' I asked.

'While they think she might have the money, they won't kill her.'

He pulled out a gun and held it to my head. 'Robbie, I've had enough killing this is a way out for you and Gloria, but don't test my patience. Have you no sense at all?'

'I just want me and Gloria, to stay alive,'

'I think you're telling the truth about the missing money But Frenchie, needed to ask you personally,

I think he's satisfied,' she pulled out a phone from her hand-bag. 'Okay, I am phoning Inspector Wyatt, you speak to him Robbie, and give him this registration number, tell him Gloria, is in this vehicle, no more no less.'

Doreen, held the phone to my ears, Frenchie, held my balls, Doreen, looked at me.

'No heroics Robbie, or you'll die still wearing your handcuffs,' said Frenchie.

'Hello, Inspector Wyatt.' I gave him the message.

He recognised my voice. Doreen, took the phone away and turned it off.

'Okay let's get these cuffs off Robbie, sooner or later he's bound to want a shit, and I don't fancy wiping his arse,

do you Frenchie? 'No way, 'You're not going to chop one of my hands off, are you?'

Only as a last resort,' said Frenchie, 'are you left or right-handed?'

'I think you've broken my ribs,' I said to Frenchie. 'Don't worry Robbie, you're still alive, and you're not coughing blood. There you go, your handcuffs are off. I've still got the knack,' said Frenchie, with a certain amount of pride.

'That should impress them down at the job centre.'

'Listen Robbie, you're lucky to still be alive.'

'Well, I'm sure I'm only alive because you need me, I need an ambulance right now. I'm in so much pain.'

A few miles away at the police station Inspector Wyatt, sat at his office desk.

'Send out this registration alert to all cars, we need to find this vehicle as soon as possible.' He sipped his coffee, admiring an old framed photograph of his school rugby team.

'Excuse me, Boss,' said Inspector Black, 'we've managed to get the make and colour on this multi- seater that Gloria, is supposed to be in.'

'Any news about Sniffer, and Perkins?' Wyatt asked.

'Nothing,' replied Inspector Black.

Back at the apartment Doreen, handed me a drink

'Take this,' said Doreen. 'Scotch and aspirin; it'll work wonders.' She poured a straight Scotch for herself and then for Frenchie.

'If you do as we tell you Robbie,

You'll be doing me and Frenchie a favour and buying us time to get out of the country. You and Gloria, will still be alive.

'Why don't you just walk into the police station yourself with this list of villains?'

'We thought of that, but we can't trust the police. We would get locked up.'

Or they would arrange it that someone would get to us before any court proceedings started. If you look at that list, there are one or two high ranking police officers involved,' said Doreen.

'What about me? They would shoot me,'

'Not necessarily, you would just be seen as the messenger. Me and Frenchie are the real ones in danger especially Frenchie, he's been involved in some big stuff over the years. I've made a deal with, Sniffer, If I can help him find, Gloria.

We will give him this list and he will allow us twenty-four hours to get out of the country.'

'When did you make this deal?' 'Just a few hours ago.'

'But Sniffer's been kidnapped, I told you that, as soon as you picked me up. 'I know,' said Doreen, 'that's really screwed things up.'

'Can I have a look at these names,' I asked Frenchie.

Frenchie, gulped his Scotch back in one go, handed me the list and poured himself another drink. 'Have they gone completely mad? Kidnapping two police officers?' said Frenchie. He looked at Doreen.

'Jesus Christ, that would explain why Sniffer, hasn't answered his phone in the last couple of hours,' said Doreen, 'if they kill Sniffer, we've got a problem.'

Nobody, spoke for a few minutes.

'Are you sure were safe here Frenchie?' Doreen, asked.

'As safe as anywhere. Do you know much about this Perkin's fellow?' Frenchie, asked Doreen. 'Not really, I've seen him, never really spoke to him, he's young, bit of a geek.'

'Well this is a surprise,' I said. 'Perkins name is on this list, geek or no geek, the little shit has deceived all of us.'

Back at the police station, Inspector Wyatt, was still finding it difficult to cope with recent events.

'Do you want to give Gloria, top priority?' asked Black.

'Not really, I'm fed up to the teeth playing nurse maid to Gloria, and her dopey husband. As far as I'm concerned, we'd all be better off if they were both shot dead.'

'With respect, Boss, I don't think that's the attitude, we need to do something,' said Inspector Black.

'I need to fill in a report said Wyatt, concerning one twat of a police officer taking a dive at a lounge cabinet and if that's not enough. I need to explain why I have two uniformed police officers fighting in the middle of a busy street allowing one handcuffed male, to escape from their car at the same time I need someone to write a logical explanation. I'll let you sort it out you seem a bright lad.'

'What fill in the report?' Black, didn't sound pleased.

'No, sort out this mess with all these people that are missing. If I was you, I'd give Perkins, and Sniffer, priority after all they are police officers I'm just going to the toilet.'

'You're sure your all right, Boss?'

'Never felt better, I'm just going to change my shirt.'

A couple of minutes later, there was the sound of a gunshot. They found Inspector Wyatt, slumped on the toilet seat he'd shot himself through the head wearing his favourite rugby shirt. As most officers were vomiting Inspector Black kept his composure, He adjusted his tie and thought if Sniffer, and Perkins get wiped out by their captives, he could be in line for rapid promotion. He was an ambitious man.

Not too many miles away, in a small old private gym with dull grey walls with no windows. Young Perkins, chewed quickly at his sandwiches. Sniffer, with his aching head looked at him with disgust.

'You'll never get away with this,' he said.

'Yes, I will, Sniffer, so just tell us were the money is.'

Every sound echoed.

'What makes you think, I have this money?' Sniffer, asked.

Perkins, stood up from his chair he gently wiped the crumbs from his hands and walked over to Sniffer, who was tied to a chair?

'I've always wanted to do this,' said Perkins, as he punched Sniffer, in the face. Then he yelled,

'I think I've broke my hand,'

Sniffers, head jolted to his right he shook his head a couple of times, and just stared at Perkins.

'If Robbie, and Gloria, haven't got the money, it's obvious you have said Perkins. You've had access to the house, and the car you probably hired a big-time solicitor for Robbie, out of guilt.'

Sniffer, looked around at the other two men in the room, Daz, and George, a couple of, well-worn hard cases. Then he looked back at Perkins.

'You had exactly the same opportunity's as me you big shit and you were always moaning about the job. I've just got a couple of years before my retirement. I'm not prepared to risk that, and besides I might bend the rules a little bit, but I'm not corrupt. You make me sick. I know you'll have to kill me, whatever happens.'

'That was a very good little speech but I don't believe you,' said a well-built young man who had just walked into the room. He was holding a white cat in his arms. Sniffer, started to laugh.

'What's so funny?' he asked.

'I didn't think cats and rats got on so well together,' replied Sniffer.

'Kill him, kill him now,' said the man with the cat to one of the other men.

'Is that wise Boss? We need this guy alive for bargaining reasons.'

'Oh, all right, Daz, shoot him in the leg or something like that.'

Daz, pulled out a gun from his pocket and shot Sniffer, in the shin. The noise was deafening the cat shrieked and jumped out of the boss's arms, Sniffer, yelled in pain and Perkins, was holding his broken hand.

'You stupid twat,' said the boss. 'Haven't you got a silencer? We've all gone deaf.

Marilyn, has scratched me too pieces.'

'Marilyn?' Daz, asked, looking confused.

'Yes, Marilyn, that's what I've named the cat. The poor little thing, you must have scared the shit out of her. And god knows how many people must have heard that noise.'

Sniffer, had passed out with the pain.

'We better put a bandage on that leg, or he'll bleed to death,' said Daz.

'There's some in the back of the multi seater,' said the boss, 'you never know when you might need some these days.'

As Daz, opened the door the cat ran out.

'Oh Bollocks, just get the bandage. You'll never catch Marilyn. I think we better move from here Perkins, you go and get Gloria, from the room next door just untie her legs, and make sure her hands are still tied and she's well-gagged.'

'Could you repeat that Boss? I can't hear a thing. There's ringing in my ears.'

'Just get Gloria,' said the boss, were off out of here. I'll go and see if I can find Marilyn, George, you just give Perkins, a hand with Gloria, make sure that sack is on her head properly we don't want her recognising young Perkins.'

The boss stepped outside into the yard, it was a small industrial estate, most of the buildings were unoccupied. He could see Marilyn across the yard, but there was no sign of Daz.

'Come on Marilyn, come to Daddy.'

Suddenly the boss was surrounded by armed police. He was handcuffed and laid spread-eagled on the floor; the officers swiftly entered the gym. Apart from Sniffer, who looked in a bad way the room was empty, there was a deafening sound of gunshots in the next room and a loud scream.

A bloodstained female with a sack on her head staggered through the doorway. she held a gun in her hand and started shooting indiscriminately.

'Don't shoot, were police,' shouted Inspector Black. Everyone had dived to the floor.

'How do I know that?'

'Is that you Gloria? We're here to rescue you, if you take that bag of your head, you'll be able to see we are police officers,' said Inspector Black.

'Don't you think I would take it off if I could? You stupid bastard.' If anybody moves, I'll shoot them.'

Inspector Black, looked round the room,

'You've already injured two of my officers'

'And I've, either injured, or killed two bastards in the other room, a few more won't bother me.' Her voice was trembling.

'Men, I hate them, they're depraved' said Gloria. She started crying, threw her gun down and fell to her knees. 'Oh God, someone help me please.'

'Let's get Gloria to hospital as quick as we can,' said Inspector Black.

'What about Sniffer.' replied W.P.C Lipinski, 'he looks like he's lost a lot of blood.'

'Oh of course, Sniffer, we need to get him to the hospital.'

After Inspector Black, was informed that Perkins, although badly wounded was still alive and the two officers that Gloria had shot, were only suffering from minor injuries. He managed to congratulate everyone for a successful operation

This should look good on my C.V., catching 'Mr Big', he

thought to himself and who knows, if Sniffers, leg wound is that bad, he may have to have his leg amputated, I could still be in line for a rapid promotion.

Sniffer, had just gained conciseness as he was put on the stretcher. He grabbed Inspector Black, by the lapel,

'Perkins, he's one of them,' he growled, 'just be careful.'

'I don't think so, 'said Inspector Black, 'Anyway this is no time to be homophobic, we need to get you to the hospital.'

'No, I don't mean he's a homo, he's bent, 'said Sniffer, angrily and passed out again.

'He's probably hallucinating,' said one of the paramedics.

'Did you hear what he said?' asked. Black.

'Not a word, but I can see he's traumatised,' replied the paramedic.

Inspector Black, walked into the other room, it was small and stunk. Perkins, was being carried out on a stretcher unconscious and on a drip, he looked as though he'd been shot in the stomach. The man lying on the floor, called George, had a bad neck wound, the medical team were desperately trying to stop the bleeding.

This is all very depressing, thought the inspector, if the hierarchy know that Sniffer, is homophobic, he's got more chance of promotion than any of us.

Christine, carried on typing,

'So, Robbie, while all this was going on, you were still held captive under the supervision of Doreen, and Frenchie.'

'That's right, Doreen, allowed me to have a wash, but only with the bathroom door open. It was humiliating having to wash with Frenchie, watching me.' Doreen, looked concerned.

'Don't you think you've had enough to drink Frenchie? We need to have our wits about us.'

The pain in my ribs didn't seem to be so bad, maybe the effect of scotch and aspirin was doing its job.

I just hope that with too much whisky inside him Frenchie, doesn't find the sight of my wet torso irresistible.

'Hurry up, you, fat get,' said Frenchie, 'We haven't got all day.'

Oh well that's one less thing to worry about, I don't think I'm his type! I sat down on the settee, slightly refreshed, 'It must be difficult,' I said to Frenchie.

'What's difficult,' he replied.

'You've been a gangster all your life and now you want to leave all that respect, people fearing you, that bonding between fellow gangsters, that feeling of power.' Frenchie, looked at me.

'It's just a job at the end of the day.'

Frenchie, was a thick set man, with several scars on his on his face, he looked a tough character.

'When I was involved in that shoot out at Martin's old cottage,' I said, even though I was scared and felt like vomiting for a short time when I had a gun in my hand, I could feel the excitement and the adrenaline rush.'

'You're not thinking of becoming a gangster, Robbie?' Doreen, asked.

'No, I haven't got the stomach for it.'

'Neither have I anymore,' said Frenchie, 'don't get me wrong, it wouldn't bother me to bump you off, but it's not as appealing as it used to be.

This new boss is a right prat. That's one of the problems with this job. You can't take your boss to a tribunal or go through the grievance procedures one verbal warning, and then your shot dead.'

'That's enough Frenchie,' said Doreen, 'this is getting us nowhere, we need to see if Sniffer, is still alive, I'll give him a call.'

There was no answer. I looked at Doreen.

'You don't need me; you know I haven't got the money. Send this list of villains through the post, and by the time the police receive this information you could be out of the country,' I said.

'We need reassurance. Sniffer, was going to give us that. We need to keep you hostage, until I'm convinced, we can get out of the country,' said Doreen.

'In that case I'll have another scotch,' I said, 'let me phone Inspector Black, see if Sniffer, is still alive, and maybe there's good news about Gloria.'

Inspector Black answered the phone,

'Robbie, where are you? We've got Gloria, she's a bit shook up, but she's okay.'

'Oh great, what about Sniffer?' I asked.

'He was shot in the leg, but he's alive and kicking. Oh dear, that was a bad choice of words,' he replied.

'Gloria's well,' I said to Doreen, as she took the phone off me and turned it off.

'And Sniffer is still alive, so that's good news,' I said.

'It is,' said Doreen, 'Frenchie gave me the tip off about were Gloria might be and I informed Sniffer.'

I looked at Frenchie, 'you may have kicked my ribs in but thanks, thanks both of you for saving Gloria's life. What can I do to repay this debt? I'll do anything to help.'

'Anything? I don't think so,' said Frenchie.

'Have they captured any of the Gang?' he added.

'I didn't ask.'

Perkins, eyes opened he realised he was in hospital, his stomach was hurting.

'Welcome back,' said the nurse, Inspector Black, was standing next to her.

'You've been in the wars, young Perkins, nice to see you're back in the land of the living,' said the Inspector 'Things have been moving at a tremendous pace since you've been lying in hospital. We've, managed to round up some big-time villains shortly after we rescued you and Sniffer. We had a phone call from Robbie, he sounded totally pissed.'

'Is he all right?' Perkins, asked.

'It's hard to tell, he's got a couple of broken ribs and a badly bruised jaw. We had to break down the door to find him lying on the floor with an empty bottle of whisky at his side and a gun in one hand. He wasn't making much sense.'

'In the same room was Doreen, and an unidentified male both shot dead. When asked what happened, all Robbie, would say was no comment, I need to speak to my solicitor first. That Mr Bellow has become a right pain in the arse.'

Perkins, never said a word.

'There seems to be some confusion about what happened at that old gym, before the armed response team got there and rescued you, Sniffer, and Gloria.'

'I was lucky you got there as quick as you did, said Perkins.'

'An off duty 'police officer, spotted the vehicle driving into the industrial estate and recognised the registration number.'

'There's always a bit of luck involved in these cases,' said Perkins.

'There certainly is,' said Inspector Black. 'Unless you've got a lawyer like Mr Bellow, as far as your luck is concerned, you're well and truly fucked. I think you better start telling me about your relationship with these criminals.'

In another part of the hospital, Casper stood outside the ward that Robbie was in. He waited patiently as detectives and Mr Bellow seemed to be having a fair amount of disagreement. Robbie hardly said a word.

'Who are you?' asked one of the detectives

'Just a friend, I've come to see Robbie.'

'Do you have a name?'

'Yes, Casper.'

'Well, Casper, if I was you, I'd fuck off home. Robbie, is seeing no one at the moment.'

'It's okay, inspector,' said Mr Bellow, 'Robbie is allowed a visitor, you can check Casper, out with Inspector Black, or Inspector Snipe. This man is of good character.'

'How can he be of good character if he's a friend of Robbie's?'

'I could say the same about any detective that is associated with Inspector Perkins,' replied Mr Bellow.

'News travels fast,' said the detective.'

'Nothing has been proved yet, about detective Perkins, the same with my client, innocent, till proven guilty. Now if you will kindly let Casper, in to see his cousin, thank you very much.'

'You all right Robbie?' Casper, asked.

'I'm not sure, I'm suffering with a massive hangover at the moment,' I replied.

'I've been told by Mr Bellow not to mention anything to anyone about what happened earlier on.'

'What? The fact that you were found in a room with two dead bodies, and a gun in your hand!'

'Naughty Casper, I've told you no comment. Have you seen Gloria?'

'She's fine,' said Casper, 'she's under sedation at the moment. She's had a bit of a rough time.'

'She's fine, but she's under sedation, that's a bit of a contradiction,' I said.

'She's a bit of a heroine, she managed to untie herself and shoot two of the thugs that held her captive. Robbie, you seem a bit high, have they drugged you up? Your eyes seem to be rolling about all over the place!' said Casper.

'A bit like your teddy bear,' I said, 'He looks really fucked up. Is there anyone I know who is still alive? Do you know were all that money has gone,' I fell asleep.

'Has he had a bang on the head?' Casper, asked the nurse. 'Only he doesn't seem quite right.'

'It's probably the medication,' said the nurse, 'and being in a room with two dead bodies could be rather upsetting and traumatic,'

'I would have thought Robbie would be getting used to that sort thing, taking into account what's been happening to him over the last few weeks,' said Casper. 'Everywhere he goes, some sort of disaster happens. I'll go and see how Gloria, is.'

She was asleep, and Freddie was sitting by her bed side.

'She's been knocked about a bit. 'Freddie told Casper.' Casper, looked round the ward,

'Do you think this is wise, Freddie?'

'What do you mean?'

'Well Robbie's more or less in the next ward and you've come along bold as brass to see how his wife is.'

'Oh, grow up Casper, it's not as though I'm in bed with her, giving her one.'

'Well, that's only because all the lights are on,' said Casper. At that moment, one of the nurses came along.

'How is Gloria?' she asked.

'Sleeping,' said Freddie.

'I won't wake her while she's resting,' said the nurse. 'I suggest you two should do the same, and leave right now, and come back later.'

In a nearby hospital, Sniffer, laid in his bed, thinking of retirement. he was surprised to have a visit from Reverent Percy.

'You haven't come to pray for me, have you Vicar?'

'Not really, I've come to pray for your leg and thank you for making our streets safer to walk on. Is it true about Robbie? He shot two people dead?'

'It's true, they found Robbie in a room with two bodies, with a gun in his hand. We don't know yet what happened exactly but his solicitor will probably get him off with self-defence, something like that, possibly a free holiday in Tenerife. I wasn't there at the time; I was tied to a chair in some smelly old gym where some bastard shot me in the leg.'

'I think it's the house,' said Percy.

'What house?'

'Robbie's, house, it's bad luck. I knew the couple that lived there before Robbie, bought it. He was an alcoholic, and he used to beat his wife. Do you believe that some premises possess their own kind of misery and evilness?' Percy, asked Sniffer.

'I think you've been drinking some of that wine you keep hidden in the church, you daft prat. I knew that couple. They were both mad it had nothing to with the house being evil. She was tired of all the beatings, and stabbed her husband one night in the kitchen,' said Sniffer. 'She should have killed the bastard years ago.'

'So, do you think Robbie's mad?' Percy, asked.

'What's all this interest in Robbie? He's not a churchy person.'

'No, but Gloria used to be, and we try to assist and help people who may have fallen by the wayside. Robbie, could go to prison for a long time if found guilty of murder.' Sniffer, stared at the vicar for a while.

'Well, it's up to people like me to make sure that doesn't, happen,' replied Sniffer. 'I think he's a complete idiot, but let's say he's been a little unlucky. He may have had a complete breakdown in that room but at least he didn't shoot himself in the head like Inspector Wyatt. But Robbie, does seem to bring the worst out in people. I've never been in hospital so much and suffered so many injuries in my life, since the day I met him. If you're trying to introduce him to god, you're wasting your time.'

'The Lord moves in mysterious ways,' said Percy. 'Has he got a bad leg like me, then?' Replied Sniffer.

14

I looked at Christine, as she typed away on her computer. 'I think that's enough story telling for today,' I said.

'What you can't leave it at that,' she replied, 'what happened in that room with you, Frenchie, and Doreen?'

'It's getting late' I said, 'After four years in jail I'm still programmed to go to bed early. I told you that before, I wouldn't mind another drink just before I go.'

'Did you really have a break down?' Christine, asked.

'Full blown,' I replied, 'if it hadn't been for Reverend Percy, with his support and help for the first year I was in prison I don't think I would ever have got my head together. He was very good with Gloria, but she was a lot stronger than me, she held up well in court. 'She was very brave in that gym; I was just mentally falling apart.'

'Do you still love her?'

'No, I think I just needed her more than loved her. I never trusted her; she only came back to me when she thought I was rich I think once there's no trust in any relationship that's the end.

Freddie, left her last year, for some young slapper and Gloria, went back to live with her sister. They're happy running people down all week, and then going to church on Sunday and having their souls cleansed.'

'No bitterness there then,' said Christine,

I smiled,

'You have a nice face when you smile' said Christine, 'you should try it more often,'

'Thank you, Christine, give me time, it hurts when I say it, but smiling doesn't come naturally to me anymore. Let's change the subject, I'm going home, we'll continue with Doreen, and Frenchie, another day.'

'You could always stay here for the night.'

'I didn't know you had a spare bedroom,' I replied.

'Don't play dumb, Robbie, I want to fuck you.' Somehow, I knew she was going to say that but, maybe not quite so directly. I was expecting something like, let's make love, or sleep with me tonight.

'I know this may sound corny,' I said, 'But I'm not ready for a relationship yet.'

'Who said anything about a relationship?'

'You and Casper, are good for each other,' I said.

'Oh, don't be so old-fashioned. Casper, and I know we won't be together forever. I'm twenty years older than he is. When he's fifty, he won't be wanting a seventy-year-old relic like me hanging round his neck. I just like my cock and I'm determined to get plenty before I wake up one morning, look down the bedclothes to discover my fanny has dried up like an old prune.'

'You have a way with words Christine, I can see why you enjoy writing kiddies' books. I should imagine your biography is very good;

Christine, was born and educated in the Midlands, and has written several kiddies books, loves flower arranging and plenty of cock.'

'Oh, don't be such an old-fashioned chauvinist pig, sexually

273

adventurous would have been far more appropriate,' she replied.

'Thanks for the offer Christine, I think you are very attractive but I couldn't do this to Casper, you're his girl. I'm going now, and I'll speak to you in the morning. That's if you're still interested in finishing the book.'

Robbie. You've been flirting with me the last few days, you've been leading me on, how can you refuse sex after four years in jail?'

'It's nothing against you Christine, it's been so long, the thought of sex is beginning to frighten me. I am an old-fashioned guy, I'm not able to fuck em, and leave em, If I made love to you I would probably fall in love. If it's okay with you there are things I need to do tomorrow. I'll see you the day after, is that okay?'

'I suppose it will have to be,' said Christine.

'I'll give you a call tomorrow don't get bitter on me,' I replied, I left Christine's house. I must start a new painting I thought to myself.

The next morning, I gave Reverend Percy, a visit. He seemed very pleased to see me.

'Hello Robbie' you just missed Rosie.'

'You keep some bad company, Vicar,' I said.

'It's part of my work, to help rehabilitate people, Rosie's, never quite got over murdering her husband,' said Percy.

'That was over ten years ago, I believe it was pretty gruesome,'

'Very,' I think she took a shine to you ,' said Percy.

'I'm relieved to hear that Vicar That's how we bought the house so cheaply. Twelve thousand less than market price the thought of somebody being knifed to death in the kitchen just put people off.'

'Did they ever find that body you disposed of in the river?'

'There was a rumour, a couple of years ago, Fergal, found a naked body near the river. The pigs and any other sort of creatures that were into that sort of cuisine, had been nibbling at it,' I replied.

'So, what happened?' Percy, asked.

'Nothing officially, Fergal, didn't tell the police. He'd been in enough trouble when he splattered that gunman across the path at the cottage with his shotgun.'

'Yes, I remember that, you were lucky that night.'

'I suppose I was, anyway, Fergal, took the corpse to his brother-in-law's place. He had one of those tree shredders.'

'That's enough,' said Percy, 'I can visualise the scene only too well. So, who started this rumour?'

'It was the hairy travellers, they detested Fergal, for certain reasons. Nobody believed anything they said, and Fergal, died about a year ago, he drank himself to death.'

'So, how do you feel now Robbie?'

'I'm okay, I can't thank you and Rosie, enough for all the support you gave me with your prison visits and letters, it did help me a lot. I would have cracked up in those early months if it hadn't been for you and Rosie.'

'Good, said Percy. 'I think you should go and see Rosie, she's a bit down at the moment.'

'We used to have some bizarre conversations,' I said.

'I'm sure you did,' said Percy.

'You were both good for each other, being able to talk about your horrific experiences. Come with me Robbie, I'd like to show you something.' Percy, took me to a building behind his house, 'This was Sniffers, idea,' as he opened the door.

'I know he said he could find me somewhere else to live, but this place is like a shithole, and it's not much bigger than where I am living now.'

Percy, started to laugh. 'This is not for you to live in, you can use this as your new studio, what do you think?'

'Sniffer, suggested this.'

I can't believe it.'

'Well, what do you think?' Percy, asked.

'It's perfect, toilet, good lighting, running water, a big sink and draining board. It might take weeks to tidy it up but it's the dog's bollocks.'

'I do wish you'd tidy up your language Robbie, it's bad enough having to listen to Sniffer.'

'I'm sorry Vicar, I must try harder, who used this place before?'

'Oh, just the odd rapist, murderers, drug addicts, the last person to use it renovated furniture, I thought that was all a bit boring.' said Percy.

'You've been talking to Sniffer, too long. You acquired his wicked wit,' I said.

'Perhaps,' replied Percy, 'Perhaps.'

'So does the church own this property?' I asked.

'Why all these questions, Robbie? You are a very talented man you've rode the storm and have become a stronger man because of it, embrace it with both hands your paintings are unique, I think your paintings are incredible.'

'I don't think Sniffer, would agree with you,' I said.

'Sniffer, loves looking at your paintings Robbie, he said it prepares him for hell, he'll know what to expect when he dies.'

I looked around the room.

'I'm very grateful to you both 'I'll start tidying this place tomorrow, I can't wait to get started.'

I phoned Casper, as soon as I got home and told him the news, he didn't seem that impressed.

'Oh. I'm sure that'll be good for you, Mr Golden Balls, all these people looking after you,' said Casper.

'I thought you'd be pleased for me you miserable bastard.'

'Christine, phoned me earlier on,' replied Casper, she said she doesn't want to see me again, did you shag her last night? impress her with your big muscles.'

'No, I didn't.'

'I hate you Robbie,' he turned off the phone.

Oh shit, it's started again, trouble follows me everywhere.

The doorbell rang,

'Hello, Robbie,' it was Christine.

'I've just been talking to a man who's going out of his mind, because his girlfriend has just left him,' I said.

'So, does that mean you're not going to let me in? make your mind up yes or no, I can't stand here all day.'

I opened the door wider to let her in.

'This will really fuck him up, he's quite fragile really.' I told her.

'For god's sake Robbie, the guy's almost thirty, we all get our hearts broken from time to time.'

'Oh yes and when was yours broken? He thinks I fucked you last night.'

'Well that defiantly didn't happen did it? Old Mr Goody Two Shoes,' said Christine.

'So why take it out on Casper? he's done nothing wrong, it went quiet for a while. 'You still want to know what happened in that room with Frenchie, and Doreen?' I asked her.

'Not particularly,' she replied.

'There's a dark side of me you ought to know. I can tell you the events that where explained in court four years ago wasn't quite true. I just need to tell someone the truth. I can either tell you, or Reverend Percy, in complete confidence of course. If I tell you the truth, I must insist that you don't write it in the book. I just thought you ought to know the real me.'

'I've seen the real you when you told me to piss off, it was frightening,' Christine, replied.

'So, I refuse to have sex with you, and then you tell Casper, that you don't want to see him anymore and then you come around to my humble abode.'

'It's a shithole,' said Christine.

'So why are you here?' I replied, 'I shot them both in cold blood.'

'Who?' she demanded.

'Doreen, and Frenchie,' I said. It wasn't self-defence, 'There was no struggle with Frenchie, trying to get the gun off me, no accidental shooting, Frenchie, was pissed and dropped the gun on the floor. I quickly picked it up and deliberately shot Doreen, through the head, and Frenchie, through the heart, no hesitation, no remorse. I was just glad to wipe them out.'

'Why did you shoot Doreen?' Christine, asked.

'She was just a crook and a liar all this talk about laundering money, it turned out it was all bullshit. She was living in a world of fantasy; she hadn't got a pot to piss in.

So that's the sort of man I am how do you feel about that Christine? I was lucky I didn't get sent down for twenty years.

How do you feel about being in the same room as me? Please

tell me, why are you in the same room as me?'

'Just tell me you like me Robbie,' said Christine, 'something like that, I can't stop thinking about you.'

'I just told you I've killed two people in cold blood.'

'Well. we all have an off day,' said Christine, 'as long as you don't keep a gun in the house, we'll be fine.'

'We'll be fine, doing what?' I asked.

'For Fucks sake,' Christine, shouted, 'Do I have to spell it out for you, I love you.'

'What's happened to this modern, liberated, woman, who wants lots of sex with lots of men, without any sort of relationship?' I asked.

'Well, we can all change Robbie, you don't shoot people anymore.'

'I've only been out of prison for a few days, give me time. I need to think, about that, I do like you very much, but I'm having trouble enough just living with myself, I'm not sure I can spend the rest of my life living with someone. Can't we do this the old-fashioned way.? Let me take you out for a meal, a cosy drink we can talk about something other than the book If that's alright with you?'

Christine, picked up her handbag.

'Goodbye Robbie, this is your loss,'

'Don't you dare give me ultimatums, I've been decent and honest with you, and you drop Casper, just like that and you expect me to shack up with you, just fuck off and carry on writing your kiddies books and don't bother me again.'

Christine, slammed the door behind her, later on I went to the gym and had a great work out.

The next day I went to my new studio, well it's a large garden shed really but when I clean it out it will be perfect.

I didn't realise how much rubbish was in there. After about an hour, Rosie, turned up and gave me a hand. Percy, said she was on a bit of a downer. So, I quickly checked to make sure she wasn't carrying any knives. She was weak and frail but her help was appreciated. We'd both been in a dark place in our lives, and because of that we connected well, even though, very often I had to cheer the conversation up a little bit.

Rosie, didn't stay long but she seemed a little happier when she left to go to the bookies. Percy, apologised, because he couldn't find me any more help with the cleaning. We sat down in his house to have a pot of tea and some biscuits, all very civilised. He still reminded me of Rupert the Bear's dad the way he dressed.

'I still can't get over the way you and Sniffer, get on with each other,'

'Maybe it was just meant to be,' said Percy.

'Are you all right Robbie? You seem to be a little troubled.'

'Is it that obvious?' I asked.

'I was just thinking what you just said, 'maybe it was meant to be, I think that sometimes, about all that missing money. I had plenty of time to think about that when I was in jail too much time really. I used to think it might be Sniffer. I used to think it was a lot of different people.'

I took a sip of tea.

'So, do you have any theories about who did take it Robbie?'

'I used to have a good chat with Rosie, about that,' I said.

'Surely you don't think it was Rosie?

'I did, at one time she could have had a duplicate set of keys, her husband had plenty of hiding places where he kept his booze.'

'I know,' said Percy, 'I use to help Rosie, search for it. It was mostly vodka; it was difficult to tell if it was better to take it away or just let him get drunk. He used to give her some terrible beatings.'

'I know, he gave you a couple of hidings,' I said.

'Yes, he did,' said Percy. 'Would you like some more tea?'

'No thanks, you do know when the police searched my house, the forensics, found your D.N.A and finger- prints?'

'That's right,' said Percy, 'but as I said, I used to help Rosie, plus the fact I used to visit Gloria, now and again when your marriage was starting to break up. She was seeking God's help. I even came to visit you, remember?'

'Yes, I do, that was the day Martin, told you to go away.'

'I think he actually told me to fuck off,' said Percy. 'It's one of the hazards of the trade. Still he's in God's hands now.'

'I find that hard to believe,' I said. 'Unless God is trying to strangle him and if Gloria, was seeking Gods help, I think that went out the window as soon as she saw all that money,' I said.

'It must have been tempting,' said Percy. 'You don't think it was me that took the money?

'Well, I look at you and Sniffer, and wonder if you planed it between the two of you. I remember how he spoke to you at my house just before Martin, died. He disliked you immensely and now you two seem as thick as thieves, or was that just an act?'

'He became a changed man after he had his leg amputated,'

'You mean he developed a limp,' Percy, looked at me angrily. 'That's not funny.'

'I'm sorry Percy, you and Sniffer, have been very good to me, I just get so frustrated wondering what happened to all that money I could have been so rich.'

'Or Dead,' said Percy, 'and let's not forget Gloria, lost a finger.'

'Yes, she was very brave,' I said. 'I would still like to know who paid for Mr Bellow, to look after me.'

'Just let it go Robbie,' said Percy, 'move on.'

He's right there's nothing to be gained by digging up the past, I walked back to my new studio.

I can't wait to start a new painting. The next day Christine, phoned me.

'Can I come and see you? I've been doing some research on Mr Bellow, and Reverend Percy; I think you might be interested. No strings attached; I promise.'

'Are you any good at cleaning rooms? It's taking me ages to finish tidying up this studio.'

'Only if you take me out to dinner later.'

'Okay.' If your going to help me with the cleaning, wear your blue jeans.'

Christine, knocked on my door,

'Please,' she said, 'no arguments today, you must see what I've found out on the internet,' said Christine.

'Let me take you down to my studio first.'

Christine, was very impressed with my studio. She looked out of the window.

'Is that Reverend Percy, in the Garden?'

'Yes,' I replied, it looks like he's coming over, he must have seen you.'

'Hello, Robbie, I see you brought some help with you today,'

'Yes, this is Christine, she writes books,'

'Mostly children's books,' said, Christine, 'but I'm writing one about Robbie, at the moment.'

'What, a book about his prison sentence?'

'No about the events that happened before that.'

Just then Sniffer, appeared.

'Let me guess, you must be Christine?' she looked at his walking stick.

'And you must be Mr Snipe?' Sniffer, looked at both of us.

'So, how's the book getting on? and, by the way, just call me Sniffer.'

'It's going very well,' said Christine, 'we've just got to the part when the police found Robbie, in the room with Doreen, and Frenchie.'

'You mean Doreen, and Frenchie, deceased, when Robbie, handed the list of villains over to Inspector Black.'

'Oh, the infamous Black list', said Christine.

'Robbie, was well and truly pissed that day,' said Sniffer.

'He wasn't even certain who he handed the list too, he took a bit of persuading to get the gun out of his hand. Robbie, was seen as a hero by some, a villain by others. We rounded up a few crooks that week. I was sorry I missed it all, I was lying in a bed in hospital.'

'Yes, I was sorry to hear about your leg', said Christine. 'It would be nice to hear your side of Robbie's story, and yours, Reverend Percy.'

'Why don't we go inside?' asked Sniffer. 'it's getting a bit chilly out here, and my leg is aching. Percy, get that idol bastard of a house- keeper to make some tea.'

'Language Sniffer,' said Percy. Sniffer, looked at Christine, as we all sat down,

'Percy, thinks the more I swear, the more likely I am to go

to hell. I asked him the other day if I stopped swearing would I grow a new leg?'

'He told me not to be so ridiculous, the Lord doesn't work that way. Well how about a couple of inches on my dick? That shouldn't be too difficult.'

Sniffer, and Christine, started to laugh, I smiled, and Percy, looked disgusted.

'I don't think it's wise to write this book,' said Percy. 'It involves a lot of suffering; I think it's best to leave things as they are.'

'I would like this book to be written,' I said.

'Robbie, said he would make me sound suave and hand-some,' said Sniffer.

'Is that with or without the extra two inches on your dick?' Christine, asked jokingly.

Sniffer, looked at Christine, for a few seconds and then they both burst out laughing. I thought they were actually flirting, with each other.

'Were did you find this woman? If I had two legs, I'd give you a run, for your money.'

'I think we ought to go Christine, we've got loads of cleaning to do.'

'Oh relax, Robbie,' said 'Sniffer, 'since when have we had the time to sit down and enjoy ourselves and not worry about being kidnapped, or shot? you of all people should be able to appreciate this situation.'

'Sniffers right,' said Percy. 'You should be able to appreciate the situation you're in. Tell me Christine, are you hoping to make money from this book?'

'We both are,' I said.

'Don't you think you're doing all right with your painting?' he asked.

'Whatever profit we make, we'll give It to Charity,' said Christine.

'Hang on,' I said. 'I never agreed to that.'

'I'm just checking with Percy, would that be okay, would you be able to sort that out for us?' she said.

'We're always happy to receive donations for charity. As we speak, some child's life is being saved from cancer because of the generosity of the public. We have been lucky lately we have had some incredible donations. Many of them anonymous.'

'So, if someone came along and gave you a million pounds in cash, would you accept it without any questions?' Christine, asked.

'There are some cases we would refuse, if the donor was well-known and associated with the criminal element.'

Sniffer looked at Christine,

'Where are you going with this?' He asked her, then he looked at me.

'You haven't got a load of cash you want to get rid of, have you Robbie?'

'No, I haven't,' I replied.

'I think you better make your point, Christine,' said Sniffer.

'Why would the church be prepared to pay a top-class solicitor?' said Christine, to represent someone who is possibly a criminal and a murderer.'

'I don't know what you mean,' said Percy.

'Mr Bellow, the solicitor who represented Robbie, was on the payroll of a company that was associated with the churches finances.'

'Okay, I'm a vicar, but I don't know anything about Mr Bellow, and his connection with the church.'

'Let's change the subject,' said Sniffer, 'I thought we were all having a cosy chat,'

'Did you know Percy, had a spare set of keys that Rosie, gave him,' I said to Sniffer.

'What's this, good cop, bad cop day? Percy, been very good to you Robbie,' said Sniffer.

'Did you know Percy, had a set of keys to get in the house?'

'Yes, I did, so what?'

'You knew it was Percy, that took the money he had the keys; he knew all the old hiding places where Rosie's husband used to hide his drinks.'

'That's all circumstantial,' said Sniffer.

'What about the large amounts of money that have been donated to hospitals over the last three and a half years? Christine, asked.

'What about it?' said Sniffer, 'has that become a criminal offence?'

'No, but where did it all come from?' Percy, stood up from his seat and walked over to the lounge cabinet. As he took out a bottle of Scotch and four tumblers, he shouted to his house-keeper, that for the next hour he didn't want to be disturbed.

Everything went quiet, he poured out the drinks and sat down.

'You know, I haven't had a drink since I had my leg off,' said Sniffer.

'Just drink it,' said Percy. 'You might grow a new leg, or even two inches on your dick.'

'Leave the bottle with me, said Sniffer.'

Percy, looked at me and Christine.

'I knew one day this would happen, yes I took the money. Sniffer, didn't know, at the time, but like you Christine, he discovered Mr Bellow, was indirectly being paid by the church. I thought it was the right thing to do, being as Robbie, supplied the church with this money.'

'How did you know it was in the house?' I asked.

'I didn't,' said Percy, 'I could just sense it was there. It was just luck really, as you said, I knew all the hiding places, I just felt compelled to look for it. I knew both you and Gloria, were out that day.'

'So, where's the money now?' I asked.

'There's no money left. It's all gone.'

'What all of it?'

'Yes, all of it,' said Percy. 'We have helped to build new hospital wings, research for the mentally ill, homes for victims of domestic abuse.'

'That money could have set me up for life, it was money you stole from me.'

'Would you have given any to charity?' Christine, asked.

'Well maybe a little. I thought you were on my side. I spent four years in jail, almost going out of my mind. Give me another drink. You must have bought something for yourself Percy?'

'I must admit I did weaken. I bought myself a new bicycle.'

'A new bicycle, all that money and you buy a new bicycle. My wife lost a finger and left me. Sniffer, lost a leg, I lost my mind, and Inspector Wyatt, shot himself. I shot Doreen, and Frenchie, Fergal, blasted some criminal all across the cottage pathway, one man died in my taxi, and one passenger died in Martins, car. Don't you think I deserved a little bit of that money?'

'No, you don't,' said Sniffer.

'Did you know it was Percy, that stole that money from my house?'

'That was money you stole from a dead man,' said Sniffer. 'As we speak, lives are being saved, because of that money, women half out of their mind are being looked after and protected from there violent partners, they didn't have a choice. I didn't realise Percy, had stolen the money, but like you Christine, shortly after the trail I found out that Mr Bellow, was indirectly paid by the church.'

'I felt it was only right,' said Percy, 'after suppling us with all that money. We made sure you had the best solicitor in the country,'

I stood up from my chair,

'I didn't supply it, you stole that money from my house, at that time I was suffering with depression and I was financially fucked. That money would have set me up for life.'

'That's not true,' said Sniffer, 'if the vicar hadn't taken that money away when he did, the police would have found it anyway and you would have almost certainly served a longer prison sentence.'

'You should have arrested Percy,' I said.

'Why?' replied Sniffer.

'He broke the law' I replied.

'Oh, fuck the law,' said Sniffer.

'You can't say that, you're a retired copper.'

'I've told you before Robbie, I couldn't care less about hardened criminals killing each other. That money was like poison, even to this day, nobody was actually sure whether it was money for drugs, or stolen goods. Nobody has actually reported that they lost loads of   money, I've never been able to judge you Robbie, but I've never considered you to be evil and selfish, what good would it do to bring this all up again?'

'But you lost a leg Sniffer, surely you must think you deserve a share of that money?'

'Maybe, but when I was having my leg amputated, all I could see was young soldiers, young women and children suffering. What this crafty old goat did, was breaking the law, but I bet when he goes to bed at night, he sleeps well with a clear conscience. All my life, I've been banging people up, evil bastards, I'm not too sure about this God thing, but I know Percy, is a good man. What he has done with this money makes me feel good to know him.'

'You speak of him as though he was a God,' said Christine.

'Well he certainly isn't the Devil,' said Sniffer, 'and I've met a few of his disciples in my time.

I think I'll have another drop of Scotch,' said Sniffer.

'I don't know what to think, 'I said, in despair. Christine, started to cry,

'I'm sorry Percy, I did some research on you and the church finances. I was hoping to nail you to the wall about all these so-called anonymous donations. I feel so bad about it, you are a good man and what you have done with this money is wonderful.'

'Thank you, Christine,' said Percy.

He looked round the walls,

'I think there's enough crucifixions on this wall without nailing me on there as well,'

'Don't push it Percy, she's not saying you're Jesus Christ,' said Sniffer.

'I can't believe it', I said, 'I am surrounded by a bunch of born-again Christians who have squandered a shit loads of money.'

'I think it's brilliant,' said Christine.

'Will you be finishing the book?' Percy asked.

'Oh yes,' said Christine, 'I'm just not certain how to finish it. But don't worry it won't involve you two!'

'Thank you,' said Percy.

Christine, and I walked across the garden towards the studio. Sniffer, looked at Percy,

'What do you reckon?'

'You mean, will they tell anybody?'

'No, will they fuck each other's brains out?' Sniffer, said.

'You really can be crude at times,' said Percy, 'anyway after four years in prison, it'll probably be over in twenty seconds.'

Sniffer looked at Percy.,

'There is something about her,'.

'I know what you mean,' said Sniffer. I think it's the tight blue jeans.'

'Yes, she does have a nice bottom', said Percy. Sniffer laughed.

'Lucky bastard. Fancy another drink, that's if there's any left?'

'You all right, Robbie?' Christine, asked me.

'I'm not sure. 'Can I hold your hand, Christine?'

'Of course, you can,' it felt nice.

'Try not to be angry Robbie, I need you more than ever.'

'I need you? Were you flirting with Sniffer, when you first met him today?'

'Why, were you jealous of me talking to a one-legged man?'

'Not really, I think you naturally flirt with men.'

'I've just thought, I could write a book about a one-legged detective and a vicar who go around solving murder mysteries,' said Christine.

'That sounds ridiculous to me,' I said. 'Are we going out to eat?'

'I need to change if we are,' said Christine.

'It felt nice that you were jealous; it makes me feel wanted, do we have to eat? I don't like having sex on a full stomach.'

'I can't remember, it's been that long ago,' I replied. 'but who needs food.'

An hour later I fell in love. Christine made me promise I would never leave her, and she would never flirt with another man. I had a smile on my face from ear to ear.

Then Casper, burst into the room and shot me in the left shoulder with an old shotgun he'd found on the tip. Fortunately, the cartridge was old too, and it didn't have all the energy it should have had, but the pellets hurt like hell. Trust Casper, to fuck everything up. He had really become the jealous type. I could hear Christine, screaming as I fell off the bed onto the floor, all I could see was blood everywhere. There was a second shot. Christine, stopped screaming, there was silence. I passed out with the pain. I remember thinking, *maybe my luck has run out.*

I woke up in a hospital bed, my shoulder was hurting like hell.

'How do you manage it, Robbie?'

It was Sniffer. 'You only been out of nick for a few days, and you're back to your old tricks. You've cheated death yet again.'

'How long have I been here?'

'Three days. Robbie, you had lost a lot of blood,'

Sniffer, paused. 'We thought we'd lost you a couple of times.'

'How's Christine,' I asked.

'She's traumatised, but she's okay. Casper, tried to shoot her but his home-made gun blew up in his face taking half his left hand off, Christine, slipped trying to avoid being shot and knocked herself out on the hand basin. It was just like the old days as I walked into that room, there was blood everywhere, and a few fingers. I thought you were all dead, then I realised. No one can kill Robbie Knotcutt.'

A few months later, Christine took up writing children's books again. She had developed a talent creating evil characters that scared the hell out of the kids, it gave her books that extra edge they needed. I continued with my paintings. Casper, ended up in prison, and managed to start his own Arts and Crafts workshop. Considering he had a few fingers missing he was still good with his hands, but I can't forgive him, the gun-slinging bastard.

By the way Christine did finish her book about me. It was shit.

THE END